EXCEPT YOU'RE A BIRD

PETER TINNISWOOD

D1493564

HODDER AND STOUGHTON
LONDON   SYDNEY   AUCKLAND   TORONTO

With thanks to the Welsh Arts Council

"... you cannot be in two places
at once except you're a bird."

Boyd Roche

Chapter One

Mr Brandon worked on the bowling greens.

It was his job to keep them fresh and fast.

One evening when he returned home from work, his wife met him in the hall with a hug and a kiss and said:

"Do you fancy a second honeymoon, Les?"

"No thank you," said Mr Brandon.

"Why not?" said Mrs Brandon.

"Well, I didn't reckon much to the first one," said Mr Brandon. "The breakfasts was a bloody disgrace."

He went into the back kitchen and commenced to wash himself in the sink.

Mrs Brandon followed him in.

"What was wrong with the breakfasts?" she said.

"The toast was damp," said Mr Brandon, screwing up his eyes against the harsh, sour soap and spluttering noisily as he splashed himself with tepid water.

"Maybe, but the bacon was scrumptious, and she only burst the sausages on the Thursday," said Mrs Brandon handing her husband a towel. "And you could have as much marmalade as you wanted — within reason, of course."

Mr Brandon puffed and grunted as he dried himself on the damp towel.

Then he pushed his wife to one side and walked into the back parlour, where he put on his carpet slippers, lowered himself gently into the arm chair in front of the coal fire and shook open the evening paper at the gardening page with a long, deep, contented sigh.

Mrs Brandon snatched the paper out of his hands.

"Any road, breakfast isn't the most important thing about a honeymoon," she said. "There's other considerations to be took into consideration."

"Such as?"

Mrs Brandon lowered her head and blushed.

7

"You know," she said.

"I don't," said Mr Brandon, taking the newspaper out of his wife's hands. "I haven't a bloody clue what you're talking about."

Mrs Brandon moved over to him and sat on the arm of his chair. He twitched his shoulders with irritation. She put her arms round his neck and began to stroke his gritty hair.

"Don't you remember that first night of our honeymoon, Les?" she said.

"Not particularly," said Mr Brandon, rustling his paper as he tried to free himself from his wife's grip.

"I do. I remember it well. Mrs Plimsoll was kindness personified. She were more like a mother than a landlady," said Mrs Brandon softly. "She give us ox heart and fried onions for supper and then she took us upstairs and showed us how to work the lavatory chain and then she escorted us to the bedroom door and she said: 'Well then, get stuck in.'"

"Give over," said Mr Brandon disentangling himself from his wife's embrace and standing up from his chair. "What's for tea?"

"Polony," said Mrs Brandon.

Her eyes had clouded over. A wistful smile had come to her lips. At the corners of her eyes appeared laughter creases long unused.

"I shall never forget the picture of you in the bedroom that night, Les," she said. "You looked right comical with just your socks on. I'd never seen a man before with just his socks on."

"Give over, will you?" snarled Mr Brandon.

"You got so excited. You was all fingers and thumbs," said Mrs Brandon. "If it hadn't been for me lending a hand, you'd have been all week unbuckling your suspenders."

"For Christ's sake, woman," said Mr Brandon, and he stamped into the back kitchen and began to rattle the knife drawer.

Mrs Brandon came flouncing into the kitchen. She took hold of her husband by the arm and pulled him away.

"I'll make the tea," she said firmly. "I'm not having a man tampering in my kitchen."

Mr Brandon smiled to himself and began to tip-toe back into the parlour.

Mrs Brandon snapped back at him without turning round:

"There's no use skulking off, Les. I want a definite answer from you. Do you or do you not want a second honeymoon?"

"No," said Mr Brandon.

"Don't prevaricate," said Mrs Brandon.

Mr Brandon scowled at her and returned to the back parlour and the gardening section of his evening newspaper.

Ten minutes later Mrs Brandon's brother, Uncle Mort, came in from his afternoon of cribbage at the Old Comrades' Club and grunted a greeting.

"What's for tea?" he said.

"Polony," said Mr Brandon.

"Again?" said Uncle Mort.

Outside the house the surface of the streets was streaked with sooty slime which glistened in the dull orange glow of the street lamps. The soil on the allotments was clogged.

It was a late autumn evening in the 1960s. There was fog about.

After tea was over Mr Brandon filled his pipe carefully and lit it. He took three slow puffs and then turned to Uncle Mort, tapping the evening paper with his earth-stained forefinger.

"You'll never believe it," he said. "According to sports editor they've picked Artie Shirtcliffe to play in the centre against Rochdale Hornets."

"That's Rugby League, is that," said Uncle Mort. "I'm not interested in that bloody rubbish."

"Neither am I," said Mrs Brandon, and once more she snatched the evening paper out of her husband's hands.

Mr Brandon sighed and rested his bent briar pipe carefully on the ledge of the ash tray.

"All right, all right," he said. "What *are* you interested in?"

"Our Silver Wedding," said Mrs Brandon.

"Pardon?" said Mr Brandon, and his face turned quite pale.

"It's our Silver Wedding come next spring and I've been making plans," said Mrs Brandon.

"Oh Christ," said Uncle Mort.

"On the day of the anniversary we're going to have a service of rededication in the church where we was married with full choir and organ plus floral decorations," said Mrs Brandon. "And after that we're going to have a pukka sit-down reception with an MC for the dancing and real port for the toasts. And then after that we'll have a full-scale honeymoon with all the trimmings. So put that in your pipe and smoke it."

Mr Brandon gazed at her with open mouth. His lower lip began to quiver and his Adam's apple trembled.

Uncle Mort sniggered. The snigger made him cough. He coughed so much that his cheeks turned purple, his veins stood out on his temples and Mrs Brandon had to pat his back violently.

"There, there, Mort, I knew you'd get excited about it," she said. "Particularly as you'll be giving me away."

"Pardon?" said Uncle Mort, and every drop of colour drained from his face.

"You'll be giving me away in the service of rededication," said Mrs Brandon. "Me dad can't do it owing to death so you'll have to step into the breach."

Mr Brandon rammed his pipe into his mouth and snarled at Uncle Mort through clenched dentures:

"So put that in your pipe and bloody smoke it."

Chapter Two

That evening in the local Mr Brandon and Uncle Mort drank their pints of Oughthwaite's Best Bitter silently and glumly.

Uncle Mort wiped the creamy froth off his lips with the back of his sleeve and said:

"Has she decided on the venue for the honeymoon?"

Mr Brandon shook his head.

"You went to Blackpool for the first one, didn't you?" said Uncle Mort.

"I'm not quite sure," said Mr Brandon. "It could have been."

Uncle Mort gazed into his pint pot.

"I can't stand holidays," he said.

"Neither can I," said Mr Brandon. "All that rain gets you down, doesn't it?"

Uncle Mort nodded his head. Carefully he began to pour a bottle of Jubilee stout into the beer in his glass. The sharp amber turned to warm, tumbling brown.

"I'll tell you the greatest bugbear about going on holiday— you can never get a plastic mac what fits you proper," said Uncle Mort. "They're forever flapping round your ankles and catching in your bicycle clips."

"Correct," said Mr Brandon.

"And the buttonholes always bloody rip on you, too," said Uncle Mort.

Mr Brandon puffed at his pipe gravely.

"Aye," he said. "You need great resources of character to enjoy a good holiday."

He blew a thin stream of smoke upwards at the fly-pocked ceiling.

Uncle Mort yawned.

"She says I've got to wear the proper clobber when I give her away in church," he said.

"Oh aye," said Mr Brandon. "You'll have to wear the proper clobber. It'll be a spats job, will this."

"Spats?" said Uncle Mort.

"Forced to be," said Mr Brandon. "Women are buggers for spats."

Uncle Mort drained off his glass and beckoned the waiter to repeat the order.

There were few people in the pub.

Darts thudded listlessly into the newly-oiled board in the public bar. Dominoes clacked in the snug. Popular mine host and ex Green Howard, Bert Coleridge, sat on a high stool filling in his football coupon.

The lights flickered and for an instant it seemed they might go out. They did not.

Uncle Mort paid for the drinks and gave the waiter a three-penny tip.

"What's her bloody game, Les?" he said.

Mr Brandon clicked his tongue and shook his head wearily.

"She says she wants to feel appreciated," he said. "She says she wants more affection shown her. She says she wants to go out more."

"Aye," said Uncle Mort. "We once had a sheepdog like that."

Mr Brandon shivered for an instant.

"She says she wants to shower me with love," he said fearfully.

"Struth," said Uncle Mort. "What a mess to be in."

It was half past eight.

At nine o'clock the door opened to let in an icy waft of fog. It also let in the head gardener at the park, where Mr Brandon worked.

His name was George Furnival.

He was accompanied by his wife.

Her name was Olive.

He looked across at Mr Brandon and scowled.

"Miserable sod," said Mr Brandon. "He hates my guts. And I hate his, too."

"Good," said Uncle Mort. "It's nice to have something in common with your boss, isn't it?"

George Furnival waved the waiter away and went to the bar to order his drinks personally. He scowled at the barmaid when she gave him a friendly smile, and the corners of his thin white lips drooped into the blue-grey gloss of his pointed chin.

"He's what I call lugubrious," said Uncle Mort.

"So would you be, if you had a wife as ugly as his," said Mr Brandon.

Uncle Mort looked across at Olive Furnival, and she smiled at him warmly.

"Aye, she's ugly right enough," said Uncle Mort. "She's got a face like a siege gun."

George Furnival brought the drinks to his wife and with a deliberate twist of his shoulders and a noisy scraping of his chair turned his back on Mr Brandon.

"You was dead right, Les," said Uncle Mort. "He loathes you."

Mr Brandon puffed at his pipe. He rested his elbows on the mottled table top and let the tobacco smoke dribble out over his lower lip.

"I'll not have much longer to put up with him," he said. "He's due to retire in a couple of months."

"Is he?" said Uncle Mort. "You want to put in for his job then."

"Me?"

"Aye. It'd suit you down to the ground. You're a dab hand when it comes to gardening. You can dig smashing holes."

Mr Brandon tapped the stem of his pipe against his teeth slowly.

"I've no chance," he said. "To get that job I'd have to have a recommendation from Furnival himself, and there's as much hope of that as being canonised by the Pope."

"I never knew the Pope played billiards," said Uncle Mort.

Mr Brandon knocked out his pipe on the heel of his shoe.

"I'm happy in the job I've got," he said. "I'm left to me own devices. I like being left to me own devices. You don't get no upsets and complications and disturbances in your routine when you're left to your own devices."

They had one more pint of black and tan, and then they set off for home.

The fog swirled around them. It had a peppery tang. It made them cough.

When they got home, Mrs Brandon fussed round them happily and settled them in front of the roaring fire in the back parlour with much punching of cushions.

She sang to herself as she brought in the supper of cream crackers, Cheshire cheese and pickled onions.

She sat on the rug at Mr Brandon's feet and stroked his ankles.

"I don't like these onions," said Mr Brandon. "They make me sweat."

Later that night Mrs Brandon inched her way across the cold bed and pressed her stomach into Mr Brandon's back. She ran her finger nails up his spine. She rubbed her chin on his shoulder blades.

"Les," she said softly. "Are you awake, love?"

"No," said Mr Brandon. "Go to sleep, can't you?"

Chapter Three

On Saturday afternoon Mr Brandon put on his gauntlets and went to the match with his son, Carter Brandon.

The home side won 33–7 and by way of celebration the father and son went to The Griffon public house for liver and bacon sandwiches and pints of black and tan with whisky chasers.

"By God, young Leatherbarrow made mincemeat of their defence," said Mr Brandon.

"Aye," said Carter Brandon. "And Artie Shirtcliffe played a corker, too."

"He were rubbish," said Mr Brandon. "He's forever posing and posturing, is Artie Shirtcliffe. He's the sort of bloke what changes into a fresh jock strap at half time, is Artie Shirtcliffe."

"Mm," said Carter Brandon.

"And I'll swear blind he'd shampooed his hair during the interval."

"Mm."

"No wonder he couldn't catch the ball proper," said Mr Brandon. "His fingers was probably all bunged up wi' Brylcreem."

The first of the evening revellers bound for the City Hall dance came into the lounge bar. They wore navy-blue raglan overcoats and shoes with pointed toes.

They read pink football papers and thumped each other on the back from time to time. They fingered their boil plasters tenderly.

Mr Brandon lit up his pipe.

"He can't kick with his right foot neither, can't Artie Shirt-cliffe," he said.

They finished their drinks and stepped outside into the damp night air.

A trolley bus loomed up silently out of the mist. Its tyres swished. The overhead wires hissed and were lit up briefly by a flash of palest green.

They walked down the hill towards the bus station.

Behind the cold grey mist the city muttered and mumbled to itself.

"This Silver Wedding's getting me down," said Mr Brandon as they passed the row of fishing-tackle shops in Foundry Lane.

"I bet it is," said Carter Brandon.

"I've a good mind to jack it in and run off to a South Sea island," said Mr Brandon. "I could teach the natives how to play bowls with coconuts."

They stopped off at Topley's Wine Lodge for a glass of ginger wine and whisky.

It warmed them through and through.

"You'd not get this stuff on your South Sea island," said Carter Brandon.

Mr Brandon nodded and smiled ruefully at his glass.

"You're right," he said. "It's considerations like that what have kept me married to your mother all these years."

Next day Carter Brandon and his wife, Pat, went round to the Brandon household for Sunday dinner.

"Do you like swedes, Pat, love?" said Mrs Brandon.

"No," said Pat. "They make me eyes water."

"They're very much an acquired taste, are swedes," said Mr Brandon, and then he paused and said deliberately: "Just like weddings."

They had treacle tart and white sauce to follow the roast beef, swedes, marrowfat peas and Yorkshire pudding.

After that they went into the front parlour where Mrs Brandon provided them with cups of tea and a plate of assorted fancies from Jackson and Colclough's, the high-class bakers.

"Carter was telling me about your Silver Wedding celebrations," said Pat to Mrs Brandon as she popped a slice of Battenberg into her mouth with little finger crooked.

"Load of rubbish, isn't it?" said Mr Brandon. "Do you fancy being a bridesmaid?"

"She can't," said Uncle Mort. "She's not ugly enough."

"Are you inferring my bridesmaids was ugly, Mort?" said Mrs Brandon, her face turning scarlet.

"Well, they were no bloody oil paintings, was they?" said Uncle Mort.

"Right," said Mrs Brandon. "Right."

She swished her pinnie and she stamped out of the room.

They heard her opening and shutting doors upstairs. Then after a moment they heard her feet pounding down the stairs, and she burst into the front parlour brandishing a photograph album.

"There. Have a look at the wedding photos," she said. "The proof of the album is in the eating."

The album was bound in white satin. The material had faded. There were brown smudges on the edges of the cover, and the spine had turned to listless yellow.

On the front cover in chipped gold leaf was the legend:
"Our Wedding Album."

And underneath in smaller letters was written:
"Supplied by De Reszke cigarettes."

Uncle Mort opened the album, and began to chuckle immediately.

"What are you laughing at?" snapped Mrs Brandon.

"Him," said Uncle Mort, pointing to a large group picture of the wedding guests. "Who the hell's that bloke with the big ears and the sad buttonhole?"

"You," said Mrs Brandon. "That's you before you got drunk."

"It bloody isn't," said Uncle Mort. "There's me stood next to the insurance man."

"That's not the insurance man," said Mrs Brandon. "That's Uncle Rufus from Frodsham. Look at his squint."

"Give it here," said Mr Brandon, snatching the album off Uncle Mort's knee.

There was the sound of searing linen, and the album collapsed, scattering damp black pages and curling snapshots to the carpet.

"Now look what you've done," wailed Mrs Brandon. "My dad smoked himself to bronchitis getting enough coupons for this album."

"Did he buggery," said Uncle Mort. "He bought it for ten-pence at the Boys' Brigade jumble sale. I were with him. He bought a brush for the parrot at the same time."

Mrs Brandon got down on her hands and knees and began to collect the photographs from the floor.

Suddenly she stopped, held up a photograph at arms' length and smiled.

"There you are, Pat," she said. "There's my bridesmaids. Now you can see what they was really like."

"Mm," said Pat, cocking her head sideways. "I see."

2

"Now that one with the knowing look and the buck teeth is Gertie Foreshaw," said Mrs Brandon, settling herself next to Pat. "She married a dining-car attendant on the LNER. He were an exceptionally nice man except he'd got these funny-shaped thumbs."

"Mm," said Pat. "And who's the one with the frosted lens to her glasses?"

"Cousin Marion from Burslem," said Mrs Brandon. "Poor Marion. She'd have made someone a lovely wife if it hadn't been for her feet."

Mr Brandon looked across at Pat and winked and gave her his long slow smile.

"Now the one next to Marion stroking the guinea pig is Rene Hutchinson," said Mrs Brandon, and then suddenly she began to sob.

"Here we go," said Uncle Mort. "The old waterworks again."

"Poor Rene," snuffled Mrs Brandon. "Hitler got her with a landmine at Wallasey. If only she'd lived at West Kirby."

She dried her eyes and gathered up the photographs, which she replaced carefully in the remains of her album.

"By gum, we looked a load of funniosities in them days, didn't we?" said Uncle Mort.

"Speak for yourself, our Mort," said Mrs Brandon. "I think the women looked lovely. I think our rig-outs was gorgeous, don't you, Pat?"

"Mm," said Pat. "I suppose they must have been quite fashionable in them days."

Mrs Brandon clasped the album to her bosom and said:

"We'll have another one just like this for our Silver Wedding. Only this time we'll have a stronger binding and get the photos took professional with a camera on a stand."

Half an hour later Carter Brandon helped Pat put on her three-quarter-length mock astrakhan coat, and they set off for the park, where Mr Brandon tended the bowling greens.

They were going for a constitutional before their tea.

It was a day for strong mufflers.

An east wind scoured everything in its path.

It rattled the trellis work in the rose bower and stung the sand in the pit where the children played.

It blew back spaniels' ears.

It sent the gulls reeling above the chapped playing fields. It made noses drip and finger ends tingle.

"It's better than the fog, I suppose," said Carter Brandon.

They skirted Mr Brandon's two bowling greens and made for the rustic shelter which overlooked the tennis courts.

The red shale of the courts was sodden and the nets sagged under the weight of the soggy autumn leaves blown into their meshes.

Carter Brandon lit a cigarette and handed it to Pat.

"No ta," she said. "I don't think I should under the circumstances."

"What circumstances?" said Carter Brandon.

"Can't you guess, love?" said Pat blushing and turning her face away.

"No," said Carter Brandon. "What are you on about?"

"You'll see," said Pat. "You'll see, love."

She snuggled into Carter Brandon's chest. He ran his chin over her springy black hair with its sheen of navy-blue. He placed his hands inside her coat and fondled her breasts.

She sighed.

On the wall of the shelter someone had written in scarlet paint: "Artie Shirtcliffe is a prick."

Later that night as they cuddled together in bed and the east wind rasped at the curtain rail Pat said to Carter Brandon:

"Wasn't your mother's bridesmaids ugly?"

"Aye," said Carter Brandon.

They laughed and Carter Brandon ran his hands softly over her buttocks.

She moaned gently.

"Would you like to have a second honeymoon, Carter?" she said.

"Aye. Righto," said Carter Brandon, and he tugged open the cord of his pyjama trousers.

Pat placed her hand firmly on his wrist.

"Not now, love," she whispered. "I don't think we should under the circumstances."

The east wind blew without respite for three days.

Then it veered to the south-west quarter and blustery rain swept over the allotments and blew slates off the roof of the Roman Catholic church in Quilter Lane.

One of the slates stunned a passing bus conductor.

He was a Sikh.

On Thursday evening Pat tiptoed upstairs to the bathroom where Carter Brandon lay in the bath smoking a cigarette and reading a rumpled copy of *Health and Efficiency*.

"So that's what you read when my back's turned, is it?" she said taking the book out of his hands.

She thumbed through the steam-soaked pages.

"I don't know how these women can pose for nude pictures," she said. "I wouldn't do it even if they let me keep my clothes on."

Carter Brandon flicked the stub of his cigarette into the wash basin and stretched himself back in the bath. He grunted with pleasure as the hot water rose up behind his ears.

Pat smiled down at him and said in a coy voice:

"I went to see the doctor this morning, Carter."

"Mm," said Carter Brandon.

"He give me some news, Carter."

"Mm."

"Can you guess what it was, love?"

"What?"

"The news what the doctor give me."

"What doctor? What are you talking about?"

"You rotten dog. You've not been listening to a word I've said," said Pat, and she took hold of the face cloth and slapped it hard against her husband's cheek.

"Ouch," said Carter Brandon.

He rubbed his cheek tenderly, and then he grinned and said:

"What news have you got then?"

Pat smiled and kneeled down beside the bath. The steam from the hot water glistened on her forehead as she ran her fingers through the hairs on her husband's chest and let them linger among the damp creases in his belly.

Carter Brandon took hold of her wrist and said:

"Do you fancy coming in for a bit of a splog then?"

"I don't think I should, love," said Pat. "Not under the present circumstances."

"What circumstances?"

"I'm a mother-to-be."

"Congratulations," said Carter Brandon. "Now what's this news you've got to tell me?"

When Pat told Mrs Brandon of her pregnant condition the

following day, her mother-in-law took her in her arms and hugged her.

"Smashing," she said. "Aren't you a clever clogs?"

Pat lowered her eyelids and smiled modestly.

"When did you conceive, love?" said Mrs Brandon, walking round Pat slowly and examining her stomach from every angle. "You must have been having long lay-ins on Sunday mornings. I know where you conceived. I bet it were that long weekend you spent with your cousin in Hoylake. Well, there's nothing else to do in Hoylake unless you go to New Brighton, is there, love?"

She hugged Pat again and then raced home to bring the good tidings to her husband.

Mr Brandon was in the kitchen unwrapping a winter-flowering jasmine he had just bought from Thos and Jas Humberstone, the nurserymen in the covered market.

He was whistling a happy tune.

He picked up the red name tag once more and read it aloud.

"Jas-min-um Nud-i-flor-um," he said slowly and then he smiled broadly and said: "I bet George Furnival can't pronounce it like that."

Mrs Brandon poked her head round the door and said with a smile:

"Hullo, Bompa."

"You what?" said Mr Brandon. "What are you on about now?"

Mrs Brandon tittered softly and stepped into the room.

"You're going to be a Bompa, Les," she said.

"Oh no I'm not," said Mr Brandon.

"Oh yes you are," hissed Mrs Brandon. "Pat's just this minute told me she's expecting. So unless she falls off a trolley bus and has a nasty mishap, you're going to have a grandchild."

"Mebbe," said Mr Brandon. "But I'm not having the little bugger calling me Bompa."

"Oh yes you are," said Mrs Brandon. "It's a family tradition in our family — the grandfather is always called Bompa and the grandmother is always called Nana. So from now on you're going to be Bompa, like it or not."

"Bompa!" said Mr Brandon savagely tearing the red name tag into little pieces. "I'll sound like a bloody elephant at a circus."

"What's all the row about?" said Uncle Mort, shuffling into the kitchen from his afternoon of dominoes at the Miners' Welfare.

"Pat's pregnant," said Mrs Brandon.

"Oh aye?" said Uncle Mort. "So was me mother before she had me."

When Pat's widowed mother, Mrs Partington, was told the news, she hurled herself onto the sofa and burst into tears.

Pat dashed across and leaned over her anxiously.

"This is the happiest day of my life," said Mrs Partington, catching hold of her daughter by the scruff of her neck and dragging her down beside her on the sofa.

Pat struggled to protect her hair-do. It had cost twenty-five and six at Maison Enid's.

"It's funny, isn't it?" said Mrs Partington through her snuffles. "It's funny, but a mother can never imagine her daughter going through all that ordeal."

"Oooh, it's no ordeal having a baby these days," said Pat. "They give you gas if you scream loud enough."

"I'm not talking about *having* a baby, love," said Mrs Partington. "I'm talking about the process of being *given* a baby. What a rigmarole to have to go through just to get pregnant. All that panting and grunting and bad breath. I used to make out imaginary shopping lists while your father was trying to give me a baby. I must have bought up half the Co-op wholesale warehouse before you was conceived."

Mrs Partington sighed deeply, rubbed her eyes and blew her nose.

Then she smiled and said:

"Is your bust tender?"

"Yes," said Pat.

"Well, don't let Carter play with it."

"Mother!" said Pat.

"Now don't look at me in that tone of voice, young lady. I know about these things. All you've got to say to Carter is this— 'Mammy says you're not to tamper with me whatsits, Carter.' He'll understand. I mean, how would he like it? And another thing—make him sleep downstairs on the sofa till the infant's born. It's as well to keep temptation at bay. You know what these men are like on a Saturday night if the home side's won."

"Mother, don't be so old-fashioned," said Pat. "The doctor made a point of telling me you can have sex these days right up to the eighth month."

"Sex?" said Mrs Partington. "Who's talking about sex? I'm talking about the business of having babies. Kindly keep sex out of it, if you don't mind."

Pat smiled and allowed her mother to kiss her on a cold cheek once more.

"I wonder how you'll carry," said Mrs Partington. "If you're like me, you'll keep your figure right up to the bitter end. I were just like a sylph. People couldn't believe I were pregnant. I were the main topic of conversation for weeks on end at the coal merchants."

She rested her hand on Pat's stomach and moved it round and round.

"I wonder who's inside there," she said. "I hope he wants to be a white-collar worker when he grows up."

Pat took hold of her mother's hand and removed it from her stomach.

"First things first, Mother," she said. "We've to make sure he passes his 'O' levels first, haven't we?"

Mrs Partington nodded an enthusiastic agreement.

"I'm right delighted for you, love. I'm on cloud number nine," she said. "Just wait while I tell Mr Shirtcliffe."

"Who's Mr Shirtcliffe?"

"My sweetheart," said Mrs Partington.

Pat sank back onto the sofa.

"Your sweetheart?" she said.

"That's right, love," said Mrs Partington. "We're walking out together. We're going to get married if only he'll use a bit of gumption and propose to me."

Pat turned quite pale.

She was still in a state of shock when Carter Brandon returned home from work.

He had to make his own tea, too.

Chapter Four

The subject of Mr Shirtcliffe loomed large.

"I wonder what he's like," said Pat to Carter Brandon one evening as they sat in the Chinese restaurant at the back of the Cordwainers' Hall.

"Who?" said Carter Brandon.

"Mr Shirtcliffe," said Pat. "I wonder if he's obese. I wonder if he's got a speech impediment."

The restaurant had been opened one thundery afternoon in June. It was called The Scented Lotus Garden.

There were hexagonal lampshades with tassels. The wallpaper had a pattern of peacocks and cormorants. The menu was printed by G. Fearnley & Sons, Pontefract.

Carter Brandon was eating curried King prawns with fried rice and water chestnuts. Pat was eating liver and chips.

"It's very continental in here, isn't it?" said Pat.

"Mm," said Carter Brandon, applying another sprinkling of Yorkshire relish to his shrimp crackers.

They finished their meal with lychees and custard and then they stepped outside into the autumn night.

Stars crackled in the jet-black sky. It was frosty. The frost glistened on the trolley bus wires.

Pat shuddered and linked arms with Carter Brandon.

"It all seems so vast, doesn't it, Carter?" she said.

"What does?"

"Life."

"It is," said Carter Brandon. "Or so they say."

On their way home the car skidded on an icy patch in a dip in Sherwood Road. It struck the kerb of the nearside pavement and then snaked across the road.

The engine roared.

Carter Brandon struggled with the steering wheel.

Pat screamed.

Her cry was drowned by the braying of the engine as the car

24

spun round and round. Then quite suddenly it came to rest with its rear fender gently nudging a concrete lamp post.

There was silence.

"Christ, that was close," said Carter Brandon.

Pat began to shiver.

"Bloody cars," said Carter Brandon. "Why can't we learn to walk?"

Pat was still shivering half an hour later when they went to bed. She could hardly hang onto her mug of Ovaltine.

Carter Brandon switched off the bedside lamp and wrapped his arms tightly round her.

"Oh, Carter, Carter," she sobbed. "What if you'd been killed just then? What would baby and me have done without you for the rest of our lives?"

"I don't know," said Carter Brandon. Then he patted her on the back and said: "Still, you never know, you might have been killed as well and there'd have been no problem, would there?"

Over breakfast next morning Pat said:

"Do you think Mother really will marry him?"

"Who?" said Carter Brandon.

"Mr Shirtcliffe," said Pat. "I mean, she's not bad-looking for her age, is she? I mean, there's some folk might find her quite desirable when she's just come from having her hair done by Hazel at Maison Enid's."

"Mm," said Carter Brandon spreading his slice of toast with thick, bitter orange marmalade.

"Do you still find me desirable, Carter?" said Pat. "You're not put off by my condition, are you?"

"No," said Carter Brandon.

That night he leaned across in bed and grunting softly placed his hands on Pat's breasts.

"Give over," said Pat. "I've told you before about doing that in my condition. They're not playthings, you know. If you want to find something to do with your hands, you can mend the plug on the wireless."

Carter Brandon sighed.

The gales of the autumn equinox roared.

On the great wide strands of the distant coast curling, tumbling breakers crashed and spat.

Out in the shallow seas the seine netters and the drifters and the muddy Dutch coasters fought the bruising waves, and the dunnage was wrenched from their decks.

Whooper swans beat inland to the water meadows on powerful, timeless wings. Shore larks crouched in the lee of naked sea walls. The maroons for the life boats exploded and then curled gracefully above clapboard villas and stuccoed boarding houses.

Pat sighed.

"I'd never rest easy if he married my mother," she said.

"Who?" said Carter Brandon.

"Mr Shirtcliffe," said Pat. "I mean, I just can't bear the thought of a stranger doing it in bed with my mother."

"I shouldn't mither about that," said Carter Brandon. "He'll not be a stranger to your mother once they're married, will he?"

"Not to my mother he won't," said Pat. "But he will be to me."

It took Carter Brandon the best part of a week to pluck up the courage to tell his workmates at Wagstaffe and Broome's of his impending fatherhood.

Sid Skelhorn sucked in his cheeks and nodded his head rapidly.

"What a bugger," he said. "You just can't trust this new generation of french letters, can you?"

Louis St John, the West Indian fitter, clapped him on the back and said:

"Holy Mackerel, Kingfish, dese whites are no better dan de beasts of de field wid all der breedin' and disgustin' goin' ons. Ah tell you, man, dey'll be pinching our jobs on de buses next."

"You daft nelly," said Carter Brandon.

"I'm dead pleased, kid," said Louis St John. "I'll buy you a pint on pay day."

Linda Preston expressed her pleasure by grasping Carter Brandon firmly round the back of his neck, thrusting her thighs into him and scouring the back of his mouth with her flickering, needling tongue.

"I always knew you'd got lead in your pencil, kid," she said.

"Give over," said Carter Brandon. "The canteen manageress is looking."

When the hooter blew to end the afternoon shift he went into the washroom with Sid Skelhorn to scrub down. There were puddles of cold soapy water on the concrete floor. The mirrors were chipped and cracked and the wash basins were ringed by gritty, aged tidemarks.

"We're no better than bloody pigs, are we?" said Sid Skelhorn, and he joined Carter Brandon in lathering his forearms with the pink abrasive soap powder from the mildewed dispensers.

Eric Black, the welfare committee chairman, came in and poked Carter Brandon in the ribs with his bicycle pump.

"Congrats on the imminent infant," he said. "I hope it'll be born normal."

Carter Brandon pulled the plug out of the sink and the water was sucked away with a hoarse rattling gargle. He ran in fresh water and began to rinse himself.

"You'll want something to take your mind off it, Carter," said Eric Black idly blowing drafts of air from his bicycle pump onto the underside of his chin. "Why don't you join the works football team?"

"I don't mind," said Carter Brandon. "Is it serious?"

"Course it is. We've got a set of matching jerseys and we're going to employ tactics," said Eric Black. "Are you any good at catching?"

"Not bad," said Carter Brandon.

"Grand," said Eric Black. "You can play in goal."

Carter Brandon dried himself on the sodden dirty roller towel. Then he licked down his eyebrows and went into the front yard to collect his car.

There was a thin bank of yellow-tinged mist above the canal. Through it the distant railway signals glowed a fuzzy, splintered red.

Dusk was settling shiftily among the tall chimneys and the hump-backed warehouses.

Starlings rippled over the gaunt frame of a gasometer.

Carter Brandon was driving slowly through the crowds streaming through the main gates, when he spotted Tommy Rowley from the Draughtsman's Office.

He tooted his horn and beckoned him inside.

"Ta," said Tommy Rowley, and he squeezed his way into the front seat and promptly fell asleep.

There were deep magenta bags beneath his eyes. His mouth lolled open and bubbles of saliva spread over his lower lip.

He did not wake up until Carter Brandon stopped the car outside The Tinker's Bucket. He smiled sheepishly, and they went inside for a pint.

It was a cavernous pub with sad windows.

"I hear you're expecting," said Tommy Rowley when they settled themselves at a table by the Hammond organ.

"Aye," said Carter Brandon.

"So am I. It's the third," said Tommy Rowley, and he laughed.

It was a bleak laugh that tailed off into a half-choked sob. He yawned deeply and blinked his eyelids rapidly.

"Have you got your pram yet?" he said.

"No," said Carter Brandon.

Tommy Rowley yawned again and stared into the depths of his pint.

"Take my advice then," he said. "Don't get one that squeaks."

Phyllis, the half-caste barmaid, looked at them and yawned. Her tongue was streaked with yellow.

"Have you got a dog?" said Tommy Rowley.

"No," said Carter Brandon.

"You're lucky. She'd make you get rid of it as soon as the nipper turns up. Joyce did with our first 'un."

"Did she?"

"Aye. She took exception to it licking the nipper."

"All dogs like licking nippers."

"Aye. I suppose they must taste nice to a dog," said Tommy Rowley.

His eyelids began to droop, and he had to shake his head to keep himself awake. He smiled sheepishly again.

"It were a thoroughbred, were that dog," he said. "It'd got a better bloody pedigree than the nipper."

Carter Brandon nodded sympathetically.

Tommy Rowley shook his head violently again, but he could not stifle a long, racking yawn.

"Listen to me, Carter," he said urgently, pounding his fist on the table. "I can stand owt about nippers bar the sleep."

"Sleep?"

"Aye. I've not had a good night's sleep since Joyce was two months gone with the first 'un."

"No?" said Carter Brandon. "Why not?"

"Because a pregnant woman does nowt bar scratch in bed. There's no sex. Only bloody scratching. Then once the nipper starts kicking in her belly, she's tossing and turning and grousing and grumbling, and then she's up and down for a pee every five minutes, and if she's not going to the bogs, she's nipping downstairs for brown sauce sandwiches and bottles of cream soda.

Then, bugger me, she wants to cuddle into your back, and her belly's so big, you get curvature of the spine. You'd be better off trying to sleep under a mound of bicycles."

"Mm," said Carter Brandon.

Tommy Rowley yawned deeply once more and continued:

"Then once it's born you've no chance at all of a decent night's kip. She has you lying there all night listening to it breathing. You feel like a fucking Asdic operator on a destroyer. The least bit unusual noise it makes, and it's panic stations. Phone for the doctor. Phone her mother. Phone the ambulance. Run across to Mrs Pycroft's. See if it says owt about farting in *Pears Encyclopaedia*.'

Carter Brandon took another long sip of his beer. Two off-duty firemen came in and ordered half pints of shandy.

"Even when everything's going normal she keeps you awake to watch her feeding it," said Tommy Rowley. "Bloody hell, what's so marvellous about a nipper with a fistful of tit rammed in its mouth? She says it's one of nature's miracles. She says it's the proudest moment in a man's life. Bollocks! She just wants you awake so you'll light her bloody fags for her."

He let out a long juddering yawn.

"You just wait, owd lad," he said. "You just wait while you see what's in store for you."

He slept all the way home. When they arrived outside his house, it took Carter Brandon a good minute to wake him.

He patted Carter Brandon on the shoulder and cackled.

"You're trapped now, kiddo," he said. "You're well and truly on the bloody treadmill. There's no way out now."

When Carter Brandon got home, he had his evening meal and then he sat at the table in the lounge/diner making a model warship from a kit.

It was the German heavy cruiser, *Prinz Eugen*. It had a funnel cap and a clipper stem.

Pat sat upright in one of the low-slung imitation leather arm chairs. She was working on a newspaper competition for Bassett's sweets. She had put in order her preferences for the ideal confectioner and tobacconist. Now she was struggling with the slogan.

"Carter?" she said. "Can you think of owt that rhymes with Liquorice All-sorts?"

They had cold lamb chops, sliced tomatoes and pickled walnuts for supper, and when they had climbed into bed, Carter Brandon told Pat of his decision to join the works football team.

Immediately she burst into tears.

"Now what's up?" said Carter Brandon.

She turned a tear-stained face to him.

"You could break a leg playing football," she said. "You could get an incurable infection from the showers. You could be crippled for life, and we'd have to get a special ramp for your wheelchair. Well, we haven't the money for buying a special ramp, Carter, and I can't be lugging you up and downstairs with baby on the way and risk losing the poor little mite all because you didn't look after that cut you got playing football and had to have your leg sawn off. You should be ashamed of yourself. Why didn't you use my mother's green ointment, when she told you?"

"Give over," said Carter Brandon, turning his back to her and burying his nose in the pillow.

"You see, Carter, you see, our days of pleasing ourselves are over now," said Pat. "We've got baby to think of now. We've got to be thinking of his future. I mean, do you think he'll be sensible enough to look after his own fountain pen when he goes to grammar school or shall we just get him a cheap ball point?"

"Sweet Jesus. Go to sleep, will you?"

"You should be kind and tender to me in my condition," said Pat. "You should cosset me be rights."

"All right then," said Carter Brandon. "We'll go for a piss up at the Old Comrades' Club tomorrow."

"Pig!" said Pat, but Carter Brandon was already slipping peacefully into sleep.

Three-quarters of an hour later he was wide awake.

Next to him Pat was scratching herself furiously.

"Stop your bloody scratching," he shouted.

"I can't help it," said Pat. "It's my condition."

Carter Brandon rammed his face deep into the pillow.

Pat sighed. She tossed and she turned. She groaned and she grunted. She scratched herself on the back. She scratched herself under the arm pits. She scratched herself on the stomach. The whole bed shook.

"Oh God," groaned Carter Brandon. "Oh hell."

Next morning he stumbled into work with hollow cheeks and bloodshot eyes.

"Hello, hello, been on the tiles then, kid?" said Linda Preston when she saw him in the clocking-on queue.

"No," said Carter Brandon. "Under a mound of bloody bicycles."

Chapter Five

Tuesday night was the night when Pat visited her mother.

It was a ritual.

Carter Brandon drove her there in the car.

He went into the front parlour and paid his respects to Mrs Partington who said:

"I'm just longing for the both of you to meet Mr Shirtcliffe."

"Well, why don't we?" said Pat pursing her lips. "Has he got bad breath?"

"He most certainly has not," said Mrs Partington. "He takes a special pride in his breath, does Mr Shirtcliffe. He must spend a small fortune on glacier mints."

Pat sniffed again and settled herself on the sofa among the litter of knitting patterns and child care manuals.

"You're keeping him very well-hidden, any road," she said.

"No, I'm not, love," said Mrs Partington. "Cocky's met him several times."

"The budgie?"

"Yes, and they got on like a house on fire," said Mrs Partington. "I think budgies are wonderful judges of character, and they'd put some humans to shame the way they take a bath every day and manage to sleep on one leg."

Carter Brandon hunched his shoulders and began to edge his way to the door.

"You'd be very interested to meet Mr Shirtcliffe, Carter," said Mrs Partington. "He's got a son who plays for the team."

"Not Artie Shirtcliffe?"

"Oh, you know him, do you? He's well known, is he?" said Mrs Partington smiling happily. "Is he any good?"

"Shit hot," said Carter Brandon.

"Carter!" said Pat springing to her feet. "How dare you use such language in my mother's house. You'd better not use language like that when baby comes along. They'd never accept him in the Wolf Cubs. Akela would throw a fit if she knew his father swore like a trooper."

She dismissed Carter Brandon with a nod of the head and he left and drove over to his parents' home.

His mother was out at the Co-op whist drive, but his father was in the back parlour drawing a diagram in red and black ink on a large sheet of squared paper.

"Hey up, guess what," said Carter Brandon.

"What?" said Uncle Mort who was sitting in front of the fire cutting his corns with a razor blade.

"Mrs Partington's going to marry Artie Shirtcliffe's dad."

Mr Brandon threw down his pens.

"Typical," he said. "That bloody woman hasn't got an ounce of discernment. If she wants to marry into the Rugby League fraternity, why doesn't she marry young Leatherbarrow's dad? Or what about Taffy Isaacs? What a forward. He'd trample his own mother into the ground and kick her teeth in if it meant getting a try. I bet his dad's a nice bloke."

Uncle Mort wiped the razor blade on his shirt sleeve. Then he began to massage his big toe gently.

"Bloody Rugby League," he said. "She doesn't know what she's letting herself in for getting mixed up with that. After one year of marriage she'll have a cauliflower ear and lumps on her shins the size of golf balls."

"She's getting married not playing in the bloody scrum," said Mr Brandon.

"Same thing. There's nowt to choose between the two institutions," said Uncle Mort and he began to apply the newly-cleaned blade carefully to the big toe of his left foot.

Carter Brandon let out a long, mournful yawn. Then he pointed to his father's diagram and said:

"What have you got there then?"

Mr Brandon's eyes lit up. They sparkled.

"It's a plan of the new lay-out for the back garden," he said. Uncle Mort snorted.

Mr Brandon came to sit on the arm of his son's chair. He opened his diagram with a proud flourish.

"Now, over here by the dustbins I'm going to put me Alpine rockery," he said. "Then next to the water hydrant I'll have me heather garden and just by the manhole for the drain I'll have me herb garden plus ornamental fountain plus lily pond. Now then, I'll site the orchard and the vineyard next to . . . "

"Hold on, hold on," said Uncle Mort. "You've forgotten something, haven't you?"

"What?" said Mr Brandon.

"You've forgotten to leave room for your polo pitch and your grouse moor."

Mr Brandon looked at him scornfully, rolled up his diagram silently and slowly curled his upper lip.

At ten o'clock Mrs Brandon marched into the back parlour. She was angry.

She had met Olive Furnival at the whist drive. That worthy had informed her of her husband's forthcoming retirement. Why, she demanded, had Mr Brandon not told her himself? Why, she quizzed, had he not applied for the job?

"Nonsense. Rubbish," she shouted when Mr Brandon explained the futility of such an action. "It's just bone idleness. It's just lack of ambition."

"Ambition?" said Mr Brandon, and he gave a croaky laugh.

"Ambition," said Mrs Brandon firmly. "If you'd had more ambition when we first married, we might have been celebrating our Silver Wedding now in style and comfort. We could have been running a sub post office. We could have had our own dry cleaners with a woman doing invisible mending in the front window."

"Give over," said Mr Brandon weakly.

"No, I won't give over," said Mrs Brandon. "I expect you to apply for that job tomorrow. *And* I expect you to get it. I'd get much better service at the Dinky Bakery if they knew my husband was in an administrative position. They might even save me some custard creams on a Saturday morning."

Mr Brandon's shoulders drooped. He looked across the room to his son for support. None was forthcoming. Carter Brandon was sound asleep. He was slumped askew in his chair, mouth wide open, and he was snoring deeply.

Mrs Brandon let him sleep on for half an hour, then she led him to the door gently and waved to him as he drew away in the car to collect Pat from her mother's.

He could hardly keep awake.

Pat had to nudge him in the ribs to stop him collapsing over the steering wheel.

When they arrived home, he could hardly find the strength to drag himself up to bed.

"He sounds a right rum 'un to me and no mistake," said Pat, wriggling her head on the pillow and starting to scratch her thighs.

"Who?" mumbled Carter Brandon.

"Mr Shirtcliffe," said Pat, transferring her scratching activities to the soles of her feet. "According to me mother he's got his married daughter and her baby living at home with him and according to me mother the daughter's run away from her husband and left him in the lurch, and, according to me mother, she doesn't do a thing round the house. She doesn't even know where the Ewbank is, and she's not set eyes to this day on the top shelf of the airing cupboard."

The bed began to rock as Pat's scratching grew more violent.

Carter Brandon buried his head in the pillow as the springs in the mattress creaked and twanged.

"Fancy letting her father cook the Sunday dinner for her with two veg and choice of sweet," said Pat, twisting back her arms to scratch her spine and digging Carter Brandon sharply in the ribs with her elbow. "Eee, I could fume when I think of her, the idle young faggot."

She stopped scratching.

She began to cry.

"What an humiliation," she wailed. "Fancy having a step-sister at my time of life. I've been an only child ever since I was born, and now me mother's presenting me with a total stranger as a step-sister."

"You're not going to start scratching again, are you?" said Carter Brandon.

"Why couldn't it be someone I know?" sobbed Pat. "Why couldn't it be Hazel from Maison Enid's? She'd make a lovely step-sister, would Hazel. She's got a smashing dress sense when it comes to clothes. We could go fuddling round the shops to-gether on Saturday afternoons and have a right good laugh trying on hats."

"Lie still, will you?" said Carter Brandon.

"Course, I blame it all on him," said Pat.

"Who?" said Carter Brandon wearily.

"Mr Shirtcliffe," said Pat. "Mr bloody Shirtcliffe."

And she began to scratch herself once more.

Faster and faster and faster she went, and then she got up and went to the toilet.

"Oh dear," said Carter Brandon. "Oh dear oh dear."

Chapter Six

Carter Brandon played his first match for the works football team on the ground of Pemberton Pulsometer Pumps Ltd United.

It was a Wednesday afternoon.

Two carrion crows sat on the pavilion roof and cawed.

It was a wizened pavilion.

It creaked. A smell of stale gas came from the showers, and the benches in the dressing room were splintered and covered in coke dust.

Carter Brandon yawned as he pulled off his trousers.

"Come on, Carter, wakey, wakey, owd lad," said Eric Black. "On the nest all night, was you?"

He smacked Carter Brandon on the bare bottom and chuckled.

Suddenly the smile left his face and he scurried over to a dark corner of the dressing room where a tall, pale, spotty-shouldered youth was struggling to remove his underpants from beneath a long woollen vest.

"Hey up, Rudyard, you're not wearing your bloody vest, are you?" he said.

"Yes. I've got a cold," said Rudyard Kettle.

"And you'll have a thick ear as well, if you don't take that bloody vest off," said Eric Black. "Struth, I bet Nat Lofthouse never wore his singlet when he played for England. I'd lay money on it."

Rudyard Kettle reluctantly took off his vest to reveal two small pink nipples ringed by pale-blue goose pimples.

The team trainer, Sid Skelhorn, opened the hamper and took out the jerseys. They were sky blue with red collars and cuffs.

"Now, see here, lads, these are brand new jerseys," said Eric Black. "I don't want no-one buggering them up with sliding tackles and similar showing off."

Slowly the team put on their jerseys. Slowly they filed out of the dressing room in a haze of cigarette smoke. Slowly they shuffled down the draughty corridor into the open air.

"Come on, the Sky Blues," said Sid Skelhorn. "Kick 'em up the arses."

They shivered as they stepped outside.

It was a bleak day.

The ground was on top of a hill. It was a windswept hill. It overlooked a cluttered valley with marshalling yards, strip mills and gaping outfall pipes hissing into a cramped and sluggish stream.

It was the first Wednesday in October, and the goalmouths were rutted hard.

Kneecaps stung with the cold.

The carrion crows cawed again, and the referee blew his whistle to start the game. He had lank ginger hair and a stutter.

It was a tough first half.

A passing greyhound ran off with Sid Skelhorn's egg sandwiches.

Pemberton Pulsometer Pumps Ltd United scored five goals, and Carter Brandon's team scored one.

At half time they sucked oranges and gathered round Eric Black in the centre of the field.

"We're doing champion, lads," he said. "Forty-five minutes played, and not a single jersey ripped."

Within three minutes of the resumption of the second half Ernie Cosgrove had pulled a goal back for Carter Brandon's team. He scored it with his nose. It made it bleed.

Eric Black ran up and down the touchline, flapping his arms.

"Come on, the Sky Blues," he shouted. "Use tactics. For Christ's sake, use tactics."

After ten minutes he tripped over Sid Skelhorn's bucket. A scuffle ensued.

A quarter of an hour before the end of the game Carter Brandon was bitten on the left shoulder by the opposing centre-forward.

"Don't call me Baldy again. Right?" said the centre-forward.

He turned away and Carter Brandon crept up behind him and kicked him violently on the hip.

"That's it, Carter," bellowed Sid Skelhorn. "That's what I call tactics."

"Come on, the Sky Blues," shouted Eric Black from the other side of the field. "Come on, Rudyard. Take your scarf off, man."

The referee blew his whistle to end the game, and the two teams scowled at each other and trooped off the pitch.

Pemberton Pulsometer Pumps Ltd United had won the match by five goals to two.

"Ne'er mind, eh?" said Eric Black to Carter Brandon as they trudged down the cinder path which led to the pavilion. "It's the game that counts, and their centre-forward'll not be able to ride his bike for best part of a month, I tell you."

"Mm," said Carter Brandon.

Eric Black put his arm round his waist and squeezed him.

"You played a blinder in goal, Carter," he said. "I'll try you at left half next match."

Carter Brandon limped into the dressing room and painfully peeled off his muddy kit.

Eric Black scuttled among the weary players collecting their jerseys.

"Hey up, Rudyard," he said. "Have you been wiping your nose on your sleeve again?"

"Yes," said Rudyard Kettle. "I've got a cold."

After they had been in the showers, woken up Tommy Rowley, who had fallen asleep on top of the hamper, combed their hair, wound up their watches and checked the money in their wallets the team climbed stiffly into their coach and drove to the Navigation Inn.

It was a white-washed public house that stood on the tow-path of the canal. From the windows of the snug patrons could see the lock gates and the keeper's cottage with its tangle of rambler roses. Sometimes there was the sight of a narrow boat and its buttie laden with peat.

Eric Black bought a jug of beer and the team filled up their pint pots and drank greedily.

"You played a blinder, Rudyard," said Eric Black. "But if I was you, lad, I'd wear me arch supports next time."

The team put five shillings each into the kitty and sent Sid Skelhorn for another jug of beer.

Ernie Cosgrove lay back on a bench and held a blood-stained handkerchief tenderly to his swollen nose.

Bernard Garside, Stewart Woodhead, Terry Dunphy and the team captain, Maurice Buckle, took out the dominoes and began to play fives and threes.

Louis St John sat on a high stool and ogled the barmaid.

She had a sharp nose.

Carter Brandon squirmed in his seat as he tried to find a comfortable position. Every bone in his body ached. He was covered in cuts and bruises. He found it difficult to clench his fists.

Tommy Rowley looked at him from above the rim of his pint pot.

"You look knackered, kid," he said.

"I am," said Carter Brandon. "I only had an hour's kip last night."

"Scratching, was she?"

"No. Twitching."

"What sort of twitching? Non-stop, intermittent or now and then?"

Carter Brandon scratched his chin thoughtfully.

"Intermittent mostly," he said. "Now and then sometimes and non-stop never."

Tommy Rowley laughed. It was a sad laugh.

"You've only just started, kid. That's only the tip of the iceberg," he said. "You've got the cramps to contend with yet. You'll just be nodding off one night, when she'll let out a scream, dig you in the guts and say: 'Tommy, Tommy, I've got a cramp in me toe'."

"What do you do then?"

"Pretend I'm asleep like what I always do," said Tommy Rowley. "Bloody hell, Carter, never crack on you're awake or she'll start yattering about wallpaper patterns or the cheap tumblers she's just seen in bloody Woolworth's."

"Give over, will you?" said Sid Skelhorn. "What a topic of conversation—women and nippers. This is supposed to be a happy occasion."

Eric Black came up and re-filled Carter Brandon's pint pot from the jug.

"By God, it's grand to get a bit of good healthy exercise, isn't it, Carter?" he said as he watched the beer foam and fizz in the glass.

"Mm," said Carter Brandon, wincing with pain as Eric Black slapped him on his bitten shoulder blade.

"Do you know what?" said Eric Black. "The pundits reckon that five minutes on the nest wi' a woman takes more out of you than a full ninety minutes toil on the football field."

"Mm," said Carter Brandon.

"I reckon football's more exciting, though," said Eric Black. "There's more tactics to it."

They woke Tommy Rowley at half past seven and left at eight. There was mist over the canal. Frost glinted on the slates of the lock-keeper's cottage.

When Carter Brandon limped into the lounge/diner, stiff and bloodied, Pat let out a cry of horror.

"Carter!" she cried. "What on earth have you done to your new blazer?"

"I ripped it getting out of the chara."

"Right. That's it then—no more football for you."

"Pardon?" said Carter Brandon easing himself gingerly into one of the low-slung imitation leather arm chairs.

"I've been worried sick about you all afternoon. I've listened to every news bulletin on the wireless in case you was involved in a tragedy. I've never left the phone for fear they'd ring up to tell me you'd collapsed with a heart attack. Just think, Carter, if an aeroplane had crashed on the pitch you was playing on, you wouldn't have stood a chance. You'd have been burnt to a cinder."

"Mm," said Carter Brandon. "What's for supper?"

Pat came up behind him and began to rub the back of his neck.

"It's baby I'm thinking of, Carter," she said. "I don't want to go to the Parent-Teachers' Association socials and have no one to dance with because me husband's in an iron lung. I mean, I know the head master would ask me in all the slow fox trots, but that could count against baby in grammar school if they thought his mother was having favours shown her even though he is a terrible dancer and can't reverse for toffee."

"All right, all right," said Carter Brandon.

"Please, Carter. Pack it in, love. For my sake, love. For baby's sake. For the sake of your blazer," said Pat.

All through the night she tossed and turned.

She grunted and groaned, too, and scratched herself furiously. Carter Brandon lay next to her, rigid and taut. He craved sleep, but every fibre in his body fought it, and his mind raced and spun and skidded from image to image.

He punched the pillow hard and then dragged himself upright.

Muscles were twitching in his left arm. His eyes stung with fatigue. A dull metallic pain throbbed deep inside his chest.

"All right," he bellowed. "I'll pack up the bloody football, if that's what you want. Just let me get some bloody sleep. Please. Please. Please."

Pat turned to him.

"Stop screaming down my ear," she snapped. "You've woken me up with your screaming. Don't be so selfish."

Chapter Seven

On the following day Pat developed a craving for silver cocktail onions.

"I just can't get enough of them," she told her mother.

"Well, try not to eat too many, love, or baby'll be born with terrible bad breath," said Mrs Partington.

It was eleven o'clock in the morning.

A watery sun pattered at the french windows of the lounge/diner. It glinted on the unpainted mainmast of the heavy cruiser, *Prinz Eugen*. It cast tiny arthritic shadows over the flight deck of HMS *Ark Royal*.

Pat's knitting needles click-clacked. She was knitting a matinée jacket.

Mrs Partington stretched out her hand and placed it on her daughter's stomach.

"Eee, aren't you slim?" she said. "If you go on at this rate, you'll not be needing no maternity dresses at all."

"Oh yes I shall," said Pat sharply. "I want everyone to know I'm pregnant. I'm proud of it."

Mrs Partington nodded doubtfully.

"In my day it wasn't considered proper for women to flaunt their condition," she said. "It was only the Irish what had got big tummies. The rest of us stopped indoors and tried to look decent."

Pat stood up with a flicker of a smile on her face.

"I thought you told me you kept your figure right up to the bitter end," she said.

"Oh, I did, love, I did," said Mrs Partington. "They couldn't stop talking about me in the gas showrooms."

Pat allowed herself a chill little smile.

The watery sun persisted.
It heralded the start of a spell of mild weather.
The sun beat down. The skies were cloudless.

Roses bloomed fiercely, thrusting back winter; taunting it.

The moors shimmered on great waves of pink and purple heather. Pipits sang.

In the gardens of the sandstone mansions on Mosscroft Edge the maples blazed scarlet and gold and the fuchsias spread lazy carmine shadows over sun-bleached walls.

Mr Brandon leaned on his fork and pointed round the park.

"And look at the riot of colour here," he said. "Sweet bugger all."

"Aye," said Uncle Mort. "The only splash of colour here comes from the bus tickets in the rubbish baskets."

They were on the bowling greens in the park where Mr Brandon worked.

Mr Brandon was spiking the turf.

The parkscape was bleak. The horse chestnuts had already lost their leaves and the blighted roses stood gnarled and naked in rigid ranks.

"Bloody George Furnival," said Mr Brandon. "He hasn't got a clue."

"Aye," said Uncle Mort. "His park's just like his wife — too much of it and bloody ugly as well."

"If I could get me hands on this lot, I'd have it looking like the Garden of bloody Eden," said Mr Brandon, spitting on his hands and resuming his work.

Uncle Mort watched him silently for a moment.

"Apply for the job then," he said.

Mr Brandon spat on his hands again.

"I might just do that," he said. "Aye, I might."

He worked hard for an hour. His movements were fluent and smooth. He had rhythm and balance. He had grace. He whistled as he worked.

Half an hour later as they sat in the greenkeeper's hut drinking tea and eating corned beef sandwiches Uncle Mort said:

"You'll be looking forward to your honeymoon then, eh?"

"I'm not mithered," said Mr Brandon.

Uncle Mort looked at him closely as he flicked through the pages of a gardening manual with a happy smile on his face. Then he said:

"I think all this consorting with Mother Nature is having a bad effect on you, Les."

"How do you mean?" said Mr Brandon blowing hard on the tea in the lid of his billy.

"Well, you spend so much of your time planting grass seed you've no more interest left in planting your own seed."

"I were never much interested in that at the best of times," said Mr Brandon taking a sip of his tea.

"True," said Uncle Mort.

"I always thought kissing were daft."

"True."

"And holding hands."

"True."

"I'd rather bath an Airedale any day of the week."

"Pardon?" said Uncle Mort.

At that moment there was a knock at the door. Olive Furnival was standing there. She was wearing knee-length boots and a faded mustard-yellow turban with purple velvet rosettes on the crown.

She smiled.

"Pardon me, Mr Brandon," she said. "But have you seen George? I've brought him his dinner, you see."

She held out a blue and white bowl covered with muslin. It steamed.

"Steak and kidney pudding with Bisto," she said. "His favourite."

Mr Brandon wrinkled his nose appreciatively and nodded.

"Have you tried the greenhouse, Mrs Furnival?" he said. "He told me he was hardening off his pansies."

"Thank you very much, Mr Brandon," said Olive Furnival. She paused at the door, looked back at Uncle Mort and said: "It's a grand day, isn't it?"

"I've seen better," said Uncle Mort.

She smiled and left the hut.

"She'll not find him in the greenhouse," said Mr Brandon. "Skiving bugger's slipped off for a game of snooker at the Old Comrades."

Uncle Mort snatched the last of the corned beef sandwiches and took a swift bite from it before Mr Brandon noticed the loss.

"By God, though, Les, she's bloody ugly," he said. "They should make her take out a licence to keep a face like that."

Mr Brandon nodded and continued his perusal of the manual.

Suddenly he snapped the book shut and stood up.

"By God," he said. "I'm going to do it."

"Tonight? With Annie?" said Uncle Mort.

"Not that, pillock," said Mr Brandon. "I'm going to apply for Furnival's job. Aye. Why not? I'm as good as him. I'm better. I'm a damn sight better. I'd make a smashing head gardener. I'd be a bobby dazzler if I set me mind to it. Aye. I would. Aye. I'll apply right away."

He glanced at Uncle Mort shyly out of the tops of his eyes. Uncle Mort nodded contentedly.

"Aye," said Mr Brandon gruffly. "Don't tell Annie, though. Wait while they turn me down before you break the news."

The fine weather continued.

Mr Brandon worked hard on his allotment.

He finished lifting his potatoes and carrots. He sowed his winter peas and protected them with bracken. He took cuttings from his black currants and gooseberries, and he pruned back his blackberries.

Meanwhile in the house Mrs Brandon worked hard on the arrangements for the Silver Wedding.

She had received replies from Gertie Foreshaw and Cousin Marion from Burslem intimating that they would be delighted to act as bridesmaids.

She had received a reply from the Old Folks' Home assuring her that Mr Brandon's eldest brother, Uncle Stavely, would be dispatched in good time to attend the celebrations and reminding her that the authorities could accept no responsibility for old folk damaged in transit.

"Eee, Les," she said one evening as they sat in the back parlour. "Are you looking forward to your honeymoon?"

"It'll make a break I suppose," said Mr Brandon.

"Course it will, love," said Mrs Brandon. "It'll blow the cobwebs off you. It'll bring the roses back to your cheeks."

She got up from her chair and settled herself on the sofa next to her husband.

"I'll buy a special nightie, Les," she said and slowly she began to edge along the seat towards him. "I'll buy one you can see through. I'll get it transparent, too."

"Mm," said Mr Brandon from the depths of his gardening catalogue. "Wisteria sinensis—by God, you can almost hear it whispering up the walls, can't you?"

Mrs Brandon squirmed closer to him.

"We'll have long lay-ins of a morning, Les," she said softly. "We'll lock the door so we won't be disturbed. We'll bung up the keyhole with blotting paper."

"Mm," said Mr Brandon. "Mexican passion flower—I don't like the sound of that."

"Oooh, I do, Les. I do," said Mrs Brandon, and she flung her arms around him and smothered him with kisses.

"Give over, woman," said Mr Brandon, pushing her away roughly. "You can spread germs kissing at this time of year."

Pat, too, was making arrangements.

"Now what about decorations, Carter?" she said one evening. "Have you had any bright thoughts regarding the decor of the nursery?"

"What nursery?" said Carter Brandon, biting his lip with concentration as he fixed the aircraft catapult behind the funnel of the heavy cruiser, *Prinz Eugen*.

"The nursery for baby," said Pat.

"What baby?" said Carter Brandon, holding the tweezers vice-hard between his fingers.

"Our baby," shouted Pat. "Our baby."

Carter Brandon sighed deeply. He pushed his model to one side and shrugged his shoulders.

"Go on then," he said.

"Well, I was looking in Lawson Ridley's, the Economical Paint Stores, this morning and they'd got a lovely selection of nursery wallpaper," said Pat. "Who would you prefer—Micky Mouse or Goofy?"

"Pardon?"

"They're on the nursery wallpaper."

"Oh," said Carter Brandon. "Hadn't they got Pluto?"

"I didn't see it, love," said Pat. "Would you like me to ask?"

"I couldn't care less," said Carter Brandon.

"Well, you should care," said Pat. "Joyce Rowley lent me a book what said nursery decor can affect a baby's character for the rest of its life."

"I see," said Carter Brandon.

"As a matter of interest, Carter, what did you have on your walls when you was a little boy?"

"Damp patches," said Carter Brandon.

"Now what about the reception, Les?" said Mrs Brandon to her husband that same evening.

"What reception?" said Mr Brandon who was reading a nurseryman's prospectus.

"Our reception," said Mrs Brandon. "We can either have it at the Congregational Assembly rooms with only soft drinks allowed or we can have it at the TA Drill Hall with no stiletto heels."

"Mm," said Mr Brandon. "What about the upstairs room at The Whippet?"

"What a good idea, Les," said Mrs Brandon. "I'm glad you're taking an interest."

She stacked up the supper things on the tray and took them into the kitchen.

Mr Brandon looked at the pictures of the roses in the prospectus and a smile came to his face.

"Just think of them bloody gardens in Persia," he said. "Masses and masses of damask roses. Bank after bank of them. By God, that's the place to go if you want to give your conk a treat."

Midnight struck.

Carter Brandon was falling asleep.

His whole body was relaxed. There was a warm glow on his skin. A voice deep inside him crooned at him to tell him he would get a good night's sleep. It would be the first for three weeks.

He let out a soft moan of pleasure.

Suddenly Pat prodded him in the ribs with her elbow.

"Carter?" she said.

"What's up? What's up?" said Carter Brandon jumping up in a panic.

"I was just thinking, love—don't you think Clara Cluck would be more suitable than Pluto the Dog?"

Carter Brandon let out a groan.

It was a long groan.

He did not sleep that night.

Chapter Eight

It was Sunday morning.

The shipping forecast was good. The weather was fair in Viking and Cromarty.

Carter Brandon, his wife, Pat, and his mother-in-law, Mrs Partington, were to visit Mr Shirtcliffe for Sunday tea.

The weather was fair in that area, too.

"It must be an omen," said Carter Brandon to his wife as they lay side by side in the rumpled Sunday bed.

"What for?" said Pat.

"For the many sunshine hours what will follow your first meeting with Mr Shirtcliffe."

"Are you trying to take the mickey?" said Pat, popping another silver cocktail onion into her mouth.

Carter Brandon screwed up his nose.

"Bloody hell—pickled onions in bed," he said. "That's the best form of birth control known to man. What a passion killer."

He went into the shower. The hot water made his flesh turn pink.

He began to sing.

He was still singing loudly when the curtains were ripped aside to reveal Pat. She was naked.

She stepped into the shower.

She put her arms round his waist and the water streamed down her back in torrents and swirled in tumbling eddies down the smooth skin of her buttocks.

Carter Brandon put his hands round the back of her thighs and pulled her up to him.

She gripped him fiercely.

After a moment she let out a long shuddering sob.

Later in the morning Mrs Partington came round to lunch.

She was wearing a tangerine and green silk dress. She had three strings of pearls round her neck. Over her shoulder was a

4   49

fox-fur cape. When she coughed, flakes of pink powder fluttered off her rouged cheeks.

"You've gone glamorous all of a sudden," said Pat with a sniff.

"It's for Mr Shirtcliffe," said Mrs Partington. "He always insists on me looking the bees knees."

They had lamb chops, boiled potatoes and garden peas followed by apple charlotte and cream, followed by Derbyshire cheese and coffee.

Then Pat went upstairs to prepare for the visit to Mr Shirtcliffe.

When she had finished combing and brushing her hair and applying make-up to her face, she stood up and looked at herself in the mirror.

She was wearing a slip.

She ran her hands over her breasts and over her stomach. There was scarcely a hint of a swelling. She smiled.

Carefully she unwrapped the dress she had bought on Saturday afternoon at Poppy's Fashions in Wakefield Road. She put it on.

It was nigger brown with pink and orange spots on the bodice.

She went downstairs, opened the door of the lounge/diner and twirled round and round.

"Well, Carter? How do I look?" she said.

"Fat," said Carter Brandon.

"You what?"

"Fat," said Carter Brandon. "That dress makes you look fat."

"It's a maternity dress," snapped Pat. "It's supposed to make you look fat. That's the whole point of maternity."

"But you're not fat," said Carter Brandon. "You're still slim. You were as slim as owt in the shower this morning."

"I beg your pardon?" said Mrs Partington raising her eyebrows.

Carter Brandon winked at Pat and went into the kitchen to clean his shoes.

Mrs Partington stared hard at Pat.

"You don't go in the shower together, do you?" she said.

"Sometimes," said Pat.

"In the nude? In your birthday suits?"

"Yes."

"Good gracious me," said Mrs Partington, and she put her hand to her bosom and sank back into the low-slung imitation leather sofa.

Pat took a mirror from her handbag and began to tidy her hair.

"We do happen to be married, mother," she said. "Everything's quite legal, you know."

"I'm aware of that," said Mrs Partington. "But that's no excuse for looking at each other's nakedness. It's very rude to do things like that. I hope Carter puts a face cloth over his little Tommy Tinkler when you look at him."

"I don't look at him, mother," said Pat crossly.

"Well, what on earth do you do then?" said Mrs Partington. "What's the point going round naked if you're not going to look at each other? I would."

At half past three they set off for Mr Shirtcliffe's.

The sun glowed. It made the autumn sky pink.

Birds chattered. And some sang. And spring echoed in their voices.

"You really appreciate a car at a time like this," said Mrs Partington as they passed a straggling bus queue outside the park at Wilson's Bar. The people looked sad.

"I'd like to stop and give every one of them a lift," said Carter Brandon.

"Charming," said Pat. "That'd do our loose covers a world of good, wouldn't it?"

"And you'd do away with the whole point of having a car — exclusiveness," said Mrs Partington. "You can keep your privacy in a car. Say what you like, but when you're in your own car, you never get Irishmen spitting on the floor and swearing."

"I hate cars," said Carter Brandon. "I loathe them."

Mr Shirtcliffe lived in a street of three-storey stone terraced houses. They were Victorian. They had long narrow front gardens and sandstone lintels to the windows.

In Mr Shirtcliffe's garden there was a cotoneaster with waxy red berries and a laurel with unhealthy spots on its leaves.

Mrs Partington smiled nervously at Pat as they walked up the brick-paved front path.

She rang the door bell.

She had scarcely time to remove her hand before the door was opened. Mr Shirtcliffe stood there.

He was a very small man. He was much smaller than Pat.

"Come on in," he said. "You're not being a nuisance."

He ushered them inside.

"Anyone want to go to the toilet?" he said.

No one spoke.

"What about a glass of tonic wine?" he said.

No one spoke.

"My word, you're soon pleased," he said.

The hall smelled of beeswax. It was an overpowering smell. Every item of furniture glowed with polish.

The glassware on the spindly mahogany table sparkled. So did the brass pendulums on the grandfather and grandmother clocks.

There was a dazzling sheen on the lino.

A door opened at the end of the corridor and a young man appeared. He had a dazzling sheen on his pomaded hair.

"This is my son," said Mr Shirtcliffe rubbing his hands nervously.

The young man grunted and took a navy-blue donkey jacket off the hall stand and draped it over his shoulders.

Carter Brandon coughed and hunched his shoulders.

"You played a belter yesterday, Artie," he said.

"Aye. That's right," said Artie Shirtcliffe, and he turned to his father and said: "Lend us a quid while Thursday."

"I will, Artie," said Carter Brandon before Mr Shirtcliffe could answer.

He took out a one pound note from his hip pocket and handed it to Artie Shirtcliffe.

Pat scowled.

"Ta, you're a pal," said Artie Shirtcliffe. Then he patted Carter Brandon on the shoulder and said: "You can come out with me one night if you like."

"Ta," said Carter Brandon. "Ta very much, Artie."

As soon as Artie Shirtcliffe left the house his father's nervousness disappeared.

He turned to Pat and said:

"So this is Pat, is it? She's a credit to you, Mrs Partington. Isn't she well turned out? What toothpaste do you use, Pat— Colgate or Pepsodent?"

"Gibbs SR," said Pat stonily.

Mr Shirtcliffe nodded gravely and then showed his guests into the front parlour.

"Make yourselves at home," he said. "It won't make much work for me tidying up once you've gone."

The front parlour was heavily furnished. There were deep-jowelled arm chairs and a row of gloomy potted plants on top of a black upright piano.

"Sit down, sit down," said Mr Shirtcliffe. "I'll just pop into the kitchen to make a cup of tea. You're not imposing—I'd have made one meself regardless."

When he left the room, Mrs Partington turned to Pat and said: "Well, love, what do you think? Isn't he a gem? Haven't I made a catch?"

Pat looked round the room coldly before answering her mother.

"He's very small," she said. "Did he come out of a circus?"

"No, love. He works in the snuff warehouse," said Mrs Partington.

"You could have fooled me," said Pat. "He's well on the way to being a midget, if you ask me."

"Yes, but look how dainty he is," said Mrs Partington. "Look how perfect his little hands are. Look at the lovely half moons he's got on his little fingernails. He's just like a Dinky toy. He's exactly to scale."

From upstairs a baby began to cry. It was a steady howl.

Pat looked at Mrs Partington and raised her eyebrows. Mrs Partington coughed.

Just then Mr Shirtcliffe brought in the tea. He smiled.

"I do all my own baking," he said. "Have a rock bun."

At five o'clock they went into the back parlour for high tea.

The table was laden with food. There were four varieties of cold meat and nine sorts of pickle.

"Tuck in everyone," said Mr Shirtcliffe. "Don't be shy. I'd have had to make tea even if I was on me own."

All through the meal they could hear the child sobbing upstairs. Sometimes it was an aggressive noise. Sometimes it was a whimper full of woe.

At length Pat said:

"Is that your daughter's child I can hear crying all the time?"

"Yes," said Mr Shirtcliffe. "Isn't it a nuisance?"

Pat stared at him intently, and he shifted uncomfortably in his seat.

"So your daughter's not at home, I gather?" she said.

Mr Shirtcliffe glanced anxiously at Mrs Partington.

"Yes, yes, yes, she's at home," he said. "She'll be around the house somewhere. Now who's for apricots and who's for crushed pineapple?"

After tea Mrs Partington insisted that she and Mr Shirtcliffe do the washing up. Her host concurred readily and led Carter Brandon and Pat to the front parlour.

"Don't get too settled because you'll not be stopping long, will you?" he said.

Pat and Carter Brandon went into the front parlour.

A young woman was sitting on the floor with her back to them.

She had long silky golden hair which stretched down to her waist.

She turned with a start.

She had an oval face and pale green eyes with tawny flecks.

It was the most beautiful face Carter Brandon had ever seen.

"Oh," said Pat. "Oh. You must be Mr Shirtcliffe's daughter. Well, I'm Mrs Partington's daughter. My name's Mrs Brandon. Is that your child what's been crying for the last two hours?"

The girl did not speak.

She hardly blinked.

She rose to her feet and padded out of the room silently in bare feet.

She had the most beautiful body Carter Brandon had ever seen.

"Well!" said Pat. "Well! What do you think to that?"

They left the house at eight o'clock.

"Come again some time," said Mr Shirtcliffe. "You've hardly been any trouble."

The baby was still sobbing as they walked down the brick-paved front path to the car.

Carter Brandon turned and glanced up at the front bedroom window.

He thought he saw a flash of golden hair.

But he could not be sure.

Chapter Nine

"What did I tell you?" said Mr Brandon hurling his gauntlets onto the floor of the kitchen. "What did I bloody tell you?"

Mrs Brandon looked up from the pan of cow heel stew simmering slowly on top of the cooker. She was stirring in a handful of pearl barley.

"I don't know," she said. "What did you tell me, Bompa?"

"Don't call me Bompa, woman," shouted Mr Brandon.

Mrs Brandon watched the barley disappearing into the thick, glutinous body of the stew. The surface plopped and gurgled. The aroma of cow heel, leeks, turnips and carrots filled every nook and cranny of the room.

"What are you talking about, Les?" she said, and round and round went her wooden spoon in the stew.

Mr Brandon stood in the middle of the room·clenching and unclenching his fists. His face was red. Muscles were twitching in his neck.

Uncle Mort watched him silently.

Suddenly his shoulders drooped. The hard line of his jaw softened, and ponderously he lowered himself into the rocking chair.

"I applied for George Furnival's job," he said. "I went for the interview today. They turned me down."

"Today?" said Mrs Brandon spinning round from the cooker.

"Aye," said Mr Brandon. "I had to go to the Town Hall."

"Why didn't you tell me for heaven's sake?" said Mrs Brandon wagging the wooden spoon at him. "Was you wearing clean underpants? Did you change your socks? You never went in your working clothes, did you?"

"Aye."

"Good Lord, Les, no wonder they didn't give you the job. Fancy applying for a job as gardener wearing gardening boots," said Mrs Brandon.

"Leave him be, Annie," said Uncle Mort. "Give him some peace."

He glowered at his sister, who flicked her shoulders, turned back to the cooker and rattled the wooden spoon angrily against the rim of the pan.

He walked across to the rocking chair and rested his hand on Mr Brandon's arm.

"What happened, Les?" he said.

Mr Brandon shook his head slowly. He struggled for words. At length he spoke.

"Well, there was this committee, you see," he said. "And they asked me what my plans was for the park. And I said Very Simple. And they said What. And I said to make it Beautiful. And they said How. And I said By Various Methods. And they said What Methods. And I said As Per Follows—a walled garden would be the centre piece, I said. And in that walled garden I'd plant masses of lavender and honeysuckle and jasmine and rosemary and thyme to make it pong nice. And there'd be buddleia to attract the butterflies in summer and wild thistles to attract the goldfinches in the autumn. It wouldn't be all formal and rigid. It'd be a jumble of things so you'd always get surprises. And I wouldn't plant these gaudy, cocky modern roses. I'd plant the old-fashioned ones for their fragrance and their modesty. Damask, Musk, Moss, Bourbon and Rosa Alba—that's what I'd plant. And I'd have pergolas running riot with clematis and wisteria, and there'd be firethorn and climbing hydrangea covering the walls, and there'd be benches where the old codgers could have a good yarn and a good spit, and there'd be a patch of grass what I'd never cut and the kids could play there and pick aconites in the winter and bluebells and primroses in the spring, and I'd scatter the seeds all higgledy piggledy in the flower beds and came June there'd be an explosion of lupins and hollyhocks and sunflower and phlox that would make your eyes want to dance out of their sockets."

He paused for breath.

Uncle Mort coughed.

"And what did they say to that, Les?" he said quietly.

"They asked me what paint I'd use to stop the pins on the putting green from rusting."

When Carter Brandon arrived home from work that evening, he found his wife had a guest.

She was Joyce Rowley, the spouse of Tommy, and she was

lying on her back with Pat on the lounge/diner carpet. They had their arms flat by their sides and their legs wide apart.

"What the hell are you up to?" said Carter Brandon.

"We're relaxing," said Pat. "It's our relaxation exercises."

"Mm," said Carter Brandon. "What's for tea?"

"It's not made yet," said Pat. "I've been relaxing."

"He should be getting his own tea be rights," said Joyce Rowley. "I make Tommy. I don't let him get away with owt when I'm carrying."

Pat raised her legs in the air and breathed in and out deeply and slowly.

"Once I get the hang of these exercises, Carter, you need never have no fear for me when D-Day comes along," she said.

"D-Day?" said Carter Brandon, picking up the evening paper and turning to the sports page.

"The day we're longing for with all our hearts," said Pat. "The day when I'll be radiant. The day when the little body is gently eased out of the womb and at this joyous and overwhelming moment all the effort is completely forgotten and I shall have thoughts only for this tiny little fellow who belongs to me and my husband — the most beautiful baby in the world."

"Pardon?" said Carter Brandon.

"I learned that by heart from the book," said Pat, blushing slightly. "Isn't it a smashing bit of writing? It's almost like literature."

"What book are you talking about?" said Carter Brandon, and at once Pat handed him a glossy paper-backed book.

On the front cover was a picture of a young pregnant woman with dreamy eyes, a large stomach and a prominent wedding ring.

It was entitled:

"*Voyage Into Happiness* — Part one — The Little Mite Arrives."

"It's a smashing read, Carter," said Pat. "It's got some smashing pictures of illustrations."

"You want to make him read it from cover to cover and then he'll have no excuse for doing nowt when baby comes," said Joyce Rowley.

"Good idea, Joyce," said Pat. "Isn't she full of helpful suggestions, Carter?"

"Aye. She is that," said Carter Brandon, and he went into the kitchen to make some tea.

He had just unrolled the lid off a tin of sardines, when the serving hatch shot open and Pat threw in the book.

"Joyce has made another helpful suggestion, Carter," she said. "She says why don't you read the book while you're having your tea, paying particular attention to the chapter on Happy Fatherhood?"

She shut the hatch and Carter Brandon picked up the book and idly began to thumb through its glossy pages.

His eyes alighted on a poem entitled "Precious Fulfilment". by Winifred J. Thornthwaite.

He began to read it.

> Baby dear, asleep in your cot
> Is there anything I have forgot?
> Nappies?—well, yes, we've plenty of those,
> And cotton wool swabs for your dear little nose.
> And as for the bottles they're lovely and clean,
> Cos we know how important is domestic hygiene.
> Your new plastic dribbler is . . .

Carter Brandon groaned and swept the book off the table. It skidded across the floor and came to rest under the spin drier.

"Sweet God," he said, and he rammed four sardines into his mouth and slunk out of the house.

An hour later he met his father and Uncle Mort in the billiard room of the Liberal Club in Strachey Gardens.

They were sitting in a haze of cigarette smoke and green chalk.

Billiard balls clicked. Pint glasses clinked. There were four green gashes in the gloom where the fierce overhead lights shone on the tables.

Carter Brandon climbed onto the raised bench at the side of the room and nodded to his father and uncle.

They nodded back.

They spoke in a low murmur.

Mr Brandon told his son of his lack of success in the interview that afternoon. Carter Brandon told his father of the relaxation exercises and Winifred J. Thornthwaite.

Mr Brandon told his son of the latest developments regarding the arrangements for the Silver Wedding, paying particular attention to the altercation over Gertie Foreshaw's bust measurements in respect of the broderie anglais dress she was to wear as principal bridesmaid. Carter Brandon told his father of the high tea with Mr Shirtcliffe and of his encounter with Artie.

Uncle Mort told his brother-in-law and his nephew about the newly-installed tea machine at the foot hospital.

Mr Brandon nodded sagely and tapped his pipe against his bottom teeth.

Uncle Mort rubbed the stubble on his chin thoughtfully.

"It's a boring old life, isn't it?" he said.

"It is that," said Mr Brandon. "Thank God."

They took their drinks into the lounge bar with its portraits of William Ewart Gladstone, Clement Davies, David Lloyd George, and Councillor Cecil Makepeace, donator of the cycle shed annexe.

They drank three pints of best Oughthwaite's bitter each, and then George Furnival and his wife, Olive, came in.

George Furnival glanced across at Mr Brandon and smirked.

Uncle Mort scowled at him and stared at him savagely as he bought drinks and brought them across to his wife.

"You're not going to give up about the job, are you, Les?" he said. "You're not going to take it lying down, are you?"

Mr Brandon blew out a long stream of tobacco smoke through his nostrils and said:

"What else can I do? Furnival's put his oar in, so I've no bloody chance, have I?"

Uncle Mort looked across at Olive Furnival.

She smiled at him.

He smiled at her.

"Do you know, Les," he said. "She's not as ugly as all that, is she?"

"I suppose not," said Mr Brandon. "Nobody could be as ugly as that."

Chapter Ten

October progressed.

It always did.

Mr Brandon planted his bulbs.

He planted winter aconites, snowdrops, scilla muscari and three varieties of crocus.

Pat lost her craving for silver cocktail onions. It was replaced by a craving for Cadbury's chocolate buttons and bottles of Vimto.

She entered another competition. It was sponsored by Unsworth's pies. The first prize was a weekend in Skegness and a year's free supplies of cornish pasties.

She gave Carter Brandon the entry form to put in the post. He steamed open the envelope and read the slogan she had written on the bottom.

It said:

"Large or tall, big or small

"With Unsworth's pies you'll have a ball."

Carter Brandon crossed it out neatly with red ballpoint pen and in its place wrote in capital letters:

"Unsworth's pies give you the shits."

He posted the envelope with a deep smile.

It was a day of sneaky squalls and damp starter motors, and in the evening he took Pat to the Trocadero Grill for supper.

"Give over yawning," said Pat as they handed in their coats at the cloakroom.

"I can't help it," said Carter Brandon. "You kept me awake all night with your bloody scratching."

The Trocadero Grill was Edwardian.

It had red plush benches and gas mantles. A string trio in dinner jackets and grey woollen socks was playing selections from "The Land of Smiles".

"I like this place," said Carter Brandon. "I hope they don't start hacking it around."

"I do," said Pat. "It's right old-fashioned. I like to be bang up-to-date. That's the whole point in being the modern generation."

They were shown to a table in the far corner. It was almost hidden by a large fern in a bulbous terracotta pot.

Pat displayed her pregnant figure proudly as she followed the waiter.

Carter Brandon hunched his shoulders, coughed and slouched four paces behind them.

"You should get a kick out of people seeing me pregnant," said Pat as they settled themselves at their table. "It means everyone knows you know how to do it proper."

Pat ordered grilled pork chops, garden peas and creamed potatoes.

Carter Brandon ordered entrecote steak with mushrooms, celery hearts, tomatoes, fried onions and a treble portion of chips.

He spread mustard thickly on the meat. He plunged his knife into the flesh, and the blood ran. It was a juicy steak.

He munched it contentedly.

Pat hardly ate a thing. She just nibbled and kept her eyes on her husband.

"What's up with you, Carter?" she said after a while. "Aren't you happy?"

"Course I am," said Carter Brandon. "It's a bloody good lump of steak, is this."

"I'm not talking about your steak. I'm talking about your attitude to life," said Pat. "I mean, you don't seem to be the least bit excited about baby."

"I am. I can't sleep at nights through thinking about it," said Carter Brandon. "Do you want them peas?"

"You never show any interest in it."

"I do," said Carter Brandon. "Have you finished with them spuds?"

"What about names? You've never so much as mentioned names. I mean, do we want to call him after a film star or shall we wait while he's born and see who's in the news on the day?"

"I couldn't care less," said Carter Brandon. "You can call it what you like."

"See what I mean?" said Pat. "No interest whatsoever."

Carter Brandon cut a large welt of sappy fat from the steak. He chopped it into small squares. He dipped them one by one in the rich juice of blood, butter and mustard and popped them into his mouth.

He chomped on happily.

When he finished, he belched softly into the starched depths of his napkin. He leaned back in his chair, called to the waiter and ordered another pint of bitter beer in a pewter tankard.

Pat watched him attentively all the time.

"You're always miles away these days," she said. "You seem to be walking round in a dream. I just can't get through to you. You don't want to know reality. We could have had a red telephone last month, if only you'd have come down from the clouds and made a decision."

Carter Brandon pursed his lips round the foaming beer in the cold tankard. He closed his eyes and sucked. The beer was cool. It was sharp. It was best Barnsley Bitter.

"You spend all your time wrapped up in silence," said Pat. "I like silence."

"I don't. It's too quiet," said Pat. "I like to be spoken to. Why don't you speak to me?"

"I did when we come in. I said I'd forgotten to change me socks."

Pat wiped her mouth rapidly on her napkin.

Then she snatched up the menu and scanned it angrily. Pancakes with strawberry jam were two and six each.

"Just look at the price of these pancakes, Carter," she said. "Isn't it scandalous?"

"Pardon?"

"You see. You don't even take an interest in the cost of living," said Pat. "I bet you haven't a clue how much you have to pay for sprouts this week."

They had apple pie and clotted cream for dessert. Carter Brandon followed it with Leicester cheese, radishes and sweet pickle.

"Do you fancy a brandy to wash it all down?" said Carter Brandon.

"Not in my condition," said Pat briskly.

They moved out from the dining room and into the lounge bar, where Carter Brandon bought a Babycham for Pat and a pint of bitter for himself.

Pat sipped rapidly at the drink and shifted around on her seat impatiently.

She was wearing a maroon and green striped maternity dress. It was made of nylon, and static electricity crackled every time she moved.

They drank silently.

After ten minutes Artie Shirtcliffe came into the bar. He had a plump girl on his arm. She had dimples on her knees.

He caught sight of Carter Brandon and winked at him broadly. His companion hauled herself onto a high stool, and her breasts wobbled.

Next to Carter Brandon there was a crackle of electricity.

"Go on then," said Pat. "I'm waiting."

"What for?" said Carter Brandon.

"I'm waiting for you to say something to me."

Carter Brandon thought hard for a moment. He scratched his chin. He tugged at the lobe of his left ear. Then he said:

"Hasn't that bird with Artie Shirtcliffe got a gynormous pair of knockers?"

Pat puckered her lips angrily. But then she giggled and leaned across and whispered into Carter Brandon's ear:

"My bosom will get big, too, Carter. It's forced to. As the weeks go by it'll get bigger and bigger. It'll become an object of passion. It'll swell and tremble when you fondle it. I'll have to buy a special maternity bra. One pound two and six in Edmundson's, the draper's. Isn't it an outrageous price, Carter? Don't it make you think?"

"Aye," said Carter Brandon, and he downed his pint in a gulp and went to the bar to order another.

"How are you diddling, professor?" said Artie Shirtcliffe.

"Not bad, ta, Artie," said Carter Brandon. "You played a blinder on Saturday."

"That's right," said Artie Shirtcliffe. "Lend us a quid, will you?"

"Certainly, Artie," said Carter Brandon. "You can have two if you want."

"You're a bramah, old ducks," said Artie Shirtcliffe taking the two one pound notes and stuffing them into the breast pocket of his jacket. "Remind me to take you out with me one night."

When Carter Brandon returned to the table with the drinks, Pat said:

"Was you looking down the front of that girl's frock, Carter?"

"No," said Carter Brandon. "Honest. It never occurred to me."

Pat snuggled into him.

"Good," she said. "I'll let you look down the front of mine tonight when I take it off."

"Ta very much," said Carter Brandon and in the mirror behind the bar he saw Artie Shirtcliffe's companion lean forward and expose two crescent-shaped slivers of nipple.

He coughed and gulped.

"How much did you say sprouts cost?" he said.

"Sixpence a pound," said Pat. "Isn't it outrageous?"

On the Saturday morning before the match Carter Brandon went round to the bowling greens to collect his father.

He found him in the greenkeeper's shed drinking a mug of tea and reading a nurseryman's catalogue.

Mr Brandon welcomed him cheerfully and gave him a mug of tea. It was sweet and strong.

"You can't beat these things for reading matter," said Mr Brandon tapping the catalogue with the stem of his pipe. "I've only got to start reading one of these and, bugger me, in an instant I'm transported into realms what are bloody light years away from the life of drudgery I lead now."

"Mm," said Carter Brandon. "Mm."

"I keep getting this dream. A bloke comes up and says: 'Hey up, Les, we've had a bit of an accident with the Amazon rain forest. Some silly chuff's chopped it down by mistake. We want you to replant it.'"

He took the pipe out of his mouth and slowly leaned back in his old cinema tip-up chair. His eyes clouded over. A wistful smile came to his face.

"Aye. I'd replant it all right," he said, and he held up the catalogue. "I'd order me stuff from these people C.O.D. There's some right good stock in this catalogue only what you've got to remember is that most of it's designed for the temperate zone. I mean, you'd have to be a right bloody fool to plant dwarf conifers and flowering currants in the middle of the Amazon basin, wouldn't you?"

"Yes," said Carter Brandon. "You'd be a pillock."

Mr Brandon leaned forward. He tapped Carter Brandon on the knee.

"George Furnival would. That's just the sort of cock-up he'd make. That's why they asked me instead of him."

"Well then," said Carter Brandon. "Why don't you put in another application for the job? You know you'd do it well. You know it'd suit you down to the ground. Why not give it another try?"

Mr Brandon tapped out his pipe, snapped shut the catalogue and stood up.

"Come on. We'll be late for the match," he said.

October was drawing to a close, but the weather was still mild. It was warm enough to linger.

People lingered.

No one was in a hurry. Young women with push chairs and string shopping bags gossipped. Schoolgirls with eager Saturday bosoms talked to schoolboys who concealed their Players Weights and Park Drives in cupped and guilty hands. Pensioners smoked pipes in the lee of the bandstand, where dogs yapped and sparrows squabbled and robins sang in the thickets of laurel and holly.

"I'd root out all that holly, if I was in charge," said Mr Brandon.

"Why?" said Carter Brandon. "I like holly."

"Do you? I didn't know that," said Mr Brandon. "Right then. I'll bloody keep it."

They walked slowly down the path which skirted the tennis courts.

It was warm enough to play. Two young girls in white shorts were playing. They squealed and giggled.

"If I had my way, I'd dig up them tennis courts and build a bloody great hot house for tropical plants," said Mr Brandon. "You'd have no objection, would you?"

"No," said Carter Brandon. "I can't stand tennis."

"Neither can I," said Mr Brandon. "It encourages young women to show too much of their arses."

They strolled through the main gates into Derwent Road. They were just about to step onto the bus, when they saw two people going into the pub opposite.

One was Uncle Mort. The other was Olive Furnival.

Uncle Mort was smiling at Olive Furnival.

Olive Furnival was smiling at Uncle Mort.

Uncle Mort took off his cap with a courteous flourish as he held open the door of the lounge bar for her.

"Well, I'll be buggered," said Mr Brandon. "I'll go to the foot of our stairs."

The home side lost the match by eleven points to two.

"Artie Shirtcliffe took some hammer," said Carter Brandon to his father as they sat glumly in The Griffon staring at their untouched liver and bacon sandwiches.

"Aye," said Mr Brandon. "It made a proper bugger of his hair-do, didn't it?"

Carter Brandon took a listless sip from his pint of black and tan.

"Life can be a bit of a devil at times, can't it?" he said.

Mr Brandon said nothing. He took out his pipe and began to fill it carefully, kneading each strand of tobacco between forefinger and thumb. He took a trial suck of the pipe and grunted his satisfaction. Then he said:

"I know what's wrong with you, lad. You're feeling trapped, aren't you?"

Carter Brandon nodded.

Mr Brandon lit his pipe and puffed at it rapidly to get it burning evenly.

"I felt exactly the same before I married your mother," he said. "Did you?"

"Aye. And before you was born."

"I'm sorry."

"That's all right," said Mr Brandon, and he puffed at his pipe and then laid it carefully in the ash tray. "You see, lad, I'd always wanted to travel. I'd always wanted to see the world and have adventures."

"You?"

"Aye. I thought that would surprise you. But I was like your Uncle Stavely, only he went to sea and did the travelling, and I stopped at home and married your mother. While he were gadding about the world in his tramp steamers, I were papering the back bedroom and lagging the cock loft."

"Mm."

"When I were a youngster, I nearly emigrated. I'd loved to have seen all them wolves in Canada and all them wallabies in Australia. I'd have gone to a non-English-speaking part of the world, if needs be. I'd have gone to Timor or the Dutch West Indies."

"I didn't know the Dutch had got any West Indies."

Mr Brandon picked up his pipe and puffed at it fiercely.

"Do you know what my greatest ambition was before I married your mother?" he said.

"No."

"To be in half a dozen places at once," said Mr Brandon. "Aye, to be in half a dozen places at once and to lead half a dozen different lives."

Carter Brandon stared at his father with amazement.

Mr Brandon's eyes sparkled through the blue haze of tobacco smoke. His hands quivered. His mouth twitched.

Then suddenly the sparkle disappeared. His shoulders drooped.

"And what happened to all them dreams?" he said. "I married your mother and settled for a life of drudgery."

"That sort of thing must run in the family," said Carter Brandon, taking another sip of his pint.

Mr Brandon patted him gently on the shoulder.

"There's a lot to be said for drudgery, Carter," he said. "It doesn't make no demands on you. It doesn't cause no disturbance in your routine. It causes no distress."

He snatched up his pint pot and took a long savage pull at the black and tan.

At the very moment he slammed the glass onto the table Uncle Mort walked into the bar with Olive Furnival.

He smiled at Mr Brandon and said:

"This is Olive Furnival, Les. I don't know if you've been introduced, but it doesn't matter either road, cos we're going to sit on our own to discuss some personal matters personally in person."

Olive Furnival smiled at Mr Brandon.

It was a warm smile.

Uncle Mort led her away.

"Well, I'll be buggered," said Carter Brandon. "I'll go to the foot of our stairs."

"So will I," said Mr Brandon.

Chapter Eleven

Uncle Mort was late down to breakfast on the Sunday morning.

Mr Brandon waited until Mrs Brandon chivvied them out of the kitchen with her duster, and then he invited his brother-in-law to take a walk on the allotments.

Uncle Mort concurred readily.

"It'll clear me head, will a good walk," he said. "Me and Olive had quite a hectic evening last night."

It was still mild.

The dew sparkled on gossamer threads entangled in the thickets of briar and blackberry. The last of the buttercups cowered in the lank grass on the allotment paths. Yarrow and hawkweed flowered.

The two men did not speak until they reached the shed on Mr Brandon's allotment.

Mr Brandon pumped up his primus stove and prepared to mash a pot of tea.

When he had finished, he smiled at Uncle Mort. Then without warning he grasped him by the lapels of his jacket and shook him until his shoulders were covered with dandruff.

"Right," he said. "What's the game?"

"Game?" said Uncle Mort. "What game?"

"The game you're up to with Olive Furnival."

Uncle Mort wriggled free of Mr Brandon's grip. He straightened his lapels, dusted down his trousers and grinned.

"By God, she's ugly, is Olive Furnival," he said. "If she was hanged for being beautiful, she'd die innocent."

Mr Brandon raised his fists once more and advanced towards him.

"What's the game?" he snarled.

"It's not a game," said Uncle Mort blandly. "It's serious."

"Serious?" said Mr Brandon. "You're not having an affair with her, are you?"

"Yes," said Uncle Mort.

68

"Bloody hell, man, George Furnival'll murder you if he finds out. He worships her. He thinks she is more beautiful than the Rugby League Challenge Cup."

Uncle Mort smiled.

"That's right," he said.

Mr Brandon's face turned scarlet, and there was a high pitch to his voice as he screamed:

"And what about me? If George Furnival finds out you're knocking about with his missus, he'll have me out of the job as soon as look at me. It'll be an arse over tit job in double quick time. You selfish bugger, all you're doing is thinking of yourself. What about me? What about thinking of my interests?"

"I am," said Uncle Mort. "That's why I'm knocking round with Olive."

"You what?" said Mr Brandon.

Uncle Mort chuckled.

"I'm knocking round with Olive so's I'll get her in a compromising situation in front of George. Then, when I do, I'll tell him I'll spread the news of his wife's unfaithfulness all over the neighbourhood unless he recommends you to take over from him as head gardener."

"You what?" said Mr Brandon, and the pitch of his voice grew higher. "You what?"

"It's a cracker of an idea, isn't it, Les?" he said. "It's in the Manchester United class, is that idea. It'd walk it in the FA Cup."

Mr Brandon sank back onto a mound of upturned seed boxes. He mopped his brow and groaned.

"You bloody fool," he said. "You bloody great pillock."

Uncle Mort smiled again and tapped a bag of John Innes potting compost with the toe of his boot.

"They tell me Artie Shirtcliffe played a blinder yesterday," he said.

The mild weather continued, but there was heavy frost in the mornings, and in the evenings there were icy haloes round the bulbs in the street lamps.

There were fleeting snowfalls on the highest moorland crags, and bus conductors began to wear mittens on the country routes.

Uncle Mort's friendship with Olive Furnival prospered.

Teddy Ward saw them eating rock salmon, chips and a bag of peas in the launderette in Bessemer Terrace.

Emrys Tattersall saw them sharing a programme at a brass band concert in the Cordwainers' Hall, and popular mine host and ex Green Howard Bert Coleridge saw them admiring gold fish bowls in the covered market.

"He'll get me the sack sure as eggs are eggs," said Mr Brandon to Mrs Brandon one evening.

"Rubbish. I think it's right romantic," said Mrs Brandon. "Our Mort's following in our footsteps — he's having an Indian summer of love."

Mr Brandon looked at her over the top of his gardening magazine.

"Aye," he said. "And you know what Indian summers bring?"

"What?" said Mrs Brandon.

"Drought," said Mr Brandon.

As the days went by and Uncle Mort's ardour grew, so did George Furnival spend more and more time watching Mr Brandon at work on his bowling greens.

He would stand there motionless and silent. His gaze would be intent, and his face expressionless.

One morning, however, after Uncle Mort had been seen with Olive Furnival trying on surgical sandals in Dr Scholl's, he drew back his lips and bared his teeth at Mr Brandon.

"You bloody fool," said Mr Brandon to Uncle Mort that night in the smoke room of the Liberal Club in Strachey Gardens. "He grinned at me today, did George Furnival. He only grins when there's trouble in the offing, does George Furnival. I bet he were pissing himself the day Hitler invaded Norway."

"Don't panic, Les. Keep your nerve, lad," said Uncle Mort. "Everything's proceeding as per plan. I'm getting on like a house on fire with Olive. Bloody hell, I'm taking her to have her ears syringed tomorrow."

As the nights drew in, so did Mrs Brandon's affection for her husband expand.

One evening, when he returned from a fixture committee meeting of the Lacey Street Bowls Club, she kissed him full on the lips and gave him a plate of Cheshire cheese, cream crackers and pickled onions.

The cream crackers were damp. Their crumbs stuck to the

roof of his mouth and the vinegar off the onions ran in dribbles down his chin.

"Eee, Les, isn't life romantic?" said Mrs Brandon. "I mean, don't you feel romance in the air with our Silver Wedding in the offing? Don't it make you go all funny inside? Don't it make you go all tingly and gooey-eyed?"

"No," said Mr Brandon. "How long have you had this bloody cheese? There's little green things crawling round on the crust."

Mrs Brandon closed her eyes. The shadows from the fire flickered on her cheeks. She sighed.

"I feel exactly now as what I felt before we got married all them years ago," she said.

"Christ, you're not getting another attack of lumbago, are you?"

"I'm not talking about bodily functions. I'm talking about mental functions. I'm talking about emotions," said Mrs Brandon. "I'm talking about being starry-eyed and all of a flutter. I'm talking about how it was twenty-five years ago with me rushing round making all the arrangements and you sitting on your BTM doing nowt."

"Me? Doing nowt?" said Mr Brandon. "Who was it mended your Dad's chain guard? Who was it tarpaulined his bloody rabbit hutch for him?"

Mrs Brandon's eyes sparkled. Her skin glowed in the gentle firelight. The creases in her neck were smoothed away in the mellow orange glow.

"Les?" she said quietly.

"What?"

"Did you ever get second thoughts about getting married? I mean, did you ever get cold feet or owt like that?"

"No," said Mr Brandon after a moment's thought. "Once we'd bought the stair carpet there was no going back, was there?"

Chapter Twelve

November broke the long and lazy spell of mild weather.

It came in with roaring gales from the north.

Auks were blown far inland.

Ducks of the open sea took shelter on placid Cheshire meres.

A sand hopper was driven aground in Liverpool Bay, and the draughts that whistled under the door of Carter Brandon's lounge/diner whined through the rigging of the heavy cruiser, *Prinz Eugen*.

Pat was knitting a pair of leggings.

Carter Brandon was working on his model aeroplane. It was a Boulton Paul Defiant.

There was a smell of glue and contentment.

"Eee, Carter, isn't it nice to be on our own together, you and me in our own home sitting in the firelight's glow?" said Pat.

"We haven't got a fire," said Carter Brandon. "We've got central heating."

"Don't be so argumentative," said Pat. "You know very well what I mean."

She slipped one and purled two.

"Eee, Carter, love," she said. "I can just imagine the scene when baby comes. You'll be sat on the hearth rug next to the red setter and the drinks tray with whisky provided, and you'll be wearing your chunky, manly cardigan with matching cravat and your tailored cavalry twill trousers from Austin Reed's, and you'll have your Bulldog pipe clenched firmly between your lantern jaws and . . . "

"I can't smoke a pipe," said Carter Brandon. "It makes me tongue throb."

There was a ring at the front door, and gratefully Carter Brandon scurried out to answer it.

It was Mrs Partington who was standing at the doorstep. She pushed her son-in-law aside, dashed into the lounge/diner, took Pat in her arms and said:

"He's proposed to me. He asked me to marry him. I said Yes.

I accepted him. I said, I says: 'Eee, what a surprise. It's a bolt from the blue. Thank you for your very kind offer, which I have the greatest pleasure in accepting.' Eee, Pat, love, I'm going to marry him."

"Who?" said Pat coldly.

"Mr Shirtcliffe, love," said Mrs Partington. "I took a taxi round special to tell you. It cost five and six. Isn't it outrageous? I didn't give him no tip. I said, I ses: 'You must be joking if you think I'm going to give you a tip after that. I've a good mind to report you,' I ses."

Mrs Partington beamed at Pat and then turned to Carter Brandon.

"And, Carter love, it's good news for you, too—you're going to give me away," she said.

"Who to?"

"Mr Shirtcliffe. At my wedding. You'll hand me over all unsullied and pure in the dress what I married the late Mr Partington in, if the dry cleaners don't make a hash of it and knowing them, they will. You'll walk me arm in arm down the aisle, and you're not to wear shoes what squeak and make rude noises. And, listen to me, Carter, you're not to walk me too quick otherwise I'll be panting all through the responses and people might get the wrong impression."

"All right," said Carter Brandon.

"And I've got another treat for you, Carter," said Mrs Partington. "You can wear the late Mr Partington's collar studs as a memento if you like."

"Ta," said Carter Brandon.

The memory of her deceased husband's collar studs brought a tear to her eye, but it was gone in an instant and she turned to her daughter and said:

"And what about you, Pat, love? What do you feel about the news? I bet you're over the moon about it. I bet you're absolutely overjoyed about it, aren't you?"

"No," said Pat. "Quite the reverse."

Chapter Thirteen

"Pardon?" said Mrs Partington.

"No," said Pat. "Quite the reverse."

Mrs Partington gasped.

She staggered backwards into Carter Brandon's arms.

"Oh dear," she said weakly. "Oh dearie me."

Carter Brandon helped her to the sofa. She clung to him tightly as he made her comfortable. Her whole body was shaking. Her mouth sagged. Hollows had come to her cheeks.

"There's no point in keeping it from you," said Pat. "You might as well know where I stand. I don't approve of the match one iota. As far as I'm concerned, the marriage will take place over my dead body."

"Oh dear," said Mrs Partington feebly. "Oh dearie dearie me."

"What do you want to get married for, any road?" said Pat. "You're far too old to get married at your age. Why can't you be content with what you've got? You've got your budgie to keep you company. Why can't you settle for him and grow old gracefully?"

"Steady on," said Carter Brandon.

"You keep out of this," said Pat, her face reddening. "It's my mother what's wanting to marry this here Mr Shirtcliffe, not you."

"I wouldn't marry him if he was the last man on God's earth," said Carter Brandon.

"There you are," said Pat to her mother triumphantly. "Even Carter wouldn't marry him, and you couldn't call him fussy about the company he keeps."

Mrs Partington seemed to shrink into the sofa. She seemed to age ten years in an instant.

"He's only after what he can get from you," said Pat. "He's after your brass curtain rails, is that one."

"Oh Pat," said Mrs Partington softly. "How could you say such a thing? You hardly know him."

"It's a woman's instinct."

"But I'm a woman, too, love. I've got an instinct just like you."

"I know," snapped Pat. "But you're older than me. My instinct's younger than yours. It's more up to date."

Mrs Partington's eyes filled with tears.

"Now there's no use in crying," said Pat. "Crying's not going to change my mind. You'd best reconcile yourself to it here and now—you're too old to marry, and I forbid the wedding to take place."

"Oh Pat, love. Oh Pat," sobbed Mrs Partington.

"One of these days you'll thank me for stopping you marrying a midget," said Pat. "And so will baby. If he had a midget for a step grand-father he'd be a laughing stock when he becomes Professor of Arithmetic at Sheffield University."

Mrs Partington sniffed. She fought hard to hold back her tears. She ground her handkerchief into a damp little ball in the palm of her hand.

"Come on, ducks, I'll run you home," said Carter Brandon, and he took hold of Mrs Partington by the elbow and led her out of the house.

Pat followed them to the door and watched them get into the car. She began to speak.

"Shut the window, Carter," said Mrs Partington firmly.

Carter Brandon wound up the window, and they drove off. There was a heavy frost. The roads were slippy.

Carter Brandon went into a slight skid. He got out of it quickly and cursed.

"Bloody cars," he muttered. "Bloody awful things."

Mrs Partington said not a single word on the journey home. She stared straight ahead through the windscreen, but she saw nothing.

She did not see the icicles hanging from the girders of the iron railway bridge. She did not see the fearful hare crouched in the gutter. She did not see the stiff dead dog in Wakefield Road.

"Would you like me to see you to the front door?" said Carter Brandon, when he drew up outside Mrs Partington's house.

She shook her head. A salty tear splashed on the dash board.

Carter Brandon turned to her. He saw that the tears were pumping out of her eyes and cascading down her cheeks.

He raised his arm to put it round her shoulders. Then he lowered it, coughed, hunched his shoulders and said:

"Aye. Well. Mm."

Mrs Partington turned to him suddenly.

"Did you mean that about not wanting to marry Mr Shirtcliffe, Carter?" she said.

"Course not," said Carter Brandon.

She nodded her head rapidly and gripped his arm. She had hard fingers.

"Thank you for your support, Carter. It's very much appreciated, love," she said, blowing her nose and wiping away her tears. "Come what may, Carter, I shall always remember your kindness to me tonight."

"Aye. Well. Mm."

She kissed him on the cheek.

"And don't worry about my brass curtain rails, love," she said as she got out of the car. "Promise me you'll not lose no sleep over them."

"Righto," said Carter Brandon, and he drove home to be greeted by a disturbed and irate Pat.

"There's not one of you trying to understand my position," she said. "You're all too selfish to try and see my point of view. All mother is thinking about is her own happiness. Well, what about my happiness? What about baby's happiness?"

"Mm," said Carter Brandon, settling himself down to his Boulton Paul Defiant.

"Poor little mite. I don't want him having to share his grannie's affections with another child what isn't even his own flesh and blood."

"Which other child?"

"That Mr Shirtcliffe's grandchild. The one what's always yowling. The one with the mother what won't shift herself round the house. Fancy baby having to have that one as an auntie. I bet she'd never remember his birthday. I bet she'd be jealous of him walking so early and being so prompt on the pottie."

"Mm," said Carter Brandon, and delicately he affixed the gun turret to the Boulton Paul Defiant.

"It's not fair," said Pat. "You're all trying to steal my thunder. There's your mother with her Silver Wedding. There's my mother with Mr Shirtcliffe. There's your Uncle Mort with Olive Furnival. Well, what about me and baby? Why can't we have the field clear for ourselves? Why can't we have all the limelight?"

Carter Brandon looked at her out of the corner of his eye. She was knitting furiously. Her lips were white.

When they got into bed, she turned to Carter Brandon and said vehemently:

"As far as I'm concerned, the subject is closed. The wedding will not take place—and that's final."

"Mm," said Carter Brandon. "Go to sleep."

"Any further upsets in my condition, and I could have a premature baby on my hands."

"Mm," said Carter Brandon pressing himself into the pillow. "Go to sleep."

He felt sleep rising through his body. It nibbled at his toenails, dallied round his ankles for a moment and then stretched itself languorously into his loins.

He grunted with pleasure.

Next to him Pat lay still, but the tension crackled all over her body. It tingled the sheets and tautened the springs of the mattress.

The sleep wound itself round Carter Brandon's waist and sent out gentle probing fingers stroking his belly and caressing his chest.

Next to him Pat began to twitch. Then she scratched. Then she twitched again.

Suddenly she sat bolt upright and shook Carter Brandon violently by the shoulder.

"What's up? What's to do?" he cried in a rumpled panic.

"They'd have to put him in an oxygen tent," shouted Pat.

"Who? Who?" said Carter Brandon, and the sleep bolted away from him, and he was wide awake once more.

"Baby," said Pat. "If he's born premature, they'll be forced to put him in an oxygen tent. Poor little mite, won't he look helpless, Carter? Won't he look vulnerable? I hope they remember to feed him proper. I hope they're not too strict about visiting hours."

Carter Brandon let out a long, long wail.

"Oh fuck me," he said. "Another night's sleep gone for a Burton."

Next morning Carter Brandon dragged himself wearily into work.

Tommy Rowley saw his pale, deeply-lined face and cackled.

Eric Black watched him silently as he fumbled clumsily with the taps in the washroom.

"You want to take up football again, lad," he said. "It'll either kill or cure you."

"I'd rather it killed me," said Carter Brandon, and wearily he reached up to the roller towel and began to dry his hands.

Eric Black tapped him on the shoulder and told him that the draw had been made for the Tufton Cup for works, office and business house football teams.

The side had been drawn to play away against Inland Waterways Wanderers.

"It's a tough 'un, Carter. They're a class side. They've got experience," he said. "Their left back once had a trial with Doncaster Rovers."

"And was he convicted?" said Sid Skelhorn.

Eric Black snorted at him scornfully and shuffled away, slapping his bicycle pump against his thigh.

Carter Brandon and Sid Skelhorn went back to the maintenance shop and spent the rest of the morning stripping down the potato-peeling machine from the canteen.

"They've got machines for everything these days," said Carter Brandon.

"Aye," said Sid Skelhorn. "I wish they'd invent one for kissing my missus."

When the midday hooter went, Carter Brandon did not go to the canteen. He walked slowly across the yard and began to stroll along the tow-path of the canal that ran behind the factory.

It was a friendly path.

He had walked along it with Linda Preston in the days before he married Pat. He had wheeled Uncle Mort's baby, Daniel, in his pram down it. Daniel was dead.

"Poor Daniel," said Carter Brandon. "Poor bugger."

Someone laughed. He jumped with shock. He turned.

Linda Preston was sitting on the wall at the back of the steam laundry. She was eating chips.

"Do you fancy one?" she said holding out the bag.

"Ta," said Carter Brandon and he hoisted himself up on the wall beside her.

"You was talking to yourself like a good 'un," said Linda Preston, rummaging in the newspaper for the crispy pieces of batter off her slice of fish.

"Mm," said Carter Brandon. "I always do when I'm worried."

Linda Preston raised her eyebrows. They were pencilled purple.

"Baby getting you down, is it?" she said.

Carter Brandon shook his head.

She moved closer to him. She ran the greasy fingers of her left hand over the sleeve of his donkey jacket.

"Not getting your ration, are you?" she said huskily. "Pat keeping you without, is she?"

Carter Brandon shook his head again.

Linda Preston laughed and threw the remains of her fish and chips to the two swans which were snuffling in the scummy water.

"You're a funny bugger, Carter," she said, and she linked his arm tightly, rested her head on his shoulder and said : "Okay then, tell us what's up."

Carter Brandon began to shake his head, but suddenly he found himself talking. He could not stop himself. He told Linda Preston of Mrs Partington's excitement over the proposal of marriage. He told her of Pat's implacable opposition to it. He told her of Mrs Partington's grief. He told her of the guilt he felt in doing nothing to help.

"What the hell should I do?" he said.

"Simple," said Linda Preston. "Tell your mam-in-law and her bit of stuff to stick up for themselves. They should go round to Pat and tell her to sod it. And you should go round to the bloke and tell him you're on his side. You should tell him to show a bit of gumption and stick up for hisself."

Carter Brandon looked down at her. There was anger in her eyes. Her cheeks quivered.

"Right," he said. "I will. I'll go round there now."

He jumped down off the wall and began to walk rapidly towards the factory.

Linda Preston called out to him, and he stopped. She smiled and winked.

"If the other thing starts to bother you, kid, I'm always here," she said. "Any time. Any place."

Half an hour later Carter Brandon drew up his car outside Mr Shirtcliffe's house.

He ran down the front path.

He could hear the child crying.

He was just about to knock on the front door when the crying changed to screaming. The screams were loud. They were relentless. Intense. Cold. Without feeling.

He knocked on the door.

No reply.

He waited and knocked again.

No reply.

The child was still screaming.

He knocked again and waited. He shrugged his shoulders and, squeezing his way past the cotoneaster and the laurel, looked in through the window of the front parlour.

The girl with the silky blonde hair was lying curled up on the sofa.

She was reading a book. She was wearing a man's denim shirt with the sleeves rolled up almost to the shoulders. Her arms were tanned. They were smooth.

He tapped on the window.

She looked up.

He pointed to the front door and mimed that she should open it for him.

A wisp of a smile came to her face. Then it vanished. She closed her book and left the room.

Carter Brandon dashed back to the front door. He straightened his tie and smoothed down his hair.

He waited.

The door was not opened.

He waited for five minutes, and then he knocked again.

Still no reply.

He brushed past the laurel bush and the cotoneaster and looked in at the front parlour. It was empty.

The child's screaming had stopped.

Carter Brandon beat his fists on the front door. He kicked it.

There was no reply.

Slowly he walked down the brick-paved front path.

He opened the door of his car.

And then he turned quickly and looked up at the front-bedroom window of the house.

He thought he saw a flash of golden hair.

But he could not be sure.

Chapter Fourteen

It grew colder.

The soil on Mr Brandon's bowling greens froze solid.

Mrs Partington's morning visits to Pat ceased.

Uncle Mort's nights out with Olive Furnival increased.

One morning after he had been seen with her eating individual tartlets in the buffet of the Midland Station, George Furnival stopped Mr Brandon outside the tennis courts.

He looked him up and down for a moment.

Then he said:

"Cold, isn't it?"

"Yes," said Mr Brandon.

"It'll get a bloody sight colder, too, before the winter's done."

"That's right," said Mr Brandon.

George Furnival nodded his head. Then he drew back his lips and bared his teeth.

"Think on then," he said. "Just think on."

It grew colder and colder.

Sea lochs froze over in the north of Scotland.

Weather ships plunged and reared in Atlantic gales. Coal tips creaked with frost in Welsh valleys. Rudyard Kettle's auntie caught a chill in Hunslet and died in Batley.

One evening Carter Brandon called in for a pint at The Tinker's Bucket on his way home from work.

Artie Shirtcliffe was in the bar.

He was in the middle of a group of market traders and second-hand car salesmen with tight buttocks.

When he saw Carter Brandon he pushed his way through the crowd and joined him at the bar.

"How do, professor," he said. "What are you having?"

"I'll have a pint of bitter, please, Artie," said Carter Brandon. "Ta very much, Artie. Very kind of you, Artie."

Artie Shirtcliffe ordered a pint of bitter for Carter Brandon and a double brandy for himself. He did not offer to pay the landlord.

"Stick it on the slate, Edgar," he said.

"You're all right, Artie," said the landlord. "Have it on the house."

Artie Shirtcliffe grinned at Carter Brandon.

"He's just like all the other punters," he said. "A bloody sucker."

Carter Brandon took a long sup at his pint. Then he said:

"I were round at your house the other day, Artie."

"Oh aye?" said Artie Shirtcliffe and he winked and nodded a greeting to Larry Fenton, the bookmaker.

"I went to see your dad."

"Mm," said Artie Shirtcliffe and he half raised his hand to acknowledge the greeting of a stout middle-aged lady with hellebore red lips and peroxided hair.

"He were out," said Carter Brandon. "I saw your sister, though."

Artie Shirtcliffe turned to him.

"Oh aye?" he said sharply.

Carter Brandon took another sup of his beer and nodded.

"She's very good-looking is your sister, isn't she, Artie?" he said. "She's right attractive, isn't she?"

Artie Shirtcliffe smiled and put his arm round Carter Brandon's shoulders.

"I'll give you a word of advice, professor," he said. "Steer clear of her. Don't start sniffing."

"I'm not sniffing, Artie."

"No?" said Artie Shirtcliffe with a grin. "No?"

Carter Brandon hunched his shoulders and coughed.

"Aye. Well. Mm," he said.

Artie Shirtcliffe laughed and gave him a friendly punch on the chest.

"She's very dangerous to blokes, is my sister," he said. "Take heed of the warning—keep away. Savee?"

He laughed again and tickled Carter Brandon under the chin.

"I better be off, professor," he said. "Them stupid bloody punters I'm with are clamouring to buy me more drinks."

"Righto, Artie," said Carter Brandon. "See you again some time."

"Aye," said Artie Shirtcliffe. "I might take you shooting with me one Sunday morning."

It grew colder and colder and colder.

There was a shortage of firelighters. Plumbers were at a premium, and there was a heavy run on cough linctus.

Pat entered more and more competitions.

She spent hours poring over pictures of glamorous grannies' ankles, film stars' chests, sports stars' elbows and television announcers' nostrils.

She dreamed of the prizes that would bring her weekends in Bermuda and Porthcawl, hampers of citrus fruits, crates of diabetic pineapple crush, motorised caravans, Japanese motor cycles, a night on the town with Percy Thrower, a trip to Royal Ascot with champagne lunch and Donald Zec included, a lifetime's supply of plastic watering cans, a fortnight in Europe for two with Corbishley's Travel.

She sucked the end of her pencil, furrowed her brow and filled up sheet after sheet of paper, thinking up the slogan that would give her victory over the thousands who thought that tenacity of character was a more desirable virtue than easy social charm in the ideal postman.

Carter Brandon steamed open the envelope containing one of her entries and read the following slogan:

"Large or tall, big or small

"With Chadderton's Currant Loaf you'll have a ball."

He crossed it out carefully and wrote in its place in capital letters:

"Chadderton's Currant Loaf gives you droopy tits."

He did not have time to tamper with the entry for Corbishley's Travel.

Pat also gained another interest in life. She began to go to the ante-natal clinic in Malthus Street.

"You meet some lovely people in ante-natal clinics, Carter," she said. "What I like about it is that all the patients are pregnant, too. Well, it would be awful if they were all old people with hacking coughs and bad legs, wouldn't it?"

"That's right," said Carter Brandon.

One evening after work they went to buy a new pram.

"And what sort of model would you be thinking in terms of, sir?" said the assistant.

"One that doesn't squeak," said Carter Brandon.

They bought the de luxe St Tropez Babycoaster model. It had navy-blue bodywork with red and gold piping, white-walled tyres, double interlock safety brake, jumbo strength cat net, non-slip handle grips, lightweight chrome luggage rack and multi-position sun shade with patent kiddiproof klicker klasp.

"I'm not pushing that bloody thing," said Carter Brandon.

"Why not?" said Pat.

"People'll look at me."

Later in the week they paid a visit to Carter Brandon's parents to show them the baby bath and the pottie Pat had bought that afternoon.

"Which is which?" said Uncle Mort pointing at the articles.

"Pardon?" said Mrs Brandon.

"Which does he bath in and which does he piss in?"

"Mort!" said Mrs Brandon. "I won't tell you again about swearing in front of baby."

"It's not born yet," said Mr Brandon. "It's still in her belly."

"Precisely," said Mrs Brandon. "And that's the vital time in his development. You can set up trends now that'll stay with him all his life. Any more of this bad language, and he'll be born swearing like a Liverpool stevedore."

"If he's owt like a Liverpool stevedore, he'll not be born at all," said Uncle Mort. "The day she's due to drop him he'll be out on bloody strike."

It grew colder and colder and colder.

The snow was thick on the moorlands outside the city.

It coated the high crags. It had driven the sheep into the valleys. It had disrupted the bus services of the North Western Road Car Company.

One Sunday morning Carter Brandon went shooting with Artie Shirtcliffe.

They went out into the pit country to the south of the city. The hills were gentle.

The fields were white with frost, and the hummocks were brittle. Rooks cawed in the copses. Fox tracks led to a peeled hedgehog skin and droplets of blood.

"Do you like shooting, professor?" said Artie Shirtcliffe in the pub after they had come in from the crackling, stubbled fields.

"No," said Carter Brandon. "I think it's cruel."

Artie Shirtcliffe cackled with laughter and slapped Carter Brandon on the thigh.

"By God, you're a rum bugger," he said. And then he tickled him under the chin. "I like you, though, sweetheart. You're out of the run of the ordinary punter. Aye, you're not half bad. You'll do."

"Ta," said Carter Brandon. "Do you want to borrow another quid?"

Artie Shirtcliffe took the pound note and stuffed it in the breast pocket of his waterproof jerkin.

"Be careful of me, professor," he said. "I'm a right dangerous bugger to have as a mate."

It grew colder and colder and colder. And colder still.

One Saturday morning Pat stood naked in front of the dressing table mirror and examined herself closely.

"I'm getting right fat," she said.

"No you're not," said Carter Brandon sleepily.

"Yes I am. Don't be so argumentative," said Pat. "I'm getting a right pot on me."

Carter Brandon rolled over in bed and looked at his wife's reflection in the mirror.

"It suits you," he said. "There's more flesh to grab hold of."

"Don't be so rude," said Pat.

Carter Brandon smiled and Pat sighed.

She turned her body sideways to the mirror and ran her hands slowly down her body.

Her breasts were full. Blue veins stood out on them. Her nipples were turning brown. Her stomach swelled. It shadowed her loins.

"Come into bed for five minutes, eh?" said Carter Brandon, and he drew back the bedclothes.

Pat's face hardened. She drew back her shoulders sharply, and her breasts quivered with indignation. She turned and began to walk towards the door.

Then suddenly she stopped.

A smile came to her face. It was a soft smile. She looked down on her husband tenderly and said:

"Get Thee behind me, Satan."

"I thought you said you didn't like it that way," said Carter Brandon.

Swiftly and softly Pat slipped into bed alongside him.

He was gentle, and she received him with a long, fluttering groan.

The snow from the north was moving nearer the city.

Lorries that had crossed the high Pennine passes arrived in the city encrusted with snow. Parties of hikers set out from the bus station to help the farmers bring down the sheep trapped in the upland blizzards. Newspaper photographers flocked to take pictures of them.

"What are we going to do about Christmas then?" said Carter Brandon an hour later as they sat in the kitchen eating breakfast.

"What we always do," said Pat. "We'll spend Christmas Day with your folks and Boxing Day with my mother."

"I'm not talking about duty," said Carter Brandon. "I'm talking about enjoyment. I'm talking about going out and having a good time."

"I'm not going out anywhere, thank you very much," said Pat.

"Why not?"

"Because I'm fat. Because my face is going podgy. Because I'm getting a double chin. Because I'm fed up carting this lump around in me tummy. Because I'm ugly. Because, because, because, because."

She began to weep.

Carter Brandon looked at her. He made to touch her neck, but instead he coughed, hunched his shoulders and said:

"There's the football club dance on the twenty first. You could go to that. They'll all be too pissed to notice how fat you are."

Pat shook her head rapidly. She scattered her tears over the tea cups and the packet of Shredded Wheat.

"Oh Carter, Carter," she sobbed, and she dashed upstairs and locked the bedroom door behind her.

Three hours and five pints of Oughthwaite's best bitter beer later Carter Brandon stood on the terrace of the rugby ground with his father.

It was half time.

The home side was winning by thirteen points to four, and Artie Shirtcliffe had scored two tries and kicked two conversions.

"Jammy bugger," said Mr Brandon.

It was bitterly cold.

The east wind rasped along the girders of the grandstand and scattered onto the shoulders of the crowd below flakes of rust and the debris of sparrow's nests.

It drummed against the canvas awning of the pie stall. It gnawed into the hip joints of the man in the scorebox. It sent icy furrows running over the surface of the water in the trainer's bucket.

Carter Brandon and his father stamped their feet and blew on their hands.

"She'll apologise to you as soon as you get home," said Mr Brandon, when his son told him what had occurred that morning.

"Do you think so?" said Carter Brandon, and he took a firm bite out of his pork pie. The jelly was ice cold and the meat was livid scarlet.

"Course she will," said Mr Brandon. "Forced to. She'll realise she's not took into account the state of your condition."

"What condition?"

"Your pregnancy," said Mr Brandon. "Men can go very funny during a pregnancy, you know. Have you developed any cravings yet?"

"No," said Carter Brandon.

"You soon will," said Mr Brandon. "When your mother was carrying you, I developed a terrible craving for pear drops. Well, they bloody near took the roof of me mouth off. I lost all sense of taste. It played havoc with me supping. By the time of the eighth month I couldn't tell a pint of Bass from a grapefruit cordial. But I got no sympathy from your mother. She said I could stop at home and distemper the front parlour."

"What colour did you use?"

"Primrose yellow," said Mr Brandon. "You had to wear sun glasses to sit in it even in the depths of winter."

Carter Brandon broke up the crust of his pork pie and threw it to a group of scuffling pigeons.

"Then I got these depressions about the fourth month," said Mr Brandon. "You'd only got to look at me crooked, and I'd burst into tears."

"Get out?"

"Aye. I bloody near cried me eyes out the day we lost in the cup to Wakefield Trinity. Seven-nil up with five minutes to go, and we bloody well lose it!"

The two teams trotted out onto the field, flapping their arms and running backwards and forwards in sharp bursts with their knees held high.

The referee blew his whistle to restart the match.

A nervous skein of gulls flying overhead broke ranks and scattered as the crowd roared. The geyser in the pie stall hissed. Someone threw half an eccles cake at the touch judge (yellow flag).

The match ended with the home side winning by thirty-five points to seven.

Artie Shirtcliffe scored one more try and kicked three conversions and two penalties.

"Flukey devil," said Mr Brandon as they wended their way to The Griffon.

Chapter Fifteen

The snow hit the city without warning.

One minute the sky was robin's-egg blue. Next minute it was whipped by savage black clouds, and the blizzard swept in.

It blew for eight hours. It was deafening.

Then it stopped and within minutes the snow froze solid, and the sky turned to deepest mauve and grey.

The city cowered beneath the snow.

Buses slithered sideways down the steep hills in the suburbs. Trolley bus wires sagged and snapped.

Blue lights flashed on the cabin tops of grit lorries, red lights flashed on the cabin tops of snow ploughs fighting their way through the drifts on the main roads into the city.

There were accidents. Limbs were broken in tumbles. A narrow boat rammed the frozen lock gates by the Navigation Inn. Hen coops were buried to the eaves.

That evening Carter Brandon drove Pat and Mrs Partington to Mr Shirtcliffe's to take supper.

At first Pat had refused the invitation.

Mrs Partington had pleaded with her.

Her happiness was at stake, she said. Her whole future was in the balance. Misery, despair, and utter wretchedness stared her in the face, if Pat would not yield. There was not the slightest need to worry about the welfare of her brass curtain rails.

"Just come and see us together, Pat, love. See how contented we are in each other's company. Give us a chance to put our case proper," she had said.

Pat had tightened her lips and shaken her head adamantly.

Mrs Brandon had taken up the case a few days later.

Love, she had said, was the paramount issue at stake. The question of Mr Shirtcliffe's minikin stature was of no importance. Love could prosper in the smallest of vessels. Love could bloom on the stoniest of grounds.

"I mean, look at Mr Brandon," she had said. "You couldn't get more stonier than him."

Pat had shaken her head firmly.

Mrs Brandon was undaunted.

"You need a man to love you when you get to your mother's and my age," she had said. "When you're young and first married you're too busy painting the house and having babies to bother about being in love. But then as you get older and you gradually discover you've got nowt whatsoever in common with each other you begin to feel the need for a bit of love. Well, who's the obvious choice to give it to you? Your dad and your favourite uncles will be long since dead. Your old sweethearts will have got married or emigrated to Australia like Wesley Spooner and got run over in Brisbane. Your old heart-throbs will have long ago stopped throbbing. So who do you turn to? You have to make the best of a bad job and settle for your husband. And that's why your mother should get married, Pat. I mean, I know Cocky does some very comical tricks with his cuttle-fish bone, but a budgie's no substitute for a man when it comes to untidiness and downright lack of consideration."

Pat had shrugged her shoulders.

"The least you can do, love, is go and have supper with him. Let him put his case, love. And, if he gives you too many baked beans with the fish fingers, you've only to say No."

Reluctantly Pat had consented to make the visit.

Now she sat silent and erect in the car alongside Carter Brandon as he drove cautiously over the rutted, hard-packed snow.

"We must be bloody mad turning out on a night like this," he said.

"That's just what I say," said Pat.

Mrs Partington sat in the back. Her demeanour was tense. Her lipstick was scarlet.

As they stumbled through the snow on Mr Shirtcliffe's front path they could hear the baby crying.

The cries were shrill, but at the core was a deep, piteous echo of pain.

Mr Shirtcliffe answered the door.

"Come in," he said. "You're not being an inconvenience." They stepped inside.

"Now then, would anyone like an aspirin?" said Mr Shirtcliffe. No one spoke.

"Well, what about a Setler's powder in a glass of warm milk?" No one spoke.

"My word, you're soon pleased," said Mr Shirtcliffe, and he ushered them into the front parlour.

Upstairs the shrill cries of the baby changed to choked, gurgling sobs and then to faint and weary whimpers.

Mr Shirtcliffe smiled nervously at Mrs Partington. She smiled nervously at him.

Pat sat bolt upright in her chair and curled her upper lip.

Carter Brandon hunched his shoulders and coughed.

"Is Artie at home by any chance?" he said.

"No," said Mr Shirtcliffe. "No, he's not at home. He's gone out. He's gone out with his sister. As a consequence she's not at home neither."

Pat turned slowly to him and said imperiously:

"Not at home? Do you mean to tell me she'd leave you on your own to cope with a fractious child what's constantly howling its head off?"

Mr Shirtcliffe licked his dry lips rapidly.

"It's not quite like that," he said.

Then he invited them into the back parlour for supper.

There was pig lung's soup followed by chaps and chitterling followed by prunes and custard.

When they were halfway through their herbal tea, Mrs Partington squared her shoulders and said:

"Right. Let's take the bull by his horn and get down to brass tacks. Shall I hold the horn, Mr Shirtcliffe, or will you hold it yourself?"

"I'd rather you held it, Mrs Partington," said Mr Shirtcliffe meekly.

"Right," said Mrs Partington. "Right."

And straightaway she launched herself with fervour into the presentation of Mr Shirtcliffe's case regarding the proposed nuptials.

He was an excellent proposition, she said.

He owned his own house. It was freehold. Not a scrap of furniture was on hire purchase. His washing machine was still under five months' guarantee. He had an excellent position in the snuff warehouse with two weeks annual paid holidays. He had a policy with the Royal Liver which matured when he was sixty-five. Apart from a wart on his left index finger he was in excellent health and took three morning newspapers.

"Mm," said Pat. "Mm."

Mrs Partington renewed her pleading with increased vigour. Mr Shirtcliffe was an honest, upright man, she said.

Probity was his middle name. He had collected for the missionaries all his life. His political sympathies were with the Independent Ratepayers. He was a staunch supporter of the Royal Family, the scouting movement and the Cyclists Touring Club. He had numerous hobbies. Among them were fretwork, jig-saw puzzles and flower arranging. He loved Mrs Partington with all his heart. He begged Pat to take the view that she would not be losing a mother, but rather gaining a father.

"We'll see," said Pat. "We'll see."

Mrs Partington smiled at her and began to stroke her left forearm.

"Why don't you and Carter go into the front parlour and have a chinwag about it while me and Mr Shirtcliffe do the washing up?" she said.

Mr Shirtcliffe jumped out of his chair.

"That's all right," he said. "Me and Carter'll do the washing up. It won't be no nuisance."

He pushed a surprised Mrs Partington out of the back parlour, smiled sweetly at Pat and then, when they had left the room, bolted the door and stared wild-eyed at Carter Brandon.

"She's got it all wrong," he said. "I don't want to get married."

"You what?" said Carter Brandon.

Tears began to stream from Mr Shirtcliffe's eyes.

'The last thing in the world I want to do is get married to Mrs Partington," he said. "I don't like women. They're too bossy. They've got too many relations. Their clothes smell funny. They've got hairy legs. They talk too much. They get butter stuck under their fingernails."

Carter Brandon coughed.

"Aye. Well. Mm," he said.

Mr Shirtcliffe's tears showed no signs of abating. He moved towards Carter Brandon and clutched the hem of his jacket.

"I don't want to get married. I don't want to have to share my vacuum cleaner with another after all these years," he said. "I don't know what I'd do, if I couldn't have my half hour's contemplation over my Hoovering every morning. I don't care what anyone says, a Ewbank's not the same. And then there's me dusting and me baking and me dress-making — a man can't be expected to give all that up just for the sake of a woman."

His tears began to soak through the material of Carter Brandon's trousers.

Mr Shirtcliffe clutched him more tightly and sobbed.

"She proposed to me while I were doing the Hoovering," he said. "It were making such a noise I couldn't hear what she were saying. I just said Yes in the hope of shutting her up."

"You'd have been better off with a Ewbank then," said Carter Brandon.

Mr Shirtcliffe nodded. Then he tugged hard at Carter Brandon's jacket.

"You've got to help me," he said. "You've got to intercede. Don't let Pat change her mind now. I don't think I could stand the nuisance of that."

Carter Brandon coughed, hunched his shoulders and said:

"I'll see what I can do."

Mr Shirtcliffe regained his composure with remarkable speed. Within five minutes the redness had disappeared from his eyes and there was a springy chirpiness in his step as he led Carter Brandon into the front parlour.

"Don't get too comfortable, lad. You'll not be stopping long, will you?" he said.

On their way back to Mrs Partington's Carter Brandon drove with extreme caution. He had to, for the roads were treacherous. They were littered with abandoned vehicles. Just by the Amy Carpenter Memorial horse trough there had been an accident. A small black car was embedded in a stone wall. There were two fire engines, an ambulance and an assortment of police vans all with flashing lights.

A policeman stopped them and said:

"Go careful, lad. It's a bugger of a night."

By the time Carter Brandon reached Mrs Partington's house his eyes were throbbing and little nerves were quivering in his arms and shoulders.

"You'd best stop the night here," said Mrs Partington. "Carter can't drive any further in this lot."

"Ta," said Carter Brandon.

Mrs Partington and Pat made up a bed. It was in the same bedroom that Pat had occupied before her marriage. She and Carter Brandon undressed quickly and slipped into bed.

Pat turned to her husband and whispered:

"Shall we have a bash?"

"Aye. All right," said Carter Brandon.

Pat guided Carter Brandon into her and let out a long low moan.

"Shush," said Carter Brandon. "You'll wake your mother up."

Pat giggled.

"She's probably awake already," she said. "She'll be listening out for the bedsprings."

The bedsprings began to creak rhythmically. Faster and faster they went.

Pat looked down on Carter Brandon and thrust herself at him more violently.

"Hey up, steady on," gasped Carter Brandon. "You'll have her coming in with a bucket of water."

They finished. They lay on their backs exhausted. Pat giggled and said:

"Fancy doing it in the bed I were brought up in. I had mumps and scarlet fever in this bed."

"Mm," said Carter Brandon.

He looked up at the ceiling. The snow lit it up so that it shimmered white and cold.

He looked at the motionless curtains. In their patterns he could see the flow and fall of silky hair. In a knot in the dressing table he saw an oval face. In the faint haze of the wallpaper he saw two pale green eyes with tawny flecks.

Pat cuddled up close to him.

"Carter?" she said.

"What?"

"If baby has to have glasses in later life, what sort of rims would you want him to have — tortoiseshell or self-coloured?"

Pat snuggled closer into Carter Brandon and gently rubbed his stomach with her kneecap.

"Mother hasn't said nowt about this evening," she said. "She knows I've not changed my mind, you see."

"Mm," said Carter Brandon, and he let his eyes wander over the smooth silky whiteness of the ceiling, and the pale green eyes flecked with tawny stared out at him from the wallpaper.

"What was you and Mr Shirtcliffe talking about while you was doing the washing up?" said Pat.

"Nowt," said Carter Brandon. "Bugger all."

Pat began to stroke the smooth skin behind her husband's ears.

"I think baby's bringing us closer together than ever, don't you, Carter?" she said.

"Mm," said Carter Brandon.

"I wonder if baby'll invite us round to his house for Christmas when we get old with varicose veins?" she said.

"I don't know."

"It depends what his wife's like, of course, doesn't it? She might insist on spending every Christmas with her own folks, mightn't she?"

"Mm."

"Well, she can insist all she likes," said Pat stiffening with indignation. "It wouldn't wash with baby. He'd put his foot down. He'd say 'Fair's fair. We'll do it on rota. One year with your folk. Next year with mine. And so on and so forth.' Isn't he thoughtful, Carter?"

"Aye."

Pat took hold of his hand and placed it on her stomach.

"Can you feel him kicking?" she said.

"No."

"Oh," said Pat. "He must have stopped."

The clock struck one. The fridge turned itself on with a click and began to rumble wearily.

Pat made tiny twittering noises in the back of her throat as gradually she was overcome by sleep.

Carter Brandon let his eyes wander round the room. The face had disappeared from the dressing table, there was no silky golden hair in the motionless curtains, and the eyes were gone from the wallpaper.

He propped himself up on one elbow and looked down at his wife.

There was a smile on her face.

She was sleeping peacefully.

A wisp of hair on her temple fluttered in time to her deep breathing. She had a dewdrop on the end of her nose. It quivered and fell without a sound onto her moist upper lip.

Carter Brandon leaned forward and gently licked it away with the tip of his tongue.

"Aye. Mm," he said. "I'm quite looking forward to being a dad."

Chapter Sixteen

On the following day Carter Brandon was told of Pat's accident.

He was in the canteen eating a cold sausage sandwich, when Sid Skelhorn came rushing up to him and said:

"I've got a spot of bad news for you, Carter. Do you want me to break it to you gentle?"

"Aye. Go on," said Carter Brandon, taking another bite from his sandwich.

"Your missus has been in a car crash. They say she's copped her lot."

Carter Brandon's face went white. His heart began to pump wildly.

"It's a bit of a bugger, isn't it?" said Sid Skelhorn.

Carter Brandon dropped the cold sausage sandwich onto the floor. He began to shiver.

"Oh dear," he said. "Oh Christ."

Sid Skelhorn picked up the sandwich and dusted it on the seat of his boiler suit.

"Is it pork or is it beef, this sausage?" he said.

"Pork," said Carter Brandon.

Sid Skelhorn nodded.

"You're all right then," he said. "There *is* an R in the month."

Carter Brandon did not move. He sat in his chair and stared straight ahead.

Sid Skelhorn took hold of his shoulders and said:

"They asked me to tell you because we're mates. They knew I'd handle it tactful, you see, Carter."

"Mm," said Carter Brandon, and his knees began to tremble.

Sid Skelhorn took hold of him by the elbow and raised him to his feet.

"The cops are outside to take you to the hospital, Carter," he said. "Shall I come with you to cheer you up?"

Carter Brandon nodded.

Sid Skelhorn led him downstairs to the lodge at the factory

gates where the police car was waiting. They got inside and roared off.

"Hey up, not so bloody fast," said Sid Skelhorn. "You don't want to bring on my car sickness, do you?"

When they got to the hospital, the police sergeant helped Carter Brandon out and said:

"Shall you be all right, lad?"

Carter Brandon nodded.

An orderly with laddered stockings led him to the ward where Pat lay.

The doctor met him outside and gripped his arm tightly.

"She's still alive, Mr Brandon, but ... but ... I'm sorry, Mr Brandon. I'm truly sorry."

He opened the door for Carter Brandon, and he looked inside at Pat.

She looked peaceful. There was not a mark on her face.

From out of the pattern of the curtains round her bed two green eyes flecked with tawny stared at him.

And one winked.

Chapter Seventeen

For the next four days Carter Brandon was constantly at Pat's bedside.

They took her for three operations, and each time she returned from the theatre the doctor looked at Carter Brandon and shook his head sadly.

"We're doing all we can, Mr Brandon," he said.

Mrs Partington came to visit each evening.

She would sit by the side of the bed next to Carter Brandon, holding his hand tightly and staring at the motionless, blank pallid face of her daughter.

"It's retribution," she said one night.

"Pardon?" said Carter Brandon.

"It's fate stepping in to punish me for going against Pat's wishes," she said snuffling into her handkerchief. "The wedding can never take place now. I've lost Pat, and now I'll have to lose Mr Shirtcliffe as well."

She began to sob bitterly, and Carter Brandon patted her hand and said:

"Don't cry."

On the following evening Mrs Partington never took her eyes off her daughter's waxen face.

"Doesn't she look peaceful, Carter?" she said. "Doesn't she look contented?"

Carter Brandon nodded, and Mrs Partington crushed her handkerchief to her eyes once more and said:

"Well, she's no right to look contented. She should be gritting her teeth and showing she's fighting for life what like the late Mr Partington did so unsuccessfully."

The night nurse rose from her chair, took hold of Mrs Partington's elbow and led her gently outside.

Mrs Brandon, too, was a daily visitor.

Each afternoon she brought her son sandwiches, Smith's potato crisps, flasks of Bovril and fresh clothes.

"Does Pat never put your undies in the airing cupboard after ironing them?" she said to Carter Brandon one afternoon.

Carter Brandon shook his head.

"Well, she should, Carter. You could catch terrible consumption going out in damp singlets."

On another afternoon she said to her son:

"I went round to your house this afternoon to get some clean socks. I washed down all the woodwork for you and I boiled all your face cloths. Does Pat never think of boiling your face cloths, Carter?"

Carter Brandon shook his head.

Mrs Brandon gazed down at the recumbent form of her daughter-in-law and said softly to Carter Brandon:

"Looking at her there lying so peaceful, you wouldn't think she was the sort of girl what never boiled her face cloths, would you?"

Mr Brandon coughed. He was standing at the door, fingering the brim of his cap and shifting from foot to foot.

"Come on in, Les," hissed Mrs Brandon. "Come in and pay your respects. By the look of Pat there might not be much time left to do it."

Mr Brandon looked across at his son with embarrassment and then slowly he shuffled across to the bed and stared down at Pat.

His lips began to quiver.

His cheeks trembled. His eyes filled up with tears.

"Mm," he said. "Mm."

On the fifth day of Pat's internment the senior registrar called Carter Brandon into his room.

It was a sunny room.

It had french windows which overlooked a snow-carpeted lawn.

Two coal tits and a greenfinch shivered by the frozen bowl of water on the bird table.

The registrar was brief and concise.

Pat was deeply unconscious. It was improbable that she would recover. Even if she did, it was a near certainty that her brain had suffered irreparable damage.

"Mm," said Carter Brandon. "Mm."

The coal tits and the greenfinch were joined by a starling. They began to squabble, but then the biting cold silenced them and they hunched their shoulders, fluffed out their feathers and closed their eyes.

The registrar continued.

The baby was still alive. As far as they could see, it was undamaged. So long as Pat lived, the baby could be saved. The situation, however, was perilous. There was not much to hope for.

He shook Carter Brandon's hand as he opened the door for him.

"There's nothing more you can do here, old chap," he said. "Go home and try to lead as normal a life as possible. The odd pint of wallop wouldn't come amiss, you know."

"Mm," said Carter Brandon.

He went to the ward and took a last look at Pat.

She was still pale. She was still peaceful. There were tubes attached to her body. There was a bottle, too, which dripped.

He coughed and hunched his shoulders.

"Tarra then," he said softly. "Aye, Tarra."

His mother met him in the vestibule, and they took the bus into town where they had tea in the UCP restaurant at the side of the covered market.

Carter Brandon chose tripe fried in batter with potato scallops. Mrs Brandon chose pressed beef and brawn with pickled beetroot and horse radish sauce.

"Now then, Carter," she said as the waitress brought them their pot of tea at the end of the meal. "There's no point in sitting back and moping. You've got to come to terms with facts."

"Mm," said Carter Brandon.

"You see, love, if a miracle should happen, and Pat comes through, it's odds on she'll spend the rest of her life as a helpless cabbage. Now then, that being the case, you can either put her in a home where she'll be well-looked after with no expense to you, or you can try to manage at home with all the inconvenience. Now then, I don't mind doing your washing and your cooking and your shopping and your ironing and cleaning out your toilet, but I do draw the line at looking after pets. So if you're thinking of getting a canary or a Bedlington terrier to keep you company, you'll have to look after them yourself."

"Give over," said Carter Brandon.

"Then there's another thing—don't leave things while the last moment and be caught on the hop regarding your funeral arrangements," said Mrs Brandon. "Now I don't mind doing the catering for the party, but I think for decency's sake it should be held at your place and not mine."

"For Pete's sake," said Carter Brandon.

"Now then, we can have boiled ham or tongue, but we're not having both," said Mrs Brandon. "And what about the carriages for the mourners? I prefer Humbers meself. I mean, let's face it, love, but Pat's not exactly in the Rolls Royce class, is she?"

"Hell's bloody bells," said Carter Brandon, and he pushed back his chair and stamped angrily out of the restaurant.

Later that evening Mrs Brandon was full of resentment, when she told her husband of her son's behaviour.

"I'm not surprised he took the hump," said Mr Brandon. "You can't talk about bloody funerals when the lass is lying at death's door in hospital."

"Well, when else can you talk about them?" said Mrs Brandon. "It'll be too late, if she goes and recovers on us, won't it?"

Mr Brandon hurled down his gardening catalogue and went into the back kitchen, where he took a bottle of stout from under the sink.

Mrs Brandon followed him to the doorway and said:

"In these circumstances you've got to be cruel to be kind. There's no use brooding. That won't get the baby's bottle washed, will it? At times like this someone's got to be practical and face up to reality."

Mr Brandon muttered to himself as he yanked the top off the bottle of stout.

"Reality?" he said. "It's all a bloody cod is reality. If there were such a thing as reality, you wouldn't have that poor lass fighting for her life with tubes sticking out of her."

"Don't be so silly, Les."

"If there was such a thing as reality, she'd be sitting under a parasol in a garden with flowering peaches in full bloom and a fountain tinkling into a pond full of lilies, and there'd be the buzz of bees and the song of nightingales and beer would only cost fivepence a pint."

He poured out the stout carefully into an enamel mug and padded back into the parlour.

He prodded the fire with the poker and it flared into life and spat.

"If there were such a thing as reality, we'd turn into birds when unpleasantness cropped up and fly off to the sun till it all blew over," he said.

The fire spat out a thin sliver of burning cinder.

He watched it smoulder on his slipper.

Then it went out.

Chapter Eighteen

On the following morning Carter Brandon went back to work. His workmates were most sympathetic.

"I suppose you've lost all your appetite, have you?" said Sid Skelhorn.

"Aye," said Carter Brandon. "I'm not eating a thing."

"Good," said Sid Skelhorn. "Can I have your egg sandwiches?"

Later in the morning Eric Black came up to him in the wash-room and said:

"Now your missus is out of circulation, how about starting up football again?"

Carter Brandon shook his head.

Eric Black nodded and patted him on the back.

"Ne'er mind, eh?" he said. "Mrs Black has made a set of black arm bands for the team to wear next match. We'll have a minute's silence, too, if you like."

"We have one of those every time we score a goal," said Sid Skelhorn. "One minute's silence of sheer bloody amazement."

"You sacrilegious bugger," said Eric Black. "You want to show respect. You want to show some bloody reverence. You're the trainer of the side—you're the last one what should be running them down."

At lunchtime Carter Brandon went into the canteen and the girls at Linda Preston's table looked at him with compassion and turned their heads away from him uncomfortably.

Connie Watkinson from Packing wept copiously, and Dorothy Fearnley of Complaints pinched her knee under the table and looked fierce.

When Carter Brandon had found a table for himself, Linda Preston came across to him.

"Oh, Carter, Carter," she said. "Bloody stroll on, eh? Bloody ding dong."

Carter Brandon nodded and pushed away his plate of corned beef hash and mashed potatoes. He had taken only three mouthfuls.

Linda Preston patted him on the back of the hand.

"Is there owt I can do you, kid?" she said.

Carter Brandon shook his head.

"I'm not talking about mankin' around, Carter," she said. "I'm talking about helping you about the house. I'm no bloody good at it, but if you're took short, I'll come round and have a go, and you'll be under no obligation to get fresh with me."

Carter Brandon smiled and shook his head.

All through the afternoon he worked in a frenzy.

When the hooter blew at the end of the shift, he put away his tools, scrubbed himself briskly in the washroom and hurried across the yard in the ice-laden night air.

He was stopped by Tommy Rowley, who invited him home for tea.

"If you can stand the sound of nippers howling non stop, if you don't mind the niff of drying nappies and stale Ostermilk, and if you like the taste of fig roll and lumpy custard, you're very welcome to come home with me," he said.

Carter Brandon shook his head.

"I don't blame you," said Tommy Rowley with a sigh. "I'm only going cos' I happen to live there."

Carter Brandon nodded a farewell, and stepped out through the factory gates. He began to run, for he was late for the bus to take him to the hospital. He had hardly run a dozen paces when a large grey Jaguar drew up alongside him.

The driver was Artie Shirtcliffe. He wound down the window and said:

"Come on, professor. Hop in."

Carter Brandon got into the front, and Artie Shirtcliffe stamped hard on the accelerator and roared off with a screech of spinning, slithering tyres.

"I heard about the accident," he said. "Hard luck."

"Thanks, Artie," said Carter Brandon. "I appreciate that."

"You've no need to bother about transport from now on," said Artie Shirtcliffe. "I'll drive you to the hospital every night."

"That's very decent of you, Artie," said Carter Brandon. "Ta very much."

Artie Shirtcliffe looked across at him and grinned.

"Surprised to see your Uncle Artie in a swanky crate like this, are you?" he said as he heaved the car round the junction at Wilson's Bar.

As they sped up Dovedale Road they left behind an angry chorus of neighing car horns.

Artie Shirtcliffe chuckled.

"It's one of my skives, is this," he said. "The chairman of the club runs these second-hand car showrooms, you see. Well, he gives me a car from time to time so the punters'll see me driving around. Stupid buggers flock to the showrooms to buy a car just like mine. Bloody punters! They're as thick as shit."

He put his hand into the breast pocket of his jacket and drew out two five pound notes, which he gave to Carter Brandon.

"What I owe you, professor, and buy some flowers for the missus with the rest," he said. "I get commission, see. Money for old rope, isn't it? Never be a punter, kid, it's a mug's game."

Ten minutes later he pulled up outside the hospital.

Carter Brandon was just about to open the door, when Artie Shirtcliffe leaned across and held him back.

"Take my advice, professor," he said. "Don't let them swamp you with sympathy. They'll bloody drown you in it, if they can. Stand up for yourself and spit it back in their faces."

Chapter Nineteen

For the next three weeks there was not the slightest change in Pat's condition.

"I'm sorry," said the doctor. "I'm truly very sorry. She's so young, isn't she?"

Every evening Artie Shirtcliffe met Carter Brandon outside the factory gates and drove him to the hospital.

Most evenings, too, he was on hand to ferry Pat's visitors to their various destinations.

One evening Mrs Partington said to him:

"How's your daddy taken the news that me and him can never meet again, Arthur?" she said.

"He were thunderstruck, owd ducks," said Artie Shirtcliffe. "He's hardly stopped Hoovering since you told him."

Mrs Partington took out her handkerchief and dabbed at the corners of her eyes.

"He should use an Electrolux, Arthur," she said. "Oh dear, I'd got such plans for re-organising his domestic ablutions once we got married."

On another evening Mrs Brandon said to Artie Shirtcliffe:

"Don't think I'm not grateful to you running us round like this, but I hope you're not getting our Carter into bad habits."

"There's no such thing as bad habits, owd love," said Artie Shirtcliffe.

"I beg to differ," said Mrs Brandon.

"Now that *is* a bad habit," said Artie Shirtcliffe.

On yet another evening Mr Brandon and Uncle Mort sat silently in the back seat as Artie Shirtcliffe skidded the car round corners and roared down the snaking hills.

At length Mr Brandon said:

"You're as good a driver as you are a rugby player – bloody rubbish."

Artie Shirtcliffe roared with laughter.

"Great stuff," he said. "I like you two punters. Come and have a drink."

"No," said Uncle Mort. "And don't call me a punter again or I'll not accept another lift off you."

On Saturday evening Artie Shirtcliffe invited Carter Brandon to stop off for a drink at The Groom and Potter before going home.

Carter Brandon nodded.

It was a humped pub with high floors and marble-topped bars.

They went into the cramped, crooked lounge. In a corner was a girl. She had long silky blonde hair and green eyes flecked with tawny.

"This is my sister, Alison," said Artie Shirtcliffe.

"Oh. Aye. How do then," said Carter Brandon. "Aye. How do."

She did not look at him. She thrust her empty glass at Artie Shirtcliffe and stared straight ahead into the smokey haze.

Carter Brandon looked at her out of the corner of his eyes as Artie Shirtcliffe went to the bar to order their drinks.

Her neck was smooth and slim. Her nose was straight. There was a soft down on her cheeks and a small donkey brown mole just below her Adam's apple.

"I've not been in this pub before," said Carter Brandon. "Have you? I've not. No. I've never set foot in it before."

She did not move.

She was wearing a man's navy-blue pullover. Her arms were bare.

"Mm," said Carter Brandon. "It's not a bad pub really. I think I might come again."

She did not move.

She was wearing pale blue Levis and boots with large brass buckles. She did not look up when Artie Shirtcliffe handed her a glass of gin. She did not speak as the two men drank their pints.

Carter Brandon finished his off and stood up.

"I'll be off," he said. "Aye. I'll be off."

"That's all right, professor," said Artie Shirtcliffe. "I understand."

Carter Brandon turned to Alison and said:

"Good night then. It was nice meeting you. Aye. It were grand."

She did not look up.

Carter Brandon arrived in his empty house half an hour later.

The new pram stood in a corner of the lounge/diner.

In one of the kitchen cupboards there were cartons of baby food, packets of teats, bottles of Milton and a large tin of Johnson's talcum powder.

In the small box room there were neat piles of baby clothes.

In the front bedroom there was a large, cold, unmade double bed with a crumpled nightdress sticking out from under the bolster.

Carter Brandon picked it up. He smelled it.

On the bedside table was an entry form for a competition. Carter Brandon picked it up. He read it.

"Large or tall, big or small,

"With the Royal Marine Commandos you'll have a ball."

He began to cry.

He cried for an hour. There were few tears.

He shivered all over, and a steady low moaning sound came from his lips.

He flung himself on the bed, and in a flash was fast asleep.

In his dreams he saw silky blonde hair, green eyes flecked with tawny, long bare arms and a small donkey brown mole that warmed the tip of his tongue.

Halfway through Sunday dinner at his parents' home the next day Carter Brandon looked up from his forkful of sprouts, mashed turnip and Yorkshire pudding and said to his mother:

"Would you mind if I come and live here for a bit?"

"Course not, love. Course not," said Mrs Brandon. "What's up — are you frightened of burglars, sleeping on your own? Have you got ghosts, or do you want to be near your mammy when you hear the bad news from the hospital?"

"For God's sake, Annie," said Mr Brandon, and he leaned across the table, patted Carter Brandon's wrist and said gruffly:

"You're very welcome, lad. Stop as long as you want."

They had chocolate pudding and custard for dessert, and then at two o'clock Artie Shirtcliffe called round for Carter Brandon in his car.

Alison was sitting in the back seat.

She wore a man's bottle-green padded windcheater and round her neck she had a large navy-blue scarf.

Carter Brandon climbed into the front seat beside Artie Shirtcliffe and turned to Alison and said:

"How do. It'd be a grand day if it weren't so cold and the sun came out."

Alison slowly turned her head away from him and looked out of the window.

"Aye. Well. Mm," said Carter Brandon.

All through the journey to the hospital he could feel Alison's presence in the back of the car.

It overpowered him. It seeped into him through his pores. It burrowed into him. It bored into him. It writhed through the hair on his head.

Artie Shirtcliffe talked all the way, but Carter Brandon heard hardly a word.

All the time he was conscious of green eyes flecked with tawny searing and singeing the hairs on the back of his neck, but whenever he glanced at Alison through the driving mirror all he saw was her profile as she stared out of the side window.

It was the most beautiful profile he had ever seen.

When they drew up outside the hospital, Artie Shirtcliffe said: "Take your time, professor. There's no hurry."

The sister smiled sympathetically at Carter Brandon as he entered the room where Pat lay alone and unconscious.

"She's such a pretty girl, too," she said.

Carter Brandon sat down on the chair at the side of the bed.

"Hello, Pat," he said softly. "It's me. It's Carter."

She made no response. There was no change in the rhythm of her breathing. There was no flicker of recognition on her face.

"We had best end of neck for our dinner today," he said. "It were a bit on the fatty side, but the gravy was smashing. Aye. We had sprouts, too. Mm. Mm. I got a hole in me sock yesterday. Aye. Mm. Do you know if we've got any clean pillowslips?"

He took hold of her hand. It was limp. He began to pat it.

"Aye," he said. "Mm."

There was an electric clock in the ward. He watched the red second-hand jerk round.

A great weariness slopped over him. Sleep came. He did not fight it. He felt his chin drop against his chest. He let his whole body relax.

When he looked at the bed next, Pat was lying there peacefully. Alongside her was Alison. She smiled at him and slowly drew back the bedclothes. She was naked. She held out her arms to him.

Carter Brandon screamed.

At once he felt someone holding him by the scruff of the neck and shaking him. He opened his eyes and shook his head.

"You must have been dreaming, Mr Brandon," said the sister. "You've been asleep for an hour and a half, you know."

"Oh," said Carter Brandon. "I'm sorry."

"Go home and get some sleep, Mr Brandon," said the sister. "There's nothing more you can do here, I'm afraid."

He nodded. He looked at Pat. Her position had not changed since the start of his visit. Neither had her expression.

When he got outside to the car, he found Artie Shirtcliffe fast asleep.

There was no sign of Alison.

He woke Artie Shirtcliffe and said:

"Where's Alison?"

Artie Shirtcliffe yawned and smiled.

"She upped and offed, professor," he said. "She always runs away when she gets bored."

"Oh," said Carter Brandon. "Shall we go and look for her then? I mean, she'll not go and get lost, will she? I mean, she'll not . . ."

Artie Shirtcliffe pulled him into the car and ruffled his hair.

"I've told you, professor—don't get interested," he said. "Pay attention. Don't let me have to warn you again."

Chapter Twenty

When Carter Brandon moved into his parents' home, he was welcomed by his mother with a flurry of kisses and a mug of piping hot Bovril.

"We've got to build your strength up," she said. "You look right peaked."

She had decorated his bedroom exactly as it had been when he was a boy.

She had found the old bookshelves at the back of the garage and had dusted them down and varnished them up.

She had found some of his old books in a packing case in the cock loft, and these she had placed neatly on the shelves.

Captain W. E. Johns nestled snugly alongside Percy F. Westerman. Talbot Baines Reed and Douglas V. Duff squeezed Daphne Pardoe in a dark corner.

Mrs Brandon had discovered the large drawings Carter Brandon had made with his pantograph of Baldy Hogan, Cannonball Kid, A. P. E. Carew and Alf Tupper, 'the tough of the track', and these she had pinned to the walls.

She had wiped the mould off the handle of his William Gunn cricket bat and ironed flat the covers of his Playfair football annuals.

She had found the clasp knife and the rabbit skin woggle he had used in the Boy Scouts, and these she had placed on his dressing table along with the autographed pictures of Reg Harris, Sid Patterson and Arie Van Vliet.

On his first night home Mr Brandon said to him:

"Do you fancy a pint, lad?"

"No, he does not," said Mrs Brandon. "He's going to run along upstairs and get into bed while I make him a nice nourishing beaker of drinking chocolate. Just look at the time, Carter. It's nine o'clock. It's well past your bedtime. You know how you can't stand late nights."

Carter Brandon was already in bed by the time his mother brought him the hot chocolate.

She sat on the bed and watched him drink it. When he had finished she said:

"Now there's to be no calling downstairs for glasses of water, Carter. And are you sure you've done your wee wee?"

Carter Brandon nodded.

His mother tucked him in and said:

"Night night, love. Night night, sweetheart. I'll get you a night light tomorrow if you want."

She went downstairs to the back parlour, where her husband was polishing the silver bands on his collection of Peterson bent stem pipes.

"I'm right worried about our Carter," she said.

"Mm," said Mr Brandon.

"When I give him a hug and a kiss upstairs, he were just skin and bone. I could feel his ribs through his pyjamas," said Mrs Brandon. "I'm sure Pat's not been looking after him proper."

"Now then. Now then," said Mr Brandon.

"Since he got married he's had one cold after the other. He's never without the snuffles. I'm sure she lets him go out with holes in his boot soles. And I know for a fact she never airs his braces for him."

"Give over, Annie," said Mr Brandon. "You can't talk about the lass like that when she's in hospital fighting for her life."

"She doesn't feed him proper—that's the whole trouble. He doesn't have enough fish. She never gives him stews. It's fries, fries and more fries. No wonder he's looking liverish. No wonder he's got no resistance."

Mr Brandon sighed, shoved his pipes to one side and went into the kitchen. Mrs Brandon followed him and watched him as he took out his gardening boots and commenced to dubbin them.

"Well, I'm going to build him up while he's here. Plenty of rice pudding and fresh vegetables is what he wants. And he could do with a strong laxative every Friday night and a course of halibut-oil capsules. What he wants is a string of early nights with the windows open. And he can get his hair cut, too. Carrying all that hair around on his head—it's not good for the brain, you know. It puts a strain on it."

"Aye," said Mr Brandon, flinging his gardening boots away. "And you put a bloody strain on me."

Upstairs Carter Brandon was wide awake.

He lay still.

Baldy Hogan smiled down on him, and he could smell the dust off the yellowing pages of the Empire Youth Annuals his mother had stacked on the wicker linen basket she had used when he was a baby.

Just before midnight his parents came up to bed.

Mrs Brandon tip-toed into his room, and he pretended to be asleep. She tucked him in once more and called to her husband, who shuffled into the room, scratching beneath his arm-pits and yawning.

"Just look at him, Les," she said. "Doesn't he look vulnerable? Doesn't he look innocent?"

"I suppose some folk might say so," said Mr Brandon.

"I must get him some Lung Balsam tomorrow," said Mrs Brandon. "He looks as though he could be in for a nasty bout of coughing."

"I'd get him a pair of crutches while you're at it," said Mr Brandon. "He could easy break his leg having a piss tomorrow."

"There's no need to be sarky," said Mrs Brandon. "There's no need to be vulgar."

She pushed her husband out of the room and closed the door softly behind her.

Carter Brandon opened his eyes tentatively.

He heard his mother whisper to his father:

"We'll have a kiss and a cuddle to celebrate Carter's first night home, eh? It can be by way of memory of the night he were conceived."

"I don't think I'll bother," said Mr Brandon.

"Charming," said Mrs Brandon. "Charming. Well, if you won't show me any love, I know one person who will."

The bedroom door opened again and Mrs Brandon looked in on her son.

"It's you, love, isn't it?" she whispered. "You'll give me all the love I need."

Half an hour later Uncle Mort returned home from his evening out with Olive Furnival. He bumped into the hatstand and giggled. He tripped as he climbed the stairs. He forgot to close the door of the lavatory. He giggled again as he closed his bedroom door with a slam. Within minutes he was snoring.

Carter Brandon slipped out of bed carefully and quietly.

He was wide awake.

8

His whole body tingled.

He parted the curtains and looked out. There was a full moon. All was white. And still.

He watched and he waited. He stared out unblinkingly.

And then pictures began to form on the pure white surface of the snow.

He saw anglers hunched up against a sleeting east wind. He saw a young man pushing a baby in a pram along a canal towpath.

"It's me and Daniel," he said softly.

Then the images changed.

He saw slate-hung houses in dripping forests. He saw valleys with buzzards and stabbing herons. He saw two young soldiers sitting on a bench outside a timbered inn. They were drinking steins of beer, and in the background a water wheel raced.

"It's me and Sid Jones on National Service in Germany," he said.

The images changed again.

He saw a young woman walking along the forest path. She was swinging a black patent leather handbag. Not a hair on her head was out of place. Behind her came a young man with sombre brown eyes, moving slowly, listening to the bird song, stalking the soft butterflies, stooping to inspect the woodland flowers. The woman turned to him and pursed her lips.

"It's me and Pat," he said. "And, bloody hell, we're going to have a row."

He saw a bayonet-steep fiord. The water was blue. Kittiwakes screamed. Eider duck bobbed. A white wooden boat creamed the stillness. A girl with silky blonde hair and green eyes flecked with tawny sat in the stern. She trailed her smooth bare arms in the water. She looked up and smiled at the young man with sombre brown eyes who sat at the helm. The young man hunched his shoulders and coughed.

"I wonder who them two are," said Carter Brandon. "Aye. Well. Mm. I wonder."

Chapter Twenty-one

Pat lingered on between life and death.

There was no improvement in her condition.

Neither was there disimprovement.

She lay in bed, still and silent.

The weather grew bleaker.

There were sudden snow falls, and then the skies cleared, and bitter winds from the north and the east whined in over the city.

People reeled under the relentless cold. It began to freeze the spirit out of them.

Ice gripped the roads and the pavements. It was stained red outside the butchers' shops.

There was skating on mill ponds.

Fieldfare and redwing died. Swans were frozen into canals. Toads died at the bottom of ice-covered brooks. Kingfishers in the dales died. Wrens in bundles in dry stone walls died. Long-tailed tits hunted in scanty fearful flocks for food. There was none to be found. They died, too.

In the ropeworks of Flatman, Wrigley and Nutbrown the workers complained of the cold and went on strike for two days.

Uncle Mort bought Olive Furnival a bottle-green balaclava to keep the cold out of her gums.

Each evening Artie Shirtcliffe met Carter Brandon in the car outside the factory gates and drove him to the hospital.

On most evenings they would stop off at a public house on their way home.

Artie Shirtcliffe drank double brandies.

"Think I sup too much then, do you, professor?" he said to Carter Brandon one evening as they stood in the back bar of The Dusty Forge. "Think it's clapping me out, do you? Think it could ruin my career, do you?"

"Aye. Well. Mm," said Carter Brandon.

Artie Shirtcliffe laughed and put his arm round Carter Brandon.

"Listen to me, sweetheart," he said. "If I want to cock meself up, that's my business. Bugger the punters. They don't own me. If I destroy meself, it's none of their bloody business."

"You'd not destroy yourself, Artie," said Carter Brandon.

Artie Shirtcliffe laughed and tickled Carter Brandon under the chin.

"Don't bank on it, professor," he said. "Don't put no money on it."

Half an hour later, when Carter Brandon walked into the back parlour, his mother jumped up from the fireside chair and wrapped her arms round him.

"How is she, love?" she said. "Is she in the final decline yet?"

"There's no change."

"Bless her," said Mrs Brandon. "Isn't she persistent?"

She went into the kitchen and fetched supper for her son.

It consisted of halibut steamed in milk, thin brown bread and butter, junket and a large glass of Wincarnis.

On the side of the tray was a plate containing two iron tablets, one cod liver oil capsule and a spoonful of Gregory powder.

Mr Brandon looked at the plate and scowled. Then he turned to his wife and said:

"Why don't you give him a Bob Martin's as well? He'd likely fetch your bloody slippers for you then."

Next evening in the hospital Carter Brandon gripped Pat's hand.

"It's me. It's Carter," he said.

Pat made no move. Her face was white. Her eyes were closed.

"We had braised steak on the menu today," said Carter Brandon. "Aye. Mm. I think I'm getting another dose of chinky rot in me left foot."

Pat made no response. Her breathing was steady. The tubes attached to her body dripped steadily.

"Oh Christ, love, hang on," said Carter Brandon. "Hang on. Hang on, love."

On the following evening Mrs Partington could not contain her tears as she looked down on her daughter.

After five minutes she had to leave the room and sit on a chair in the corridor.

They took the bus into town at the end of visiting hours because Artie Shirtcliffe was playing in an away match at Whitehaven.

Mrs Partington sniffled into her handkerchief all the way to the malt vinegar factory. Then she blew her nose sharply and said:

"I got a parcel from Mr Shirtcliffe this morning. It contained all my letters to him and all the presents I've ever given him with the exception of the khaki dungarees he ripped on the fretwork machine. He wrote ever such a nice covering note with it. He didn't use ballpoint neither. He used real ink. He said he hoped the egg cups arrived in one piece and if not, I was to let him know so's he could put in a claim to the GPO. He's very meticulous about making claims, is Mr Shirtcliffe. He claimed off the monumental mason, when the frost cracked his mother's headstone. He got a refund of three-and-six in the pound."

She blew her nose again and bit her lip to keep back the tears.

"He said he were devastated I'd called the marriage off. He said he were distraught. If his ink hadn't run out, I'm sure he'd have committed hari-kari."

"Mm," said Carter Brandon.

"Happy days," said Mrs Partington. "Happy, happy days."

Carter Brandon went for a pint in The Tinker's Bucket. It was damp and gloomy. He enjoyed it.

When he arrived home, he found his father and his mother in the middle of a heated altercation.

Mr Brandon was glaring at Mrs Brandon, face flushed, fists clenched. Mrs Brandon was glaring at Mr Brandon, face white, fingers kneading the hem of her pinnie.

"It's very select, is Grange-over-Sands," shouted Mrs Brandon. "It's the ideal place for a honeymoon. It's got an annual rose show and Max Jaffa."

"I don't care if it's got port wine flushes in all the public conveniences — I'm not going there on me honeymoon, and that's that."

"Well, where do you want to go?" said Mrs Brandon.

"Nowhere," said Mr Brandon. "We should cancel it. Bloody hell, if they could cancel the match against Liverpool Stanley when the King died, surely to God we can cancel our honeymoon, when Carter's wife is lying at death's door with tubes sticking out of her?"

Carter Brandon coughed and sank lower into the fireside chair.

"Rubbish," snapped Mrs Brandon. "Life's got to go on. Whatever happens, life has to continue as per normal. You never stopped playing bowls when me dad's rabbits died. It didn't stop you going to the pub when me Uncle Gladwyn was electrocuted at the Ideal Homes Exhibition. You never batted an eyelid when war broke out in Korea. Well, there's no need to start batting your eyelids now. Life has to go on. Come what may, we have our honeymoon, plus reception at The Whippet, plus community singing and games with dessert spoons, and plus, if needs be, your cousin Danny taking his teeth out and singing 'The Shades of Night Are Falling Fast'."

Mr Brandon's fists began to work violently. He pressed them tightly to his side. He gritted his teeth. Then he pushed past his wife and stormed to the door. Once there he stopped and said:

"You don't know what you're talking about, woman. It's 'The Fishermen of England' he sings without his teeth in."

He clattered upstairs, and the toilet seat was slammed down violently.

Mrs Brandon came to her son and sat on the arm of the fireside chair.

"You know what I mean about life going on, don't you, Carter?" she said.

"Mm," said Carter Brandon.

He was staring deeply into the fire. Among the shifting coals and the flickering flames he saw clearly silky blonde hair and pale green eyes flecked with tawny.

"I mean, for argument's sake, supposing Pat goes and dies, which we hope she won't, but we can't be certain, what would you do then?" said Mrs Brandon. "You couldn't give up the ghost and throw in the towel. Life would have to go on. You'd have to find yourself another wife. I mean, you're still a young man, Carter. You've got all your own teeth. You don't get winded running for the bus. You can still shift a chest of drawers upstairs with the best of them. Well, you can't hide all that under a bushel. It's not fair. You must go out in the world and give the girls a chance to catch you."

She nestled her head on her son's shoulders and began to pat his back.

"I used to pat your back like this when you was a baby to burp you, Carter," she said.

"Mm."

"Ee, love, I hope you get caught by a good 'un," she said. "I hope she airs her tea towels. I hope she doesn't smoke when she's cooking. I hope she doesn't let your underpants get discoloured."

Carter Brandon nodded and went upstairs to bed.

He did not sleep.

At half past two in the morning he got out of bed and examined his underpants.

They were discoloured.

Chapter Twenty-two

The cold weather showed no sign of breaking.

Mrs Brandon's loving of her son showed no sign of faltering.

She inspected all his shoes for holes in the soles. She bleached all his vests and his underpants. She threw out all his nylon socks.

"Doesn't Pat realise you've got the sort of feet that cry out for wool?" she said. "Your feet can't wear nylon. They can't breathe in nylon, can't your feet. They need wool and medicated dusting powder."

She made him eat porridge with brown sugar for breakfast and in the evening she cooked him milk puddings of rice, sago, tapioca and macaroni.

She kept his blood clean with sulphur tablets, his bowels free with Gregory Powder, his complexion clear with Bile Beans, and she kept the colds at bay with daily doses of halibut oil, wheat germ oil, cod-liver oil and Virol.

"Bloody hell," said Uncle Mort. "He gets better treatment than what Golden Miller got when he won the Cheltenham Gold Cup."

Carter Brandon did not object. He merely smiled when his mother bullied him. He just nodded his head and grunted when she rubbed his chest with Vick and sat him on the side of the bath to cut his toenails.

One night as he made his way upstairs to bed his mother said:

"Listen, love, I know you can't sleep at nights, so why don't you come into my bed and cuddle up like you did when you was little?"

Carter Brandon smiled and shook his head.

After his mother had tucked him in and kissed him on the forehead he lay rigid in the ice-cold bed.

Every nerve end in his body vibrated. Every muscle fibre screamed.

Earlier in the evening the registrar had called him into his room.

"I'm sorry, Mr Brandon," he had said. "I'm sorry, but there's really very little we can do for your wife now."

Earlier in the evening, too, he had driven to the hospital with Artie Shirtcliffe, and Alison had sat in the back of the car. She had not spoken.

On the way home they had called in at The Groom and Potter. She had not taken a drink. She had not spoken. She had left suddenly and without explanation.

The clock struck one.

Carter Brandon had not moved his position since climbing into bed.

The bed was still cold.

His brain raced.

His senses were sharp.

He heard the registrar's voice drumming in the back of his mind.

"I'm sorry, Mr Brandon ... I'm sorry, Mr Brandon ... I'm sorry, Mr Brandon ... "

He heard the uneven stutter of Pat's breathing.

He heard the steady tap tap of Alison's fingers on the beer-soaked table in The Groom and Potter.

Suddenly he threw back the bedclothes and jumped out of bed. He went downstairs and sat on the sofa in front of the back parlour fire. He smoked two cigarettes.

He was just about to light a third, when he became aware of someone staring at him from the door.

It was Mr Brandon.

"Why don't you poke the fire, lad?" he said. "You'll catch your death of cold."

He stuck the poker into the hard crust of slack, and the fire burst into flames and sent shadows bounding and prancing on the wall. He sat on the chair opposite his son and took out his gardening magazine.

"I wish we had room in the garden for a magnolia tree," he said.

And then he took out his pipe, filled it, lit it and read happily in silence.

The clock struck three. It was a hoarse bronchial chime. It made the willow pattern cups in the display cabinet rattle.

Feet descended the stairs. Uncle Mort shuffled into the back parlour and said:

"Hey up, I didn't know insomnia was contagious."

He sat down on the sofa and looked closely at his nephew.

Carter Brandon made no response. He just sat bolt upright and stared into the fire with vacant eyes.

"Come on, Carter," said Uncle Mort. "Get it off your chest, lad."

Carter Brandon did not move.

Uncle Mort slid along the sofa to him and put his arm round his shoulders.

"Listen to me, Carter," he said. "I've got experience of personal bloody bereavements. I had your Auntie Edna falling off the bus and crowning herself fatally, so then I go and marry your Auntie Lil, and bugger me, she goes and snuffs it giving birth to Thingie."

"For Christ's sake, don't call him Thingie," said Mr Brandon. "Call him Daniel. Annie'll have your guts for garters if she hears you calling him Thingie. You know what a fuss women make about getting your baby's name right."

"All right, all right, Daniel it is," said Uncle Mort crossly. Then he softened his tone and said to Carter Brandon: "You was very fond of Thin ... Daniel, wasn't you? You treated him as though you was his own father. I mean, the fact that his dome was miles too big for his body was immaterial to you. You loved him for what he was—even though it was bugger all. And when he snuffed it, you grieved for him. And then you forgot all about him. That's what I've done with your Auntie Edna. I've almost completely forgotten the taste of them bloody awful maids of honour she used to make for Sunday tea. I've only the vaguest memory of the day she got electrocuted at the Ideal Homes Exhibition."

"That was your Uncle Gladwyn, you daft chuff," said Mr Brandon.

"See what I mean, Carter?" said Uncle Mort. "Memory's like a pint of London bitter—it doesn't last forever, thank God. And once Pat's been and gone and snuffed it, you'll be surprised how quick you'll forget her. I'll lay you half a bar to a tanner that a month after the funeral you'll be hard-pressed to remember a single good thing about her. So come on, lad. Snap out of it. Cheer up. Don't be such a bloody misery. If you can't do it for our sake, at least you can do it for Thingie's."

Carter Brandon stood up.

He smiled. He nodded to Uncle Mort. He nodded to his

father, and then without speaking he left the room and went upstairs.

He climbed into bed and within seconds it was warm and snug.

As soon as his head touched the pillow sleep hit him. He plunged deeply into a warm scented blackness.

Down, down, down he went.

Long silky blonde hair caressed him and slowed down his fall. A wisp of springy black hair, disturbed by his deep regular breathing, smoothed and soothed his temples.

—Hey up, Carter, how you doing, old son?

—Is that you, Daniel?

—That's right, me old wingsy bash. How's tricks?

—Not bad, Daniel. How's yourself?

—Smashing, Carter. No complaints at all. Death suits me champion. I've never felt better in me life.

—What are you doing here then?

—I've come to help you, Carter. I heard you was having a spot of trouble with Pat.

—Aye. She's in hospital. They say she's going to snuff it.

—Bollocks!

—Pardon?

—Leave it to me, Carter. Don't worry. I'll fix it up for you. Have a good night's sleep—and don't worry. Do you hear me? DON'T WORRY.

A smile came to Carter Brandon's face.

The moonlight flickered over his calm, unfurrowed brow. He began to snore.

When his mother came into the bedroom to wake him for work next morning, she could not rouse him. She shook him by the shoulder. She pummelled him on the back.

At length she had to squeeze a face cloth full of water over his head before he woke up.

He smiled broadly at her and said:

"Grand day, isn't it? I don't think I'll bother going to work. No, I'll have a day off."

He sang to himself as he washed and shaved. He smiled as he ate a hearty breakfast. His eyes sparkled as he slapped his mother on the bottom and said:

"Tarra, old ducks. You're looking right sexy this morning."

"Well!" said Mrs Brandon as her son slammed the front door behind him. "Well I never!"

She went to the mirror in the front parlour and looked at herself.

A long, slow, contented smile came to her face and she turned sideways, tightened the cord of her pinnie and thrust out her chest.

"What's up?" said Mr Brandon, looking in through the door. "Getting another dose of lumbago, are you?"

There had been a slight fall of snow during the night.

It lay loose and fretful on the ice-jammed roads and footpaths. When the east wind blew, it swirled and lodged itself in eyelashes and early morning stubble.

The temperature was well below freezing.

The cold ached and burned. It drummed and throbbed.

People were bowed beneath it. They were cowed by it. They did not look up as they hobbled over the rutted ice. Their shoulders were bent. They shuffled along in clouds of grey shifty vapour.

Carter Brandon strode along the street briskly, shoulders back, arms swinging, a broad smile on his face.

He came to the canal bridge, crossed it and then squeezed through a gap at the bottom of the advertisement hoarding for Quaker Oats and scrambled down onto the tow-path.

—You like canals, don't you, Carter?

—Aye, I do, Daniel. Canals are grand.

—Do you remember how you used to wheel me in the pram along the tow-path?

—Aye. I do.

—I bloody near caught me death of cold one day. You never put me pram cover on, you daft turd.

—Sorry, Daniel.

—That's all right, Carter. I don't hold it against you.

There were footsteps engraved in the snow on the tow-path. They were frozen solid, and they had splintered black hearts. They had expanded, too, and they were mis-shapen with raised, smoothed and slippery edges.

Carter Brandon stumbled and slid and tripped on them.

Then as the canal left behind the warehouses and the mills and the factories and turned its back on the artisans' terraces and the suburban semis and the willow-fringed back gardens of mock-Tudor mansionettes and began to stretch lazily into the open countryside the snow was undisturbed on the tow-path.

The going was tough.

Carter Brandon plunged up to his thighs in the snow once or twice, but he kept forging ahead relentlessly.

—You're not running away, are you, Carter?

—No.

—You could do if you wanted. If Pat died, you'd be as free as a bird.

—I know.

—There'd be plenty of women sniffing round after you. Linda Preston would be there.

—I know.

—And Sharon Boot and Sandra Bullions and Thelma Thurlow from Ventilation.

—Mm.

—And what about Alison, Carter? Aye. What about her, lad? Now there's a woman for you. There's real class. By God, Carter, with a bird like that you'd be set up for life, lad.

Carter Brandon clambered over a baulk of rotting timber and pressed on.

The snow grew thicker. There were deep drifts into which he tumbled without warning. He had to thrash wildly with arms and legs to drag himself out of them.

—If Pat snuffs it, Carter, the trap's burst wide open. No more bars. No more padlocks. An open gate and freedom.

—Mm.

—You could be off and away. You could go to Germany. Aye, you could go to that village you went to when you did your National Service.

—Aye, I could. It were a smashing place, Daniel. It had these funny houses what were hung with slate. And it had an inn where you could get a bloody gynormous plate of cold meat with Russian eggs and beer in bloody great stone mugs.

—I know, Carter. It were grand.

—I could go to other places, too, Daniel. I could go to that place where they have that railway what runs hanging on rails above the ground.

—Wuppertal.

—That's right and I could go to that forest where Sid Jones got his end away with that bint from the NAAFI what smelled of egg and chips.

—Sauerland.

—Aye. I could go anywhere I wanted.

—You could see things you've never seen in your life before, Carter.

—Aye. Sampans.

—That's right, Carter. And you could meet women the like of which you've only dreamed of.

—Aye. Samoan beauties with big smouldering eyes. Arab dancers with jewels in their navels. Big randy Swedes and slim willowy Indians with long hair twined round their waists. And birds with ginger hair and birds with no hair. And birds with slanty eyes and birds with green eyes flecked with . . .

He stumbled.

He fell forwards into the snow. He lay still. He began to sob.

Pictures danced before his eyes on the white surface of the snow.

He saw a maternity dress of maroon and green stripes.

And he sobbed.

He saw a navy-blue pram with red and gold piping and a kiddi-proof klicker klasp. He saw a wisp of dark hair quivering on a temple. He saw three packets of Ostermilk and a wad of nappy liners.

And he sobbed.

He saw full breasts with ice-blue veins. He saw a rounded belly with shaded loins. He saw water pouring in eddies and runnels over smooth buttocks. He saw an entrecôte steak with celery hearts and a treble portion of chips.

And he sobbed and he sobbed.

He was shivering violently when at last he hauled himself to his feet. He brushed the snow off himself. He stamped his feet.

—Cold isn't it, Daniel?

—Freeze the balls off a brass monkey, Carter.

He climbed over a stile and waded waist deep through the snow until he came to a narrow country lane which led to a public house called The Assheton Arms.

It had stone-flagged floors and scrubbed pine tables.

A coal fire roared in a fireplace of rich deep red brick. A wall-eyed collie thumped its tail.

He bought a double whisky and ginger wine.

It warmed him through and through.

Chapter Twenty-three

When Carter Brandon returned home from his walk along the canal bank, he ran himself a bath.

It was a piping hot bath scented with half a bottle of his mother's best bath salts and a treble helping of Radox. He lay in it wreathed in billows of slothful steam.

He soaked himself.

He smoked two cigarettes.

He dive-bombed the loofah with the pumice stone. He made a convoy with the nail brush, the soap bowl and the back scratcher and torpedoed it with a slippery sliver of Pears soap.

Then he went to bed with a hot-water bottle and Mr Midshipman Easy.

It was four o'clock in the afternoon. At half past four the phone rang. It was the hospital. He was to go round there immediately.

—Don't panic, Carter. Now don't panic, lad.

He ordered a taxi and sat rigid in the back, tight-lipped and numb.

—Oh Christ, Daniel. Oh bloody hell.

He hurried across the vestibule and down the green-tiled corridor to Pat's ward.

The registrar was waiting for him by the door.

He held out his arms.

—Oh God, Daniel. Oh God.

The registrar wrapped his arms round Carter Brandon and hugged him.

"Congratulations, Mr Brandon," he said. "It's a miracle. It really is, old chap."

Chapter Twenty-four

Carter Brandon tiptoed nervously into the ward.

Pat turned her head to him and smiled.

"Hullo, Carter," she said. "Hullo, love."

"How do," said Carter Brandon.

He stood at the foot of the bed and shuffled his feet.

"How have you been keeping?" said Pat.

"Not bad," said Carter Brandon. "I've got a bit of chinky rot in me right foot, but I'm not complaining."

Pat smiled weakly.

Her face was still pale, but there was the hint of a faint bloom on her cheeks. There was the hint of a sparkle in her eyes, too.

"Have you been looking after yourself, love?" she said.

"Aye," said Carter Brandon. "Me mum's bought me a new pair of underpants."

Pat patted the side of the bed next to her, and he cleared his throat and moved over.

She took hold of his hand and began to stroke it.

"I had ever such a funny dream, Carter," she said.

"Oh aye?"

"I dreamed I were inside my own womb talking to baby. And then do you know who walked in?"

"No."

"Daniel."

"What?"

— It's true, old son. I were just passing by so I thought I'd drop in out of politeness and pass the time of day.

"And we had a party, Carter. We had greengage jelly and funny hats."

— We didn't have no cream soda, though, Carter. In fact, the catering was bloody terrible. All we had was cocktail onions, chocolate buttons and bottles of Vimto.

"And Daniel and baby got on like a house on fire, Carter," said Pat with a smile.

—Aye, we did, Carter. Well, after we'd finished Postman's Knock and Twenty Questions, we got in the corner together, him and me, and had a bit of a yarn. He said you was going to feed him Ostermilk once he's born. I told him not to be a mug and hold out for full cream Cow and Gate. I mean, look what it's done for the present Queen, Carter. She's a right bonny lass, and you don't see her with the snuffles very often, do you?

"And when the party was over, Carter, and the guests was leaving, Daniel come up to me and he said, he ses: 'Thank you very much for a lovely party and here's a present for being such a charming hostess. Your individual bridge rolls was scrumptious.' And he handed me a parcel tied in a red velvet ribbon. And do you know what was in it?"

"No."

"My life."

She closed her eyes, and a smile came to her face. It was a smile of the deepest, most beautiful contentment.

The registrar put his finger to his lips and led Carter Brandon outside.

"Amazing, Mr Brandon. Truly remarkable," he said, and he shook his hand once more.

Carter Brandon coughed and hunched his shoulders.

"Will she live?" he said.

"Oh, rather. I should say so, old chap," said the registrar. "And baby, too. Don't forget baby, Mr Brandon."

He took Carter Brandon by the elbow and led him down the corridor.

"Of course she'll need constant attention. There's no question of her leaving here until the baby's born."

"I see."

"Not to worry, old chap. She'll be as right as rain. Go off and enjoy yourself tonight. The odd jar of wallop wouldn't come amiss."

Once more he patted Carter Brandon on the back and shook his hand.

"I'd come with you myself for a quick noggin, old chap, only tonight's my badminton night, I'm afraid."

Carter Brandon had only taken one step outside into the night air, when Artie Shirtcliffe sprang forward out of the shadows.

"I called at your house when you wasn't at work tonight," he said. "They told me. Is she . . . I mean, are you . . . I mean . . . "

"She's grand, Artie. She's come through. She's going to live."

Artie Shirtcliffe took a sharp step backwards. His mouth dropped open.

"I see," he said hoarsely. "I see."

"Shall we go for a pint to celebrate, Artie?" said Carter Brandon.

"Mm," said Artie Shirtcliffe. "If you like."

He drove to The Furnace, but he did not get out of the car.

"I've just remembered, professor, I've got other arrangements," he said.

Before Carter Brandon could speak, he had slammed the door and roared off, his tyres sending up stinging smatters of ice and grit.

Carter Brandon paused for a moment on the pavement and then went bounding up to the upstairs bar. The first person he saw was Louis St John. When he told him the news, he burst into tears and said:

"Holy Mackerel, Kingfish. Holy fuckin' Mackerel."

He slapped Carter Brandon on the back. He tweaked his ears and punched him in the chest.

"Great stuff, kid," he said. "Have a double Bacardi."

They had six double Bacardis each, and then they went to The Devonshire Arms where they had four pints of Wards' Malt ale. After this they staggered to The Griffon where they drank bottles of barley wine with vodka chasers. Then they lurched to The Corporation Tavern where they drank double whiskies and bottles of red Bass.

At eleven o'clock Louis St John dragged Carter Brandon out of the taxi by the scruff of the neck and heaved him up the front path of his parents' home, rang the bell and dropped him on the doorstep.

Mrs Brandon opened the door, and Carter Brandon fell into the hall on his hands and knees and began to giggle.

"What's the matter, Carter?" said Mrs Brandon. "What's to do with you?"

Carter Brandon rolled over onto his back and tried to focus his eyes on his mother. He giggled again as she bent over him and began to loosen his collar.

"For Christ's sake, woman, I'm drunk," he said. "I'm as pissed as a fart."

Mrs Brandon jumped back from him. She put her hands on her hips and said slowly:

"We heard the news. Pat's mother phoned. I'm very pleased for you, you disgusting pig."

Carter Brandon hiccupped and began to crawl towards the back parlour.

"You pig! You animal!" said Mrs Brandon.

"Leave him alone, Annie," said Mr Brandon, hurrying out of the back parlour. "If the lad can't get drunk on a night like this, when the hell can he?"

"Never," said Mrs Brandon. "He's got a wife and a child to support now. He's got to settle down to his responsibilities. He should be devoting all his time and money to the home. He should be reconciling himself to twenty years of hard solid graft keeping up decent standards and maintaining his guttering in good nick. He's no time for pleasure now. His gallivanting days are over."

She prodded her son with her toe and flounced off upstairs.

Mr Brandon hoisted Carter Brandon to his feet and dragged him into the back parlour.

"Congratulations, son," he said. "I'm delighted. I'm right bloody pleased."

Carter Brandon opened one eye and said:

"I think I'm going to be sick."

"I thought as much," said Mr Brandon and he dashed into the kitchen for a bucket. Once there he paused for a moment and said softly: "By God, she fought death like a demon and for what result? To give birth to a baby what she'll have to love and cherish for best part of twenty years. By God, women are buggers for punishment."

Chapter Twenty-five

The news of Pat's recovery spread rapidly.

Next day at work Linda Preston threw her arms round Carter Brandon's waist, shoved him backwards into a dark corner outside the main door to the Paint Shop and thrashed the roof of his mouth with her tongue and sucked the moisture off the roots of his tonsils.

"Bloody hell, Carter," she said, when she finally released him, panting and breathless. "Stroll on, eh? Bloody ding dong."

She smiled at him.

"Do you fancy a bash at the back of the cycle sheds to celebrate?"

"Not just now, thank you," said Carter Brandon. "I've got a lathe to strip."

That evening Pat took hold of Carter Brandon's hand as he sat next to her on the bed and said:

"What did you do today, love?"

"Not much," said Carter Brandon. "What did you do?"

"Not much," said Pat.

The red second hand clicked and jerked.

Carter Brandon yawned.

On the following day Carter Brandon met Linda Preston under the railway bridge on the canal tow-path.

"You didn't take the hump about what I said yesterday, did you?" said Linda Preston.

"No," said Carter Brandon.

Linda Preston smiled, popped a chip into his mouth and said:

"Good. We'll wait till the shock's worn off, shall we?"

"Pardon?" said Carter Brandon.

Linda Preston laughed and sauntered off in the direction of the factory.

"Remember what I said, Carter," she said. "Any time. Any place."

When Carter Brandon visited Pat that evening, he found her sitting up in bed.

"Hello, Carter," she said. "Hello, love."

"How do," said Carter Brandon.

She smiled at him.

"What did you have for your dinner today, love?" she said.

"Toad in the hole," said Carter Brandon.

She smiled.

He yawned.

"Are you happy, love?" she said.

"Yes," he said.

"Are you contented?" she said.

"Yes," he said.

And then Carter Brandon met Alison.

Alone.

He spoke to her, too.

Chapter Twenty-six

This is how it happened.

Carter Brandon visited Pat in hospital and she looked up at him from her box of fudge and smiled.

"What did you do with yourself, Carter, while I were in a coma?" she said. "Did you remember to change your socks?"

"Yes," said Carter Brandon.

"I hope you didn't tread dirt in on the carpets."

"No."

Suddenly she narrowed her eyes and said:

"You've not been playing football, have you, Carter?"

"No."

"Are you sure?"

"Yes."

"And will you promise me never to be tempted?"

"Course I will."

Pat smiled.

"I believe you, love. Isn't it nice for a man and wife to have so much trust in each other?"

"Mm," said Carter Brandon.

Next day Eric Black said to him in the washroom:

"Do you fancy a game of football this afternoon?"

"Yes," said Carter Brandon.

"It's in the gym. We can't play outside owing to adverse bad weather."

The training took place in the Palmerstone Street Drill Hall.

The hall was damp and dusty.

So was the caretaker.

He showed them to the changing room. He had specks of rust on the buckles of his braces.

"Here you are, and don't spit on the floor," he said, throwing open the door to an airless room that smelled of mouse droppings and bad coughs.

They changed silently and glumly.

"Come on, lads, let's have a bit of a spring in your step," said Eric Black as they trudged along the corridor to the gym. "Hup, two, three. Hup, two, three."

"Piss off," said the team captain, Maurice Buckle.

"That's what I like about Maurice," said Eric Black to Carter Brandon. "He's a real enthusiast for the game."

A blast of chill air met them as they opened the door of the gym. They edged in and pressed themselves to the wall bars muttering.

"Come on then, you bloody skivers, get running round in a circle," said Eric Black. "Chests out, shoulders back, knees up — hup, two, three. Hup, two, three."

Reluctantly the members of the team began to jog around the gym.

"Come on, Rudyard, take your cardigan off," shouted Eric Black.

The men circled the gym slowly and sullenly.

Suddenly Bernard Garside stopped, turned to Maurice Buckle and said with a deep bow:

"Can I have the pleasure of this dance?"

"Certainly," said Maurice Buckle. "Can you chassis?"

The two men grabbed hold of each other and began to dance around the gym.

The other members of the team immediately found partners and joined them in the dance.

"My dear, you dance divinely," said Louis St John as he swung Sid Skelhorn round the floor.

"Hey up, don't get fresh with me," said Sid Skelhorn. "I don't approve of mixed dancing in public places."

Eric Black, purple in the face, clung hold of the wall bars and shrieked:

"Watch out for injuries. Mind you don't wrench yourselves. Hup, two, three. Slow, slow, quick, quick, slow."

After a while they tired of the dance and sat down on the floor mats to smoke cigarettes and regain their wind.

"Bloody hell, there's still an hour to go before the pubs open," said Phil Kenny.

"Come on, lads," wailed Eric Black. "We're shelling out seven and a kick an hour for the use of this gym. Let's get our moneysworth, lads. Hup, two, three. Hup . . . ah, sod you."

They finished their cigarettes. The musty dampness seeped all around them. Stewart Woodhead blew on his hands and rubbed them together. Then he suggested they play a game of five-a-side football until opening time.

Two sides were selected, and play commenced.

Carter Brandon threw himself into the game in a frenzy.

Twice he sent Bernard Garside crunching head first into the wall bars. He up-ended Phil Kenny and sent him spinning backwards into the vaulting horse.

"That's it, Carter," shouted Eric Black. "Use tactics. Kick 'em up the flaps."

The more Carter Brandon played, the more heated he became.

He flung himself through a flurry of ankles and shins to head home a centre by Stewart Woodhead. He hurtled into a sliding tackle to rob Maurice Buckle just as he was about to shoot.

He yelled encouragement at his team mates and abuse at his opponents.

After half an hour the perspiration was pouring out of him and his face was flushed with the heat of battle.

—What's up with you, Carter? You're behaving like a bloody lunatic, man. What's to do with you?

—Nothing. Everything's fine, isn't it? I'm happy, aren't I? I'm contented, aren't I? I had toad in the hole again for dinner, didn't I?

Savagely he launched himself at Rudyard Kettle and hit him squarely with the meat of his shoulders. Rudyard Kettle shot into the wall bars, and the crack of his head against the wood stopped everyone dead in their tracks.

"Oh hell, you've done it now," said Sid Skelhorn.

They gathered round Rudyard Kettle who lay in a limp heap. His face was deathly white and there was a blue flush on his lips.

—You've killed him, Carter.

—I haven't. I've not. I can't have done.

Eric Black cradled Rudyard Kettle's head in his lap and began to tap his cheeks gently.

"Has anyone got any smelling salts?" said Sid Skelhorn.

"You're the one what should have smelling salts," said Eric Black. "You're supposed to be the trainer, aren't you?"

"Damn," said Sid Skelhorn. "I forgot all about that."

The team looked on anxiously as Eric Black pinched Rudyard Kettle's cheeks and began to rub his wrists.

"Will they have to hold an inquest?" whispered a pale-faced Stewart Woodhead.

Presently Rudyard Kettle began to twitch. His right leg twitched. Then his left leg. His nose twitched. Then his ears. His right eyelid twitched. Then his left one. He opened his eyes.

"I never touched him, ref," he said. "It were self-defence."

Within two minutes he had recovered.

The colour returned to his cheeks. The bloom returned to the nicotine stains on his thumbs.

"No hard feelings, eh, Carter?" he said as they changed in the dressing room. "I just got carried away."

"You're all right, Rudyard," said Carter Brandon. "Think nowt about it."

After they had changed they went out into the perished night air and struggled and jostled each other to get into the warmth of the coach.

Carter Brandon was just about to step inside when he saw Alison.

She was wearing a navy-blue duffel coat and tartan slacks. On her head was a white tam o'shanter, and her silky blonde hair streamed from under it.

She turned the corner into Halifax Road and disappeared.

Carter Brandon did not hesitate.

He spun round, knocked Maurice Buckle to one side, shouldered Phil Kenny out of the way, shoved Stewart Woodhead in the chest and chased after her.

At first he could not see her among the crowds of workers streaming out of the pickle factory. Desperately and fiercely he pushed his way through them straining his eyes and his neck to catch a glimpse of Alison.

He was just about to give up, when he saw her twenty yards away staring into a shop window. He began to walk rapidly towards her, but when he was ten yards away, he stopped.

—Go on, Carter. What are you waiting for?

—I don't know, Daniel.

—You stupid berk. Get yourself over and give her the big How Do.

He dithered for a moment. He took two steps towards her, but then he stopped again.

—What's up with you, you barmy pillock?

—I don't know, I tell you.

She moved on and stopped to look in at another shop window. It belonged to a travel agent. It was full of coloured posters.

—Come on, Carter. It's easy, man. Straighten your tie, lick your eyebrows, go up to her and say How Do, ducks, fancy a pint of bitter and a sausage roll? Come on, Carter—hup, two three. Hup, two, three.

Alison turned her head slightly, and Carter Brandon dodged back into a shop doorway.

His heart was pounding.

—Don't be a bloody fool, Carter. Here's your great chance. You'll never get another like this. It's on a plate. It's . . .

Carter Brandon stepped out of the shop doorway and walked across to Alison.

"How do," he said. "Parky, isn't it?"

Alison turned round sharply. She smiled. Her green eyes flecked with tawny sparkled.

"Aha," she said. "It's you."

"That's right," said Carter Brandon. "Looking in the window, are you? You see some interesting things in windows sometimes, don't you?"

"Aha," said Alison. "Aha."

She had a deep voice. It vibrated on the smooth skin behind the lobes of his ears.

"They're nice, these posters, aren't they?" said Carter Brandon. "I mean, they're right colourful, aren't they? I mean, there's more colour to them than if they was in black and white."

"That's right," said Alison.

She smiled. It was a slow smile that sent tingling ripples over the surface of his chest from nipple to nipple.

"Do you like looking at pictures of distant places?" he said.

"Yes," she said. "The more distant the better."

He looked over her shoulder at the posters.

There were snow-capped mountains and sun-tanned bellies. There were cable cars and gondolas. There were Sellotaped forests and azure seas bobbing with rusty drawing pins.

—I bet she's a traveller, Carter. I bet she's knocked around. I bet she's been on more gondolas than you've had bottles of glucose stout. And just imagine her stretched out in a bikini, Carter.

—Mm.

—I bet her navel's as cool as the Cheddar Gorge.

She turned away from the window and began to walk away slowly.

Carter Brandon hurried after her and fell into step beside her.

"Do you mind me walking with you like this?" he said.

"No."

After ten minutes they came to the junction with Deepcar Road.

"I get my bus here," said Alison. "Good-bye."

"Aye. Well. Mm," said Carter Brandon. "Do you mind if I wait with you till it comes? You've only to say and I'll . . ."

"Please yourself."

—By gum, Carter. She's a belter right enough. Look at them eyes, lad. By God, you could use them eyes as castors on your bed and they wouldn't make a sound.

A bus appeared in the distance.

"I think this is it," said Alison.

—Well go on, Carter. Here's your chance. Do something.

—Do what?

—You gormless, sod. Proposition her, mate.

Carter Brandon hunched his shoulders and coughed:

"Aye. Well. Mm," he said. "Do you think I could see you again?"

Alison made no response. She was peering intently at the approaching bus.

"I think it's mine," she said, and then she continued without taking her eyes off the bus's number board: "Yes."

"Pardon?" said Carter Brandon.

"Yes, the bus is mine," she said. "And, yes, you can see me again if you like."

"Tomorrow?"

"Oh no," she said. "Not for ages. I'll tell you when."

The bus drew up and Alison jumped on the platform. The conductor rang the bell and Alison climbed the stairs.

When the bus turned into Wakefield Road, Carter Brandon thought he saw a flash of golden hair from the top deck.

But he could not be sure.

Chapter Twenty-seven

And slowly Pat continued to improve.

The progress was slow, but it was steady.

She was still frail and often she would be sound asleep when Carter Brandon came to visit.

He would not wake her.

He would sit on the chair at the side of the bed, holding her hand and listening to the radio through the headphones.

He would stare at the patterns in the curtains, and sometimes he would see green eyes flecked with tawny, and he would blink his eyes till they stung.

—She hasn't been in touch, Daniel.

—Don't be impatient, lad. Give her time.

—I don't want her to get in touch, Daniel. It were a mistake. I were a fool to talk to her. I don't want to get mixed up with her. I'm happy as I am. I'm contented. I am. I bloody am and all.

He gripped Pat's hand so savagely that she cried out with pain. But she did not wake up and he leaned across and kissed her lightly on the cheek.

On the occasions when she was awake, he would sit on the bed and put his arm round her.

"What did you have for your dinner today, love?" she said on Tuesday.

"Lancashire hot pot," said Carter Brandon.

On the following day she said:

"Hullo, love. What was on the menu today?"

"Spam and chips," said Carter Brandon.

Pat snuggled into him and sighed.

"Say something nice to me, Carter," she said.

Carter Brandon patted her gently on the arm and said:

"I think we're having corned beef fritters tomorrow."

Pat closed her eyes and shook her head slowly.

"I feel so tired, Carter," she said.

Carter Brandon stroked her wrist.

"Go to sleep. Have a good kip," he said. "I'll stay with you. I don't mind. There's a boxing commentary on the wireless in ten minutes."

Pat wriggled herself into a comfortable position resting her head on his chest.

After a while she opened her eyes and said:

"Do you still love me, Carter? Do you love me even though I am an old crock?"

Carter Brandon kissed her on the forehead.

"Aye, course I do," he said, and then suddenly he clutched hold of the headphones, sprang to his feet and shouted: "Christ, he's knocked him out in the first round."

Then George Furnival struck.

It was a Thursday morning of lumbering grey skies and idle snow showers.

Mr Brandon was in the greenkeeper's shed polishing his slitter, when George Furnival threw open the door.

He pushed past Mr Brandon and stood in front of the stove warming his hands. He did not say a word.

His chest began to heave. It was a slow, measured movement at first, but then it quickened, and suddenly he turned to Mr Brandon and said sharply:

"You know why I've come."

"Now listen to me, George, there's no need to act hasty," said Mr Brandon. "If we sit down and have a quiet chat about it, maybe we can sort things out."

George Furnival slowly drew back his lips and bared his teeth.

"Now then, George, no violence," said Mr Brandon. "One false move and I'll clock you one with me slitter."

George Furnival smiled once more. The blue grey of his long pointed chin shone.

"Nay, Les, put your slitter down. I've come to give you some good news," he said. "I'm recommending you to take over from me immediately when I retire next Monday."

"What?" said Mr Brandon. "You what?"

George Furnival laughed.

"Les, you have done me the greatest favour one man can ever do to another human being, man or beast," he said. "You've got Olive off me hands after all these years."

"Pardon?" said Mr Brandon. "Pardon?"

"By God, Les, I never realised how ugly she was till I caught her in your Mort's arms in the front parlour last night," he said. "She were smiling. What an hideous sight."

"Pardon?" said Mr Brandon.

"And what a mentality," said George Furnival, his face beginning to glow pink. "Not a single interest in the world except my stomach and her indoor cactus."

Mr Brandon gaped at him. He staggered backwards and sank into the wheelbarrow, where he remained among the damp sacking and the clots of compost, his legs hanging limply over the side.

"And she's no topics of conversation neither, Les. She'd no interest in garden pests. She hadn't a word to say for herself on the subject of aphids," said George Furnival. "All she wanted out of life was to keep me happy and the front parlour free from rising damp."

Mr Brandon shook his head.

"I don't understand, George," he said.

"Listen, Les, you can kill a man with kindness. You can smother him with it. You can squeeze every drop of life blood out of him."

"Can you?" said Mr Brandon.

"I didn't want forty-two years of contentment and clean sheets every Friday. I didn't want forty-two years of regular meals with roast brisket of beef on a Sunday and savoury rissoles on a Monday. I didn't want forty-two years of never having a cross word and being kissed every time I come downstairs from the lavatory."

"Didn't you, George?" said Mr Brandon carefully pulling himself out of the wheelbarrow. "What did you want then?"

"What I'm going to have now—uncertainty, discomfort and total lack of security," said George Furnival.

Once more Mr Brandon collapsed backwards into the wheelbarrow.

"I'm walking out on Olive, Les," said George Furnival, and his eyes lit up and he laughed. "I'm going to see the world. I'm going to be a vagabond. I'm going to live by my wits and bugger the fish cakes with parsley on Friday and the boiled breast of lamb with white sauce on Saturday. I'm going to be a man of the open road, living off the country and taking life as it comes. Mind you, Les, I'll not be without. I'll have me regular pension from the council plus my annuity from the Sun Life Assurance Company of Canada plus my endowment policy with the Scottish Widows and Orphans and plus and in addition my free bag of coal each week from the Old Comrades' Pensioners' Welfare Fund. By God, Les, I'm really looking forward to living a life of uncertainty."

He bent over Mr Brandon and helped him out of the wheelbarrow.

"I've got a lot to thank you for, Les," he said.

"Have you?" said Mr Brandon. "Why?"

"Because it was you what put your brother-in-law onto Olive, wasn't it? If she hadn't fallen for him and given me the excuse to get shut of her, I'd have been doomed to an existence of incessant love and kindness until they carried me out of the house feet first."

Mr Brandon shook his head slowly.

Ice creaked on the roof of the shed.

Dogs barked. Black-backed gulls yapped.

George Furnival slapped him on the back.

"Tarra, Les," he said. "I wish you luck in your new job. Make sure your chitties and your indent forms are in good order, keep a careful check of your petty cash, don't forget to write your purchase forms in triplicate and your time sheets in duplicate, and you'll have this park looking as pretty as a picture."

He closed the door and walked down the path whistling. It was a happy tuneless melody.

Mr Brandon sat stunned and silent in his old cinema tip-up seat until it was time to go home.

When he arrived there, Mrs Brandon flung herself at him and smothered him with kisses.

"Eee, Les, the most beautiful thing in the world has happened," she said.

"What's up, woman? What are you on about?" said Mr Brandon, fighting to free himself of his wife's amorous attentions.

"Our Mort's run off with Olive Furnival," said Mrs Brandon planting another wet kiss on her husband's forehead. "She come round this morning and packed all his things for him in three pigskin suitcases. They was matching, Les, too. Then she ordered a taxi and took him round to her house to live with her for good. She told me they was going to have cottage pie with frozen sprouts for dinner and boiled bacon ribs for supper."

Mr Brandon stumbled into the back parlour and slumped into the fireside chair.

"Isn't it romantic, Les? It's just like Romeo and Elizabeth Taylor," said Mrs Brandon standing by the fire and rubbing her hands together with pleasure. "She says she doesn't care what the neighbours say about her living in an unmarried council house. She says she's just deliriously happy to be teaming up with someone what shares a common interest in nutritious cooking and indoor succulents."

"And what did Mort say?" said Mr Brandon.

"Funnily enough after all his efforts over the past month he didn't say much," said Mrs Brandon. "In fact, he looked decidedly shocked."

At this point Mr Brandon's mouth began to wrinkle at the corners. A tremor came to his shoulders. The colour rose to his cheeks and before he could stop himself he broke into wave upon wave of laughter.

Mrs Brandon joined in. She sat on his knee and ruffled his hair.

When he told her the news about taking over George Furnival's job, she spattered his neck with kisses.

"Oh Les, I'm so happy," she said. "Everything's working out so well. Pat's been snatched from the jaws of death. Carter's taking his Gregory Powder without grousing. Mort's found love and contentment. You've got the job you've always wanted, and they've knocked a penny off their custard creams at the Dinky Bakery. What more could a woman want?"

"Mm," said Mr Brandon, and he pushed her away and took out his pipe.

Mrs Brandon began to stroke his hair. It was a slow movement.

"And we've got our second honeymoon to look forward to, haven't we, Les?" she said. "Have you had any more thoughts regarding the venue, love? Do you fancy Douglas, Isle of Man, or would you rather the North Wales coast?"

"Eee, you sort that out yourself," said Mr Brandon. "I shall be far too busy with the new job to bother about things like that."

On Monday afternoon the Parks Committee confirmed Mr Brandon's appointment as head gardener, and straightaway he threw himself into the job with enthusiasm and vigour.

He made out his order for his spring bedding plants.

The parks superintendent cut it by half.

He made out his order for his old-fashioned shrub roses.

The parks superintendent rejected it outright.

He made out his order for his ornamental shrubs and his seeds of hardy and half hardy annuals.

The parks superintendent cut it by two-thirds.

He made out his indent forms for three gross of putting green score cards and two dozen 'Keep Off The Grass' signs, and the parks superintendent gave it his unqualified approval.

Chapter Twenty-eight

Two days after Uncle Mort's defection from the Brandon household he left the neighbourhood.

He paid a brief visit to Mrs Brandon and said:

"Oh hell, Annie, she's taking me on a tour of her relatives. I've seen pictures of them. They're even uglier than her. Oh hell, what ever have I let myself in for?"

"Love, Mort," said Mrs Brandon. "Love, my sweetheart."

"That's what I feared," said Uncle Mort, and his shoulders drooped and he slouched off into the winter afternoon.

It was the worst winter people had known for years.

There were power cuts.

Boats sank in shallow seas. Dykes were breached. Moorland passes were blocked. Trains were stranded in drifts. Village pubs ran dry of beer.

The snow shimmered in the aching winter sun.

One morning two old spinster ladies were found frozen to death in the bedroom of a terraced house at the back of the Moffat Street parcels depot. There was no food in the larder and no coal in the yard.

"Doesn't it make you thankful for what you've got, when you hear of something like that?" said Mrs Brandon. "That's why God sends us tragedies. That's why He gives us earthquakes in Persia and low gas pressure on Sundays."

In the public parks of the city the ground was too hard for digging and trenching.

No football matches were played on the recreation fields.

In the big greenhouse behind the children's sand pit Mr Brandon worked hard from seven in the morning until seven at night drawing up plans for his reorganisation and fretting about the welfare of the bulbs planted deep in the frozen earth.

The parks superintendent rejected his plans for turning the gents' urinals into an orangery with tropical orchids.

And still there was no message from Alison.

—She's forgotten about me, Daniel. Thank God for that.

—Go on, Carter. Pull the other one, lad. You're bloody wetting yourself waiting for her to give you the go ahead to meet her again.

—I'm not, Daniel. I'M NOT. I'M HAPPY AS I AM.

Christmas crept nearer, and the illuminations in the city centre gashed the municipal snow with green, carmine, chrysolite, amethyst, saffron and madder violet, and Pat's health continued to improve.

Her stomach began to swell, too, and she entered a competition to select the five most desirable qualities in the perfect fishmonger.

She looked up from her entry form and smiled at Carter Brandon.

"Happy?" she said.

"Mm," said Carter Brandon.

"Happier than ever?"

"Mm."

"And do you love me more than ever, too?"

"Yes."

"Good," said Pat, and she took hold of his hand and kissed it. "Jolly good, Carter."

At the end of the visiting hour he had to make his own way back into town.

Since the news of Pat's recovery he had not seen Artie Shirtcliffe.

—Good, Daniel. It doesn't mither me. The less I see of that family, the better.

—Why?

—They're dangerous, Daniel. Can't you see it? It sticks out a mile. I wouldn't touch them with a barge pole.

He went into The Tinker's Bucket, and the first person he saw was Artie Shirtcliffe. He was drinking whisky with Larry Fenton, the bookmaker, and a detective sergeant with red wrists from B Division.

Carter Brandon smiled happily. He began to make his way towards him.

When Artie Shirtcliffe saw him, however, he downed his whisky in one gulp and elbowed his way through the crowd to the side door and disappeared into the cold black night.

—See what I mean, Daniel? They don't want to know me. Neither of them. Good. Bloody marvellous.

Next day the Brandons received two postcards.

One came from Uncle Mort who was in the middle of his tour of Olive Furnival's relations. It said:

"Barrow-in-Furness is worse than Hartlepools. Hartlepools was worse than Mexborough. Mexborough was worse than Droylsden. There wasn't much to choose between Droylsden and Birkenhead."

The other card was from George Furnival. It said:

"As you can see by the Parthenon (marked with an X) I am now in Athens, the eternal city. It has many merits, principal of which is an agency of the Sun Life Assurance Company of Canada. They do not have our equivalent of the National Savings Movement hereabouts. There is a marked lack of thrift. Long live the life of a vagabond and the lure of the open road. Yours faithfully, George Furnival."

—You'll be getting a card next time, Carter.

—Who from?

—Alison. It'll be a card telling you to meet her. It'll be wrote in beautiful handwriting, and I bet it'll have a nice niff to it, too.

—I don't want a card from Alison. I don't want to see her again. Everything's grand, Daniel. I don't want it mucked up.

Christmas week opened with the worst gale of the winter.

It blew in the windows of the long room in the county cricket club pavilion and the hail burst inside and battered at the faded sepia pictures of George Gunn, J. T. Tyldesley, Lord Harris and umpires with baggy caps.

All night long the wind howled.

Mrs Brandon snuggled into Mr Brandon in bed.

"It's going to be a white Christmas, Les," she said. "Isn't it romantic, love?"

"Stop talking," said Mr Brandon. "And take your knees out of my arse, will you?"

The gale continued unabated throughout the day.

It blew up the skirt of Linda Preston as she walked along the canal tow-path with Carter Brandon at lunchtime.

"Hey up," said Carter Brandon. "I can see your knickers."

"You can see 'em any time, kid," said Linda Preston. "On or off—I'm not mithered."

In the evening Pat greeted him with a scowl.

"Just look at the length of your hair, Carter," she said. "For heaven's sake, get it cut. You're making a holy show of me in front of Nurse Booter."

"Who's Nurse Booter?"

"The dumpy one with bandy legs," said Pat. "She told me yesterday you looked very unhealthy and podgy."

"I'm not podgy."

"Oh yes you are. Don't be so argumentative. Nurse Booter's got medical training, so if she says you're podgy, you're podgy, and that's that."

Carter Brandon shrugged his shoulders.

"Nurse Booter says she'd not be surprised if you wasn't drinking too much and having late nights."

"I'm not."

Pat linked arms with Carter Brandon and rested her head on his shoulder.

"You're not out gallivanting, are you, Carter?" she said softly. "You're not getting up to mischief, are you?"

"No."

—You bloody would, if you had the chance with Alison, Carter.

—Alison? Who's Alison? I've forgot all about Alison, Daniel. She doesn't exist as far as I'm concerned, me old mate.

Pat sighed.

"You must feel very lonely at times, love," she said. "Do you miss me? Do you miss my company?"

"Yes."

"What do you miss most about me, love?" said Pat snuggling close into her husband's chest.

Carter Brandon scratched the back of his head.

"Well, come on, man—think," said Pat crossly. "What's the main thing you miss through not having me at home?"

"Getting me end away," said Carter Brandon.

Chapter Twenty-nine

Christmas Day dawned bright and clear.

"It's a white Christmas, Les," said Mrs Brandon throwing back the bedroom curtains.

"What do you expect with all this bloody snow around?" said Mr Brandon.

"Isn't it all so romantic, Les? Sleigh bells jingling in the snow, the yuletide log glowing in the hearth, a robin singing from the mistletoe and the Beverley Sisters with another Xmas hit. Eee, give us a kiss, Les. Give us a hug. Let's have a rehearsal for the honeymoon."

She threw herself onto the bed and clamped herself on top of Mr Brandon.

"Give over, you mad bugger," said Mr Brandon, wriggling away from his wife and scrambling off the bed. "I've no time for kissing and cuddling. I've got work to do down at the greenhouse."

"Oh no you've not," said Mrs Brandon and she sprang off the bed and pressed her back firmly against the closed bedroom door. "It's Christmas Day and you're stopping at home and playing your full part in the festivities. You'll put on a happy smiling face and enjoy yourself to the full with crackers and a funny hat or I'll want to know the reason why."

Mr Brandon's shoulders drooped. He hung his head.

"Bloody hell, what a life," he said. "Happy Christmas."

"Happy Christmas, Les," said Mrs Brandon. "Very many of them, love."

She kissed him long and hard.

Then she went into Carter Brandon's bedroom and repeated the performance.

"Oooh, just look at your pillow case, Carter, it's bulging at the seams," she said, pointing to the foot of the bed. "Aren't you a lucky lad? I bet poor Santa nearly ruptured himself carting all that lot down the chimney."

For breakfast they had rashers of Wiltshire bacon, thick coils of Cumberland sausage, spicy hunks of Bury black pudding and home-made potato cakes cooked in butter under the grill.''

"That's what I call a Christmas breakfast," said Mr Brandon. "Small enough not to spoil your dinner and fatty enough to absorb the morning's boozing.''

Carter Brandon nodded and then at the insistence of his mother began to examine the contents of his pillow case.

These consisted of an orange, an apple, a packet of nuts, a set of snakes and ladders, a set of ludo, a Jew's harp, a pencil sharpener, a magnifying glass, a Biggles book and a Bunkle book, a bus-conductor's set, a light blue Shetland roll collar sweater, a pair of socks, a Rupert Annual, a cream shirt, a pair of motoring gloves and a Seebackoscope.

"Now see what happens when you're a good boy, Carter, and take your turkey rhubarb root regular," said Mrs Brandon.

At ten o'clock the first guests arrived. They were Uncle Mort and Olive Furnival.

Uncle Mort looked puffed and pasty. He moved sluggishly. There was a bright yellow sheen to his forehead and he had developed a blotchy double chin.

"Just look at him, Annie," said Olive Furnival. "Haven't I done a grand job on him?"

Mrs Brandon looked her brother up and down. She pursed her lips and inclined her head.

"It's not for me to say, is it?" she said. "But are you sure you're giving him enough roughage?"

Mr Brandon showed them into the front parlour and handed round drinks. Uncle Mort took out a large bottle of scent wrapped in a rumpled copy of the *Sporting Chronicle* and threw it to Mrs Brandon.

"Catch," he said. "Happy Christmas."

Mrs Brandon caught the bottle and sniffed it.

It was a large bottle. It was only slightly smaller than a Tizer bottle. It contained a liquid the colour of the water in the deep end of public baths.

"Smashing, Mort," said Mrs Brandon. "What's it called?"

"Scent," said Uncle Mort.

"I know that, you silly devil. I'm talking about its title. Is it called Armour de Paris or is it called Moments of Passion? I mean, it hasn't got no label on it, has it? What did they call it in the shop?"

"I don't know," said Uncle Mort. "I just said to the bloke: 'Give us a bottle of that blue stuff.' And he said: 'Which blue stuff — the scent or the shampoo for long-haired dogs?'"

Mrs Brandon smiled weakly.

"I see," she said pushing the bottle away from her. "Thank you very much. It's very nearly just what I wanted, but not quite."

At eleven o'clock the Yuletide guest list was completed by the arrival of Mrs Partington.

Carter Brandon handed round more drinks. The ladies had port and lemonade, and the men had bottles of Guinness and tumblers of whisky.

They toasted each other, and then Mrs Partington began to cry.

"What's up, love?" said Mrs Brandon. "Are you still thinking about Mr Shirtcliffe? Is there still a great aching void in your heart? Are you still pining for him?"

Mrs Partington nodded and sniffed hard into her handkerchief.

"I were just thinking of them Winceyette pyjamas I were going to give him as a Christmas box," she said. "They looked ever so nice in the window. They was next to a gents windcheater with epaulets. They looked so disappointed when I didn't buy them."

She began to sob again.

Olive Furnival sat next to her and put her arm round her.

"There, there, love, don't cry," she said. "I'm sure them pyjamas will find a good loving home sooner or later."

The fire roared.

Nuts were consumed. Tangerines were peeled. Sticky dates were speared by plastic forks.

Then Mr Brandon yawned, scratched his stomach and said: "Right then. It's opening time. Pints away, lads."

Mrs Brandon looked at them scornfully as they trooped into the hall to put on their coats.

"Men!" she said. "Fancy boozing in pubs on Christmas Day. It's no wonder there was no room in the inn when our Lord was born. It was probably bursting at the seams with boozers like Les playing carts and talking mucky. They was probably having such a sing-song they never even heard the Virgin Mary knocking at the door."

The three men left the house without a backward glance at the women.

It was cold, but they trudged through the snow dauntlessly, heads bent into the wind.

"It's the best pint of the year, is this one," said Mr Brandon.

"Course it is," said Uncle Mort. "It's the one day of the year when you can guarantee there won't be a single woman in the pubs."

The Whippet was crowded.

There was an unfamiliar tang of cigar smoke. The saloon bar smelled of new gloves and unwanted mufflers.

Teddy Ward greeted them. He was wearing a new cap. It was nigger-brown and bottle-green.

"Hey up, Teddy, I like your new cap," said Uncle Mort. "It looks like a lump of cow turd."

They ordered double whiskies and squeezed their way into the saloon, where Enid, better half of popular mine host and ex Green Howard, Bert Coleridge, was handing out home-made mince pies.

"Happy Christmas, love," she said to Uncle Mort. "Have a mince pie."

"No ta," said Uncle Mort. "I were up half the night with the ones you give us last year. No offence."

They pushed their way through a hard-packed throng of temporary postmen and found a table for themselves under the pictures of the Queen Mother and Joe Davis.

Uncle Mort looked glumly at the stunted forest of new socks and said:

"That's the only thing I'll say in favour of the three wise men—at least they thought of something more original than socks to bring as a present."

The talk in the pub grew louder. Voices husky with whisky began to sing.

"You look fed up," said Carter Brandon to Uncle Mort.

"I am," said Uncle Mort. "Olive Furnival's getting me down."

"Well, run away from her," said Mr Brandon.

"I can't," said Uncle Mort. "I've grown attached to her."

"You what?" said Mr Brandon.

"Well, she's so bloody ugly I feel sorry for her. It's like that lurcher we had when I were a nipper. It were old, it were ugly, it had bad breath, its teeth was dropping out and it was forever bumping into the piano stool. Yet we didn't get it destroyed, because we'd grown fond of it, and because it were the only one in the house what wagged its tail when me dad came home pissed from the pub. Well, Olive's like that. She's so full of love, she's bloody smothering me with it. I can hardly breathe with it. And I've grown so podgy with all that rich food she stuffs into me, I haven't got the sleight of foot to dodge when she tries to kiss me."

"Don't be a mug," said Mr Brandon. "Run away from her."

"I can't," said Uncle Mort. "She needs me to pour her affection on. If she had to bottle it up, she'd snuff it."

"You want to buy her a cocker spaniel," said Mr Brandon. "They're well-known for being affectionate, and they'd make a better job of scaring off burglars than you would."

"Aye, but they're very prone to ear trouble, are cocker spaniels," said Uncle Mort, and he took a long mournful sup of his whisky. "By God, Les, love's got a lot to answer for in the history of the world's calamities."

"True," said Mr Brandon. "Too bloody true, lad."

Carter Brandon smiled, and the two older men stared balefully into their glasses of whisky.

However, as the flow of drinks increased so did their gloom begin to lift, and by the time stop tap was called Mr Brandon had smiled three times and Uncle Mort had had two good laughs at Emrys Tattersall's new cardigan and Percy Shuttleworth's new tyre levers.

The whisky had warmed them to the cockles so they did not feel the cold as they set off for home. Hunger drove them briskly through the snow and quickened their pace as they neared the house.

The smell of goose hit them as soon as they turned in through the front gate. They bustled into the kitchen stamping their boots on the doorstep to rid them of the snow.

"We're back," said Uncle Mort.

"So I can smell," said Mrs Brandon.

Olive Furnival took hold of Uncle Mort by the waist and kissed him full on the lips. It was a juicy kiss.

"Welcome back, love," she said. "I'm glad you made it."

Condensation was streaming off the inside of the kitchen windows and the heat haze made a watery blur round the light bulb.

Sprouts were simmering in a pan on top of the cooker. So were carrots and turnips in a large copper pot, potatoes in a navy-blue enamel pan and bread sauce in a pearl-grey saucepan with a dented handle and a red lid.

The Christmas pudding bubbled in its pot on top of the black-lead range. Alongside in other pots were white sauce, giblet gravy, parsnips and gooseberry sauce.

"Hey up, goosegog sauce," said Uncle Mort gleefully, and he poked his thumb into the pot.

Mrs Brandon slapped his wrist sharply with a wooden spoon and hustled him and his colleagues out of the kitchen into the back parlour, where the table was already laid out for the Christmas dinner.

"Bloody hell," said Uncle Mort. "We're having serviettes. It must be serious."

The three men drank hot rum and lemon. The smell of goose grew stronger and stronger.

A saucepan lid clattered. The colander clanked against the side of the sink. The knife drawer rattled.

Suddenly the door from the kitchen was thrust open, and the women began to bring in the dishes.

The smell of goose writhed, squirmed and purred round the men's nostrils. Their mouths watered. Their stomachs contracted and curdled.

The sprouts were juicy green and flecked with buttercup yellow. The carrots and turnips rose in a streaming mound of orange ochre from the deep chartreuse green of their bowl.

The giblet gravy gurgled in its boat. The bread sauce heaved and plopped. The butter spread itself in golden, lucent runnels over the light and fluffy boiled potatoes.

And then Mrs Brandon brought in the goose.

It was a large goose. It was enormous.

The men gasped with astonishment.

"Struth," said Uncle Mort. "It's halfway to being an ostrich, is that goose."

"Right, Les, get carving," said Mrs Brandon. "Let battle commence."

Battle did indeed commence, and many were the honours won during its course. At its conclusion the men, bloated and greasy-chinned, staggered from the table and retired to the front parlour. Before they could fall asleep, however, there was a knock at the front door.

Artie Shirtcliffe stood there with a broad smile on his face.

"Happy Christmas, ducks," he said to Mrs Brandon pointing to a large bottle-green Bentley standing in the road outside the house. "That's my present for you."

"For us?" said Mrs Brandon. "A car? Thank you very much. It's just what we wanted, only could you get it in navy-blue?"

"Nay, it's not the car what's the present," said Artie Shirt-cliffe. "The present is me. I'll be your chauffeur all afternoon. I'm running you up to the hospital."

"What a nice gesture," said Mrs Brandon. "I didn't like you when I first met you. I thought you was rubbish. I suppose I'll have to change my mind now."

She invited him inside, and Carter Brandon wished him the compliments of the season and gave him a large tumbler of whisky.

"It's very decent of you, Artie," he said. "I appreciate it very much, Artie. You're a sport, Artie."

"That's all right, professor," said Artie Shirtcliffe. "Don't spread it around, though, or the punters'll think I'm going soft."

He laughed, tickled Carter Brandon under the chin and held out his tumbler for more whisky.

On their way to the hospital Mrs Brandon said:

"And what sort of Christmas Day have you had at home so far, Arthur?"

"I've not been home today, owd ducks," said Artie Shirtcliffe. "I've been out shooting, haven't I? Well, I can't stand Christmas. It's too much of a strain trying to look grateful for your presents."

Mrs Brandon sniffed hard and twitched her shoulders. She sank back into the deep maroon leather seats in the back of the car and remained silent until they reached the hospital.

Mr Brandon and Uncle Mort prized themselves reluctantly out of the car and shuffled their feet impatiently as Mrs Brandon and Olive Furnival respectively adjusted the respective knots in their respective consorts' ties.

"I wondered what had happened to you," said Carter Brandon quietly to Artie Shirtcliffe as he waited for the older folk to adjust their dress. "I've not seen sight nor light of you since the day Pat recovered."

Artie Shirtcliffe smiled. He gave Carter Brandon's ear a gentle tug.

"Ne'er mind, eh?" he said. "I still love you."

Pat greeted her visitors warmly when Nurse Booter herded them into her ward.

The three men stood by the door scraping their toe caps on

the floor and twiddling their thumbs. The three women sat on the bed and gossiped.

The red second-hand jerked round and round. Sometimes it gave a twitch.

Then Mrs Brandon stood up and, motioning to the door, said:

"Come on, everybody, let's leave Pat and Carter Brandon on their own for a bit. They must have heaps to talk about being as how Carter's not said a word so far."

Gratefully Uncle Mort and Mr Brandon bolted out of the door. They were followed slowly by the three women.

And so Carter Brandon and Pat were left alone.

"Happy Christmas, love," said Pat softly.

"Ta," said Carter Brandon. "Same to you."

"Come and sit by me on the bed, Carter."

"Aye. If you like."

He sat on the bed beside her.

"I put on a new nightie special for you today, Carter," said Pat.

"Ta," said Carter Brandon.

"I got it from Nurse Booter's Littlewood's catalogue," said Pat. "How much do you think it cost?"

"I haven't a clue," said Carter Brandon.

"Two pounds fifteen spread over four months," said Pat. "Isn't it reasonable, Carter? Isn't it a snip?"

Suddenly she clutched hold of Carter Brandon's arm tightly, and he felt a shudder pass through her whole body.

"We'll never spend another Christmas apart, will we, Carter?" she said. "Promise me, Carter. Say Yes, Carter."

"Yes," said Carter Brandon.

Pat sighed and sank back into her husband's arms. Her body was relaxed, and her breathing was steady.

"I had ever such a funny dream last night, Carter," she said.

"Oh aye?"

"I dreamed I were in my womb again with baby and Daniel. They get on ever so well together, do baby and Daniel."

—We'd get on even better if he didn't cheat at cards, Carter. Bloody hell, last night I catches him nicking the three of hearts off the bottom of the pack to make up a straight flush for himself.

"We had supper together in my womb," said Pat. "It was lovely. We had genuine place mats and baby played mother and poured out the tea."

—I don't like the way she's got her womb done out, though, Carter. It's too modern. I can't stand these bloody Venetian blinds and Anglepoise wall lamps. I can't stand these record players with transparent tops. And as for this modern Scandinavian cutlery, well, it's a bugger trying to eat peas off them stupid bloody knives. They've no blades to them. They've no . . .

"Any road, Carter, after we'd had supper and done the washing up, Daniel took me to one side and had a few words. He said he could see all our future spread out before us, and he wanted to let us in on it."

—I never, Carter. I never said a word about your bloody future.

"Oh he did paint a lovely picture, Carter," said Pat, biting the top off a whipped cream walnut. "He said he could see you in your chunky manly cardigan mixing the food for baby's bottles and turning the teats inside out with a sterilised apostle teaspoon. He said he could see you feeding baby when he woke up howling in the dead of night, because you insisted I got all the sleep what's going and because you found feeding baby the most fulfilling thing what you'd ever done in your life. He said you'd be working all the overtime you could so's we'd have the wherewithal to maintain baby proper and buy him a new school cap when the bullies from Ragget Road throw his old one under the bus."

—What's she on about, Carter? I never said that load of old crap.

"He said you'd never go out boozing at nights, Carter, because you wouldn't want to spend money on beer what could be spent on educational toys in natural pine."

—I never said that. I never mentioned educational toys, Carter. I can't stand the bloody things. The only thing an educational toy teaches you is how to swear when you trip over the bloody thing with no socks on.

"He said your whole world would revolve round me and baby. He said you'd be our slave for the next twenty years until baby gets his degree in difficult sums at Manchester University."

—Honest, Carter, words fail me. They do. Words bloody fail me.

"Do you fancy being my slave for the next twenty years, Carter?"

"Mm," said Carter Brandon, and he began to stroke her shoulders.

"Do you fancy a life of total domesticity, love? Do you fancy pouring all our efforts and interests into the home and baby and not going on holiday till we can afford a fully-automatic washing machine like what Hazel of Maison Enid's has got even though it was bought for her by her mother-in-law?"

"Mm," said Carter Brandon.

"So do I, love," said Pat. "I can't think of nothing better."

—Hey up now, Carter, don't blame me, owd lad. I didn't put all that load of old cobblers into her mind. She must have been on the old barley wine on the quiet in that party in her womb. It's not my fault you had to tell all them lies, mate.

—But they're not lies, Daniel.

—What?

—They're not lies, Daniel. I mean what I say.

—What?

—I'M HAPPY AND CONTENTED WITH LIFE, DANIEL. I'M AT EASE WITH THE WORLD. I'M HAPPY WITH MY LOT. I WOULDN'T CHANGE IT FOR THE WORLD.

Next day he got a postcard from Alison.

It told him to meet her outside the Town Hall at eight o'clock on Saturday evening.

Chapter Thirty

"Eee, Carter, I had right terrible luck with me Polish pork products competition in *Pins and Needles* this month," said Pat.

"Did you?" said Carter Brandon.

He was in the hospital. It was the evening he was to meet Alison. It was six o'clock.

"They give you six pictures of famous comedians with masks on, and you had to say who they was," said Pat. "I only got one wrong. Do you want to know who it was, Carter?"

"Mm."

"Nat Jackley, the rubber-boned comedian," said Pat. "If only I'd got him right and not plumped for Stainless Stephen, I'd have won a weekend for two in the capital of Warsaw plus as much salami as I could eat for the next annual year. Do you like salami, Carter? I don't. It makes me burp. Does it make you burp, Carter?"

"Mm."

— Not long to go now, Carter. Two hours from now and you'll be holding Alison's hand in the back room of The Griffon megging away like a good 'un.

— Aye. Mm. That's right, Daniel.

— By God, I bet she'll have some stories to tell you, Carter. I bet she'll be telling you all about the fiords and them steamers with black and white funnels what ply up the coasts to the North Cape and Spitzbergen. And I bet she'll tell you about dark mountains and trolls dancing away like buggery in dripping forest glades. And she'll tell you about snarling bottle-green seaplanes and kittiwakes and the chug-chug-chug of fishing boats and . . .

— Hold on, hold on. How do you know so much about this?

— Imagination, son. Imagination, and burning the midnight oil over the *Children's Encyclopaedia*.

". . . and my slogan was much much better than the one what

won it, Carter," said Pat. "Do you want to hear what it was, Carter?"

"Mm."

" 'Large or tall, big or ... ' "

—By God, though, Carter, she's a corker of a looker. She's a bloody knock-out. Imagine her all dolled up, Carter. I bet she's a classy dresser. Well, knocking about Europe like that she's bound to have picked up a few tips. I bet she doesn't sleep in rollers. I bet she doesn't wear hard bras like ice-cream cartons. I bet she's all soft and slinky, Carter. I bet she wears pyjamas in bed without the tops. I bet she doesn't shave under her arms. I bet its all silky there and she'd let you bury your beak in it till your ears turned purple. Well, she's bound to have picked up tips like that knocking round Europe so much.

—Hold on, hold on, how do you know she's knocked about Europe?

—Intuition, me old wingsy bash. Intuition and a keen interest in arm pits.

". . . any road, Carter, as I was saying, Nurse Booter confirms that I'm being transferred to a public ward tomorrow morning."

"Mm."

"It's very select, mind you. There's only four people there and they've got a very good class of illness. I believe one of them's an amputee."

The buzzer sounded, and Carter Brandon jumped up from his chair and kissed Pat on the cheek.

"There's no need to go immediately the buzzer rings, Carter," said Pat. "You don't have to clock on and off for visiting hours, you know. Why can't you be the last one out like all the other husbands?"

At nine o'clock he was still waiting outside the Town Hall.

It was foggy.

The fog was chill, and its breath was acrid and sooty.

He stood by the wrought-iron railings outside the main entrance and stamped his feet to keep warm.

The black grit borne on the coils of fog pocked the white surface of the hard-packed snow. People walked splay-legged and stiffly across the uneven, slippery footpaths, and in the distance the lights from the foyer of the Odeon cinema made a dull orange bruise in the fog.

—She's not coming, Daniel. I've been back-heeled.

—Nay, nay, lad. Don't be so impatient. If a thing's worth waiting for, it's worth waiting for properly.

—No, I think I'll jack it up and go home. They're having tripe and onions for supper tonight. The old feller's got half a dozen bottles of stout stashed away under the back kitchen sink. I think the Black and White Minstrels are on the telly, too.

He was just about to turn and make his way down the hill to the bus station, when a girl loomed up out of the fog.

It was Alison.

"Hi," she said.

"Oh. Hullo. Aye. Mm. Hullo."

"I'm late."

"Aye. You are. Only a bit, though. Not much."

Alison smiled.

She was wearing a navy-blue duffel coat and tartan slacks. She had a grey woollen scarf wound tightly round her neck. Moisture glinted on her long silky golden hair.

"Aye. Well. Mm," said Carter Brandon. "Do you fancy a pint?"

"Yes."

He took her to The Griffon. They sat at a table by the fire. Carter Brandon ordered a pint of black and tan for himself and Alison said she would like a large whisky neat.

Before putting the glass to her lips she paused. She closed her eyes and sniffed in deeply. She drank it slowly in one mouthful.

"Aha," she said dreamily. "Mm. Mm."

She unwrapped her scarf and dropped it to one side. It fell to the floor, and Carter Brandon picked it up and rolled it into a neat ball.

She took off her duffel coat and before she could let that fall to the floor Carter Brandon took it out of her hand and hung it on the peg by the fireplace.

She was wearing a navy-blue roll-collar Arran sweater. The wool was thick. She rolled up the sleeves to the elbows. There was a soft golden down on her forearms.

"Does your dad know you're out with me?" said Carter Brandon.

"No."

"Oh," said Carter Brandon. "You told him you were going out on your own, did you?"

"I didn't tell him anything."

Carter Brandon ordered another double whisky for Alison and a bottle of Guinness for himself. She took a long sup of the whisky, closing her eyes once more.

"Gorgeous," she said. "Mm. Mm."

Carter Brandon topped up his pint pot with his bottle of Guinness and said:

"Is your dad looking after your nipper then?"

"Yes."

"Do you like nippers?"

"No."

"Oh."

"I detest them."

The firelight flashed in the black heart of her pale-green eyes. The tawny flecks glowed fierily.

She finished her whisky in two gulps and this time Carter Brandon did not buy a drink for himself when he ordered more liquor for Alison.

"Does Artie know you're out with me?" he said.

She turned to him sharply and for a second her face was flushed with pink.

"Why?" she snapped.

"Well, I mean, well, because ... well, he seems to be trying to warn me off you. He keeps threatening me. I can't think why, can you?"

Alison laughed.

It was a laugh that crackled with spits of ice.

She drank four more whiskies before it was time for her to catch her bus.

At the terminus she said to Carter Brandon:

"You should have a car."

"I did. It got smashed up, though, when me missus had her crash. It were a write-off. She were almost killed, were me missus. I vowed then I'd never have another car. I hate cars. I loathe them."

She smiled at him.

"That was a long speech," she said. "It's the longest of the evening, I'd say. Wouldn't you?"

"Aye. Well. Mm."

When the bus came, she hopped on it and turned to him with a faint smile.

"I shouldn't tell Artie about tonight, if I were you."

"No, I'll not," said Carter Brandon, and then he coughed and hunched his shoulders and said:

"Would you like to go out again?"

"Maybe," said Alison. "I'll let you know."

Friday dawned with an east wind driving curtains of stinging sleet across the city.

More postcards came from George Furnival and Uncle Mort, who had once again been taken on a tour of Olive Furnival's relations.

The card from George Furnival said:

"I am now in Cyprus. Had tea with the manager of the Famagusta branch of the Scottish Amicable Life Assurance Society. Remember me to my old indent forms and chitties. Yours faithfully, George."

The card from Uncle Mort said:

"Birkenhead is worse than Droylsden. Infinitely."

Mrs Brandon came into the back parlour from the kitchen, bearing two plates of rashers, tomatoes, sausages, kidneys and fried eggs.

"There's a good boy, Carter," she said. "You've eaten every scrap of your Weetabix. Do you fancy a spoonful of rose hip syrup to wash it down?"

She ruffled his hair and then she went round the table to Mr Brandon and kissed him on the back of the neck.

"Not long to go before the honeymoon, Les," she said. "Are you excited, love? Are you getting all romantic? Is the sap rising?"

"No," said Mr Brandon.

"You just wait while spring, love," said Mrs Brandon. "You'll be just like a conker tree then when it comes to blooming."

She returned to the kitchen singing happily to herself.

"My God, this Silver Wedding isn't half getting on my wick," said Mr Brandon.

"It's forced to," said Carter Brandon.

"Your mother's just bought me a new pair of pyjamas for the honeymoon night. They're yellow with black collars and cuffs. Bloody hell, they'll think it's Wolverhampton Wanderers trotting out when I go for a slash in the middle of the night."

"Has she decided on a place for the honeymoon then?" said Carter Brandon.

"Douglas, Isle of Man," said Mr Brandon. "Fancy going all that way just to get sea-sick. And what sticks in my gullet is the TT races aren't even on."

Mr Brandon pushed back his plate and lit his pipe.

"Just think of what them swallows and swifts are up to now," he said. "They're swanning it up in Africa flitting around in the sun all day. Jammy devils. As soon as there's a touch of cold weather, they're up and off and bloody migrating. By gum, I wish we could do that, Carter."

"Mm."

Mr Brandon puffed hard at his pipe.

"I've a good mind to run away like George Furnival," he said.

"Mm," said Carter Brandon, and he stood up and packed his snap tin into his brown canvas shoulder bag.

"I bloody near run away before I got married, you know."

"Did you?"

"Aye. I got as far as Froodsham then I got a hole in me sock so I come home. It wasn't much of a trip. I got lost twice in Runcorn."

They put on their coats and slogged their way through the snow to the bus stop.

They huddled together in the shelter. When the bus came they clambered upstairs and took their seats among the bronchial coughs and the damp steaming raincoats.

"If it wasn't for the job, I'd be up and off tomorrow," said Mr Brandon.

"How's it going, any road?" said Carter Brandon.

"Not bad," said Mr Brandon. "They've thrown out more of me plans."

"Pardon?"

"I had these plans for rooting up the tennis courts and building a water garden with rapids and whirlpools and bulrushes and mountain ducks and water hens, but the Parks Committee turned it down. They said they had to consider their budding Wimbledon champions."

"They're buggers, are budding Wimbledon champions, aren't they?" said Carter Brandon.

"Sods," said Mr Brandon.

*

Artie Shirtcliffe was waiting for him outside the factory gates when he clocked off at work that evening.

He opened the door of the maroon Humber and said:

"What happened to you then last night, professor?"

"Pardon, Artie?"

"I waited for you outside here and you never turned up," said Artie Shirtcliffe slipping the car into gear and drawing out from the kerb.

"Aye. Well. Mm," said Carter Brandon. "Well, you see . . . er . . . er, I was early finishing, Artie. That's it. I were early, you see, so I went to hospital early so I'd have more time there. That's it, Artie. Sorry if you was kept hanging around. Sorry about that, Artie."

Artie Shirtcliffe smiled to himself and then battered the horn fiercely at a road that was empty of both cars and people.

When they got to the hospital, he took out a hip flask and began to gulp at the whisky greedily.

"Go on then, professor. Shove off. Do your duty. Go and grovel at the altar again," he said.

It took Carter Brandon a quarter of an hour to find the public ward, to which Pat had been transferred earlier in the day.

"You're late," she snapped when he shuffled in. "I'm the last one to have visitors. That's a great start for me prestige in the ward, isn't it?"

"Mm," said Carter Brandon.

It was a small ward with four beds. The walls were painted lilac and there were mauve curtains.

"See that lady with the goitre?" whispered Pat to Carter Brandon as soon as he had settled himself on the bed beside her.

"Yes."

"Well, she's had major surgery five times in the last two years. She used to be a champion at ballroom dancing till she had the operation to her gums. She's got a nephew in the RAF Regiment in Singapore."

—Singapore! Now there's a place worth running away to, Carter. I bet your Uncle Stavely's been there many a time on his tramp steamers. I bet he's been there and to Shanghai and Foochow and Amoy and Kwangchow and . . .

". . . and the family doctor despaired of her, you see, Carter. He said he'd never seen nothing like it since he was in Egypt during the war. Any road, her eldest brother works in William

Deacon's bank, so naturally he said he wanted a second opinion and the upshot of it was they got this surgeon special from America and he . . . "

—America! You could go to America, Carter. Just think of taking a train trip there, Carter. The Denver and Rio Grande, the Southern Pacific, the Atchison, Topeka and Santa Fé—by God, them's names to roll round your tongue, Carter. And just imagine taking a train trip from coast to coast, Carter. Waking up in bed with Alison stretched out beside you and the Rockies rearing up around you and outside the carriage it's icy cold with damp mist and inside it's warm and snug and you're having waffles and strong black coffee for breakfast—by the cringe, that beats the train to Matlock Bath any day of the week.

When the buzzer went for the end of visiting hour, Carter Brandon jumped to his feet.

Pat scowled at him.

"Look at you," she said. "Last in, first out."

"That's because I'm a good union man," said Carter Brandon and he gave her a swift kiss on the forehead and withdrew.

Artie Shirtcliffe continued to drink steadily from his hip flask as he drove back into town.

"I'm feeling brassed off, professor," he said as they neared Wilson's Bar. "Do you fancy a night on the batter to cheer us up?"

"Aye. I don't mind," said Carter Brandon.

They went to The Tinker's Bucket, where the landlord bought them two pints of bitter each with double whisky chasers.

Then they went to the Corporation Tavern, where the head boilerman at the ropeworks of Flatman, Wrigley and Nutbrown bought them bottles of Jubilee stout and Phil Swindells, rugby league correspondent of *The Morning Argus*, bought them single brandies.

When they stepped outside into the reeling night air, Artie Shirtcliffe thumped Carter Brandon on the back.

"See what I mean about the punters?" he said. "Bloody mugs, the whole lot on 'em."

They went into Topley's Wine Lodge and immediately a small man in a dark grey overcoat and a greasy black Homburg scuttled over and said:

"Hey up then, Artie, what's your pleasure? You name it, Artie, and you can have it, Artie."

"Shove off," said Artie Shirtcliffe and he led Carter Brandon to the far end of the bar. "We'll buy our own from now on, professor. The punters have had their fling for the night."

They ordered schooners of sherry and drained them in a single gulp.

"Do you fancy another, Artie?" said Carter Brandon.

"Aye," said Artie Shirtcliffe. "I like sherry. It makes your balls tingle."

The floor was bare in Topley's Wine Lodge. The pine boards were springy and sweet with the smell of sawdust.

There was a large cast iron stove which rumbled from the heat deep inside its clinkered guts. There were dark alcoves and gloomy cubicles festooned with cobwebs, and champagne was sold on draught.

"One of these days I'll get me own back on these punters," said Artie Shirtcliffe. "I'll show them who's boss."

"How do you mean, Artie?"

"I'll cock 'em up, kid."

"How do you mean, Artie?"

"Think about it. You're the professor. Think how a man like me could foul up the punters."

Carter Brandon scratched his head, and Artie Shirtcliffe roared with laughter and tickled him under the chin.

"Still, life's not all that black, is it?" he said. "At least we're getting shut of that sister of mine."

"Alison?"

"That's right. She's leaving soon," said Artie Shirtcliffe taking a long slow swig from his sherry and looking at Carter Brandon intently. "Aye, she's leaving, professor. The sooner the better, eh?"

—Alison? Leaving? What's he on about, Daniel?

—I don't know. Ask him, you daft chuff.

Carter Brandon cleared his throat noisily, but there was still a flutter in his voice when he said:

"Why's she leaving, Artie?"

"Because she finds life boring like me," said Artie Shirtcliffe with a yawn. "Aye, as soon as the baby snuffs it she'll be off."

—Baby? Snuffs it? What's he talking about, Daniel?

—Ask him, man. For Christ's sake, use your tongue.

"The baby, Artie? What do you mean, Artie?"

"The baby's got an incurable disease, professor. Poor little sod—that's why it's always crying its head off. That's why she brought it back from Norway. They bunged it in hospital last night. It'll not be long before it kicks the bucket."

—Norway, Daniel. *You* mentioned Norway and fiords and seaplanes and stuff like that. How did you know she'd been there? No one said owt about it before? How did you find out?

—I don't know, Carter. I haven't a clue. It's a bit eerie, isn't it? It's bringing me out in a cold sweat.

Artie Shirtcliffe called the waiter across with a flick of his fingers and ordered two large clarets.

"I tell you what, professor—the only thing what keeps me going is the shooting," he said. "Aye, when you're feeling bleak and brassed off there's nothing in the world better than blasting it all away with a couple of barrels of shot. It's right satisfying is that."

He tickled Carter Brandon under the chin once more.

"Come on, professor, we'll go to a club, eh?" he said, and he took Carter Brandon by the arm and led him outside.

There were flecks of chill gritty snow in the air.

They cut through Shuttle Alley and just before they turned into Lower Norfolk Street, Carter Brandon stopped Artie Shirtcliffe and said:

"What was Alison doing in Norway, Artie?"

"She married this Norwegian punter, didn't she?" said Artie Shirtcliffe. "Aye, he were a punter from Norway. Makes you think, don't it?"

They moved on down the street until they came to The Royal Nelson public house. From upstairs came the sound of a drawling trombone and the steady slur of a wire brush on drums.

Artie Shirtcliffe led Carter Brandon up a narrow flight of stairs to the concert room. It was heaving.

The lights were low and tendrils of cigarette smoke hung heavily over the people pressed shoulder to shoulder at the bar and buttock to buttock at the rickety, clinking tables.

The band was called The Smokey City Stompers. They had once played on the BBC Home Service.

Artie Shirtcliffe forced his way to the bar and called to the barman with the yellow silk shirt tied at the neck with nigger-brown braid.

"Hullo, gorgeous," he said. "I like your new eye shadow."

"Get stuffed," said the barman.

"Oooh, listen to her. She's getting her kecks in a right old twist," said Artie Shirtcliffe, and he laughed and tickled him under the chin. Then he caught hold of him by the front of his collar and snarled: "Two double brandies, colonel, and quick about it."

Sullenly the barman gave them their drinks.

Artie Shirtcliffe winked at Carter Brandon.

"I like punters what are queer," he said. "They don't take life so serious, do they?"

The band struck up a quick number and immediately the room began to rock with the stamping of feet and the throbbing of the drum.

Artie Shirtcliffe surveyed the scene through the bottom of his empty glass and said:

"Aye. Life's right boring at times, isn't it, professor?"

Before Carter Brandon could reply he was poked in the ribs.

He turned round sharply to find Linda Preston grinning at him. She was with Lesley Pincheon from Packing.

"Hullo, hullo, hullo," she said. "Out on the tiles, are you, Carter?"

She slipped her arm round his waist and hugged him. She nuzzled her face up to him and nicked his neck with her teeth.

"Ouch," said Carter Brandon.

"Who's your friend, professor?" said Artie Shirtcliffe straightening his tie.

Carter Brandon made the introductions and immediately Artie Shirtcliffe took Lesley Pincheon by the hand and pulled her onto the tiny square of floor reserved for jiving.

He jived well.

People stood back to watch. When the music finished, they applauded.

"Come on, you idle buggers, let's have some more music," shouted Artie Shirtcliffe, and the band struck up again.

"He's a right shrinking bloody violet, isn't he?" said Linda Preston.

Carter Brandon laughed, and Linda Preston pressed herself into him and said:

"I'm surprised to see you in a dump like this, Carter."

"Are you?"

She put her other arm round his waist and he could feel her sharp tight breasts slowly rubbing against his chest.

"I thought you'd be at home pining."

"Did you?"

She lifted up his shirt and began to stroke the skin at the base of his spine. It was a slow expert movement.

"It's putting temptation on a plate coming to a place like this, Carter," she said, and she took him by the hand and slowly led him to the door.

Carter Brandon did not resist.

She opened the door and pulled him outside.

"A bloke like you could easy get himself into trouble with a girl like me," she said.

"That's right," said Carter Brandon.

"Wait here while I get my coat," said Linda Preston.

She gave him a short sharp kiss and disappeared into the ladies' cloakroom.

As soon as she closed the door Carter Brandon bolted down the stairs.

He ran out into the night. He ran through the streets. He fell in the snow. He ran and he ran and he ran. And then he staggered.

When he arrived at his parents' home, his trousers were soaking from the snow he had stumbled through, and his teeth were chattering from the cold.

His mother scolded him severely. She made him a drink of Horlicks laced with cod-liver oil and rum and honey. She gave him three halibut-oil capsules, a laxative, two dessert spoons of Virol and packed him off to bed with two stone hot-water bottles and a chest glistening with Vick.

She kissed him on the cheek and whispered:

"Would you like to come into bed between your dad and me, love? It's lovely and cosy there. You'd be as snug as a bug in a rug."

"I'm okay here," said Carter Brandon.

His mother kissed him again and left.

He lay in bed motionless.

— Well, you're a right hopeless lump if ever I saw one, Carter.

— Leave me alone.

— Bloody hell, man, you had it on a plate. It was all there sizzling, piping hot and spicey — *and* with a treble portion of chips.

— Leave me alone.

— You great gormless git. You've took Alison out for the night. You got on well. You fancied her. And what happens? You sit

on your arse, wait while she calls you and now you find she's
doing a bunk.

—Leave me alone, Daniel. Please.

—Here's your chance, Carter. Do a bunk with her. Clear off
now while the going's good. Take Alison while she's there for
the taking.

—I don't want her. I've got Pat. I'm happy with her.

—Oh aye, Carter? Oh aye?

—I've got used to her. I've got used to her cooking and the
way she smells when she needs a bath. I've got used to the way
she buggers up the toothpaste tubes and knots up the plughole
with her hairs. I've got used to the sound of her cutting her
toenails. Blokes like me don't run away. We stay. We're stuck,
so we have to grin and bear it. We're stuck here for good, mate.

Chapter Thirty-one

Two nights later Carter Brandon met Alison once more.

It was a Friday. His pay packet bulged in the hip pocket of his navy-blue cords. He had paid out sixpence subs to the football club, a shilling to the Welfare Buster and two shillings to the Maintenance Shop pools syndicate.

When he turned out of the factory gates, Alison was waiting for him.

"Hi," she said.

"Oh. Hullo. Aye. Mm. Hullo."

"Artie's out of town this evening."

"Oh."

He shuffled his feet in the cinnamon-coloured snow and fiddled with the buckle of his canvas shoulder bag.

"Right then," he said. "Right. I'll have to catch the bus then."

"Where to?"

"To the hospital. To see my missus. She's in hospital, you see. Aye. She's in dock, so I've got to go and see her."

"I'd rather you took me for a drink."

"Pardon?"

Half an hour later Carter Brandon led Alison into Topley's Wine Lodge and showed her to a cubicle next to the rumbling cast-iron stove.

She took a long slow sip of her Irish whiskey and closed her eyes and said:

"Mmmmm. Mmmmmm."

Carter Brandon sat opposite her. She stared at him unblinkingly as he sipped at his sherry. When she turned her head to remove her long grey woollen scarf the glow from the cast-iron stove lit up her left cheek, and Carter Brandon saw a bruise on the bone and a swelling below the eye.

"What are you staring at?" she snapped as she dropped the scarf to the floor.

Carter Brandon bent down to pick it up. He retrieved it from among the debris of sawdust and cigarette stubs and rolled it into a neat ball.

"I walked into a door," said Alison. "Any more questions?"

Carter Brandon shook his head.

He finished his sherry and ordered another for himself and a whiskey for Alison.

She was wearing tartan slacks and a navy-blue Arran roll-collar pullover. Her hair hung loose and free over her shoulders.

"How's the baby? Mm. How's it getting on in hospital? Is it getting better or is it getting worse?" said Carter Brandon.

"Worse," said Alison.

He offered her a cigarette, but she shook her head.

"Aye. Well. Mm," he said. "Aye. Artie says you're going to be leaving us soon."

"Does he?"

"Aye. Well. I mean, have you any plans regarding destination? I mean, have you decided where you're going to go?"

"As far away as possible."

"To Norway, maybe?"

"Norway?"

"Aye. To go back to your husband?"

"Husband?"

"Aye. Artie says you've a husband in Norway. Aye, he says you married a Norwegian and that's why you had to bring the baby back with an incurable disease to get it cured."

Alison stared at him silently. She took another sup from her whiskey.

"Aye. Mm," said Carter Brandon. "That's what Artie told me, any road."

"Good for Artie," said Alison, and she held out her empty glass for more whiskey.

The cast-iron stove rumbled. A small man in a long grey overcoat and a greasy black Homburg hat ordered a glass of madeira and a cheese and onion cob. The sweet smell of the sawdust mingled with the sour smell of stale champagne.

"Have you travelled much then? I mean, have you knocked about a bit as regards seeing places?" said Carter Brandon after the fresh drinks had arrived.

"Yes. I've knocked about a bit," said Alison.

"Where've you been to?"

"Most places in Europe."

"Oh. Aye. Mm. Have you been to Ostende?"

"No."

"Neither have I. They say it's got a very good beach for holidays, though. I nearly went through it when I were doing me National Service in Germany only we went by Harwich-Hook instead. It were a terrible crossing. They give us corned-beef sandwiches and I spewed the whole lot of it up. By gum, I were badly for days after that crossing."

"Were you?"

"Aye. But Sid Jones were a damn sight worse."

Alison rolled up the sleeves of her sweater and leaned her elbows on the table. She moved her head closer to Carter Brandon. He could see the tawny flecks in her pale green eyes.

"What time does visiting hour finish in your wife's hospital?" she said.

"Eight o'clock."

Alison smiled.

"It's half past eight now," she said. "I better be going."

Carter Brandon escorted her to the bus station. She would not let him hold her arm and sometimes she lagged behind him and other times she walked quickly ahead of him.

"My missus'll kill me for not turning up tonight," said Carter Brandon as the bus drew up.

"Poor you," said Alison and she climbed onto the platform and began to walk up the stairs.

"Will I see you again?" shouted Carter Brandon.

She paused and then she called without turning:

"Yes. If your missus hasn't killed you by then."

He heard her chuckle.

And then she was gone.

When he arrived home, his mother was waiting for him in the hall.

As soon as she saw him, she burst into tears.

"Oh, Carter, Carter," she sobbed. "Terrible news, love. Brace yourself for a horrible shock."

A great chill clamped itself round his neck. Every muscle in his body went rigid. The blood drained from his lips.

—It's Pat, Daniel. Oh hell, it's Pat.

—Oh hell, Carter. Oh dear.

Mrs Brandon looked up at her son with tear-bruised eyes.

"Are you ready for the shock?" she said.

"Yes," said Carter Brandon, licking his dry lips and feeling the anguished thump of his heart.

Mrs Brandon gulped. Then she said:

"I'm going to throw you out of the house, Carter."

"Pardon?"

She burst into tears once more.

"I'm going to have to turf you out," she wailed. "I want you out of this house first thing tomorrow."

She turned on her heel and bolted into the back parlour.

After a few moments Carter Brandon followed her. She was lying on the sofa sobbing vigorously. He hunched his shoulders and coughed. She turned to him. She patted the sofa beside her. He sat down, and she flung her arms around him, hugging him to her bosom.

"I wish I didn't have to do it, Carter," she said. "I wish there were some way of getting round it."

"Getting round what?"

"Your father's jealousy," said Mrs Brandon. "He's jealous of you, Carter. That's why I'm having to throw you out."

"I see," said Carter Brandon drawing himself away from his mother's chest.

"You see, Carter, you see, love, your father's jealous of all the love and affection and All Bran I'm pouring out on you," she said. "That's why he's taking so little interest in the honeymoon and his new yellow pyjamas. He's sulking, Carter. But deep down he's bursting with love and romance and mad abandoned passion, but he'll not show it just to spite me for giving you too much of my attention."

"I see," said Carter Brandon.

"Oh, Carter, I wish it didn't have to end like this," said Mrs Brandon. "Now will you promise me faithful to take your halibut-oil capsules regular?"

Later that night Mr Brandon tip-toed into Carter Brandon's bedroom and prodded him with a rolled up copy of *Amateur Gardening*.

"It's none of my doing, Carter," he said.

"I know that."

"I'm not jealous of you."

"I know that."

"I'm not showing no interest, because I've got no bloody

interest to show," said Mr Brandon. "And in any case I'm far too busy at work to bother about honeymoons and getting me spats dry-cleaned."

"How's the job going?"

"They turned down more of me plans this morning. I were going to plough up the football pitches and build a maze and a zoo with dromedaries and yaks. But they said No. By God, Carter, some people have no imagination, have they?"

"No," said Carter Brandon.

Mr Brandon patted his son on the shoulder and smiled weakly. His eyes filled up with tears.

"I'm right sorry she's slinging you out, lad," he said. "I wish it were me she were slinging out. I can't stand much more of it. If she goes on like this, I'll be forced to take action meself and do a bunk. Oh hell, Carter, I hate having to take action. It's not natural."

Next day Pat greeted Carter Brandon with blazing eyes.

"And where was you last night?" she said.

"Aye. Well, I couldn't make it, you see. I had a spot of overtime, you see. Aye. I had to do some overtime."

"Charming," said Pat. "Bloody charming. Do you know I was the only one in the ward with no visitors. Mrs Frisby with the goitre had three, Mrs Strudwick with the bulbous nose had five and even poor Miss Finch with the glass eye had got one. I've never felt so humiliated in all my life. I were bottom of the league, and Mrs Frisby's husband kept trying to stare down the front of me nightie. You should be ashamed of yourself."

"Why?" said Carter Brandon. "I were only doing it for baby."

"For baby?"

"Aye. I thought I'd get a spot of extra money in for when baby comes. We've got to look after baby, haven't we?"

Pat smiled.

"Oh, Carter, love," she said. "I've done you wrong. I've maligned you. Have a whipped-cream walnut and make up for it."

"Ta," said Carter Brandon and he bit the top off the whirled chocolate pyramid provided by his wife.

"Am I forgiven, love?" said Pat.

"Aye."

12

—You crafty sod, Carter. You clever devil.

—Not bad, was it, Daniel?

—Ten out of ten, mate. There's blokes got life peerages for lesser things than that.

Pat began to stroke Carter Brandon's thigh.

"I had another session in my womb last night, Carter," she said.

"Oh aye?"

"Yes. We had a Tupperware party."

"Mm," said Carter Brandon. "Did you sell much?"

"Only two salt cellars and a luncheon box. It was more of a social occasion really," said Pat, and then suddenly the glints of anger returned to her eyes and she said: "And do you know who turned up halfway through, Carter?"

"Who?"

"Alison Shirtcliffe."

Carter Brandon gulped on his whipped-cream walnut and a speck of chocolate lodged in the back of his throat and made him cough.

"Honestly, Carter, the cheek of it. She wasn't even invited, and it was obvious she hadn't the slightest intention of buying anything. She just looked at us all with this supercilious smile on her face. And when Hazel from Maison Enid's invited her to a corset-fitting party, she just looked straight through her. Talk about impoliteness. I mean, even if she just wears a pantie-girdle, there's no need for rudeness, is there? Would you be rude under those circumstances, Carter?"

"No," said Carter Brandon.

Pat smiled and kissed him lightly on the chin.

"Now then, love, I've got heaps to tell you," she said. "Shall I start with the incident over Miss Finch's dentures, or would you rather I do it chronological and tell you what I had for breakfast?"

—Sweet God, Carter, what are you doing with yourself, mate?

—Mm. Aye. Mm.

—Think of all the places in the world you could be right now at this very moment.

—Mm.

—You could be watching the sun go down on the Perfume River.

—Mm.

—You could be watching charr fighting the currents in Alpine rivers.

—What are charr?

—Little fishes like salmon, you ignorant bugger.

—Mm.

—Just think, Carter, you could be with Alison lying on a roadside bank in France filling her mouth with strawberries and sucking them out one by one.

—I don't like strawberries.

—All right then, we'll make it raspberries.

—With sugar?

—With sugar and saliva that tastes of bitter oranges.

—That sounds good, Daniel. By God, that sounds good, mate.

The buzzer sounded, and Carter Brandon jumped up from the bed and kissed his wife.

"Will you be doing any overtime next week, love?" she said.

"I don't think so."

"Well, you damn well should be. If you don't do overtime, where do you think we're going to get the money from to send baby to scout camp at Capel Curig with green flashes for his socks?"

Carter Brandon did not call in for a drink at The Furnace. He went straight home to his empty house.

He prowled round the rooms, picking up the items Pat had bought for the baby and then putting them down.

He gave the pram a push. It squeaked.

He went upstairs to the bedroom and changed into his pyjamas. Under the pillow he found Pat's nightie. He smelled it, and then he crumpled it up into a ball and buried his head in it.

He fell asleep at once.

He began to dream.

He dreamed he was at a party. It was in Pat's womb. The catering was excellent.

Someone put on a record. It was slow and sultry. He found himself dancing with Alison. Her mouth was full of raspberries. One by one he sucked them out.

She took him to a dark corner. He began to kiss her. He ran his hands through her silky blonde hair. He ran his tongue along her neck.

And then very slowly she began to remove her clothes.

She did it slowly. She did not blink. She stared at Carter Brandon all the time.

When she was completely undressed, she moved across to Carter Brandon and stretched out her arms to remove his jacket.

He screamed. He screamed and he screamed and he screamed.

When he woke up, he was drenched in perspiration and he had ripped Pat's nightie into shreds.

Chapter Thirty-two

"I warned you, professor. I told you not to sniff. And now I've caught you."

Artie Shirtcliffe stood in the lounge/diner next morning, legs apart, fists clenched hard at his sides.

Carter Brandon stood there in his pyjamas, scratching his chest and yawning.

"What are you on about, Artie?" he said.

"Alison," said Artie Shirtcliffe. "Bloody Alison."

"Oh," said Carter Brandon. "I see."

Ten minutes previously he had been woken by a furious pounding at the front door. He had lurched downstairs, opened the door and Artie Shirtcliffe had swept him to one side and marched into the lounge/diner.

"You need to be taught a lesson, professor," said Artie Shirtcliffe moving slowly towards Carter Brandon.

Carter Brandon stepped backwards.

"Now then, Artie, there's no need for violence," he said. "It were all innocent and above board."

"Nothing's innocent and above board with Alison," said Artie Shirtcliffe, and he brought his fists up to his chest and he advanced even closer to Carter Brandon.

"Well, there is with me," said Carter Brandon.

The harshness in his voice halted Artie Shirtcliffe.

"What?" he said. "Pardon?"

Carter Brandon squared his shoulders and thrust out his chest.

"There's nowt guilty between Alison and me," he said, and he took two steps forward. "And I tell you summat else—you come barging into my house like this again and I'll bloody give you such a kick in the balls you'll need a wheelchair to play outside half for the rest of the season."

"You what?" said Artie Shirtcliffe, and he dropped his fists.

"I don't care if the punters think you're the best thing since sliced bread. I don't care if you've pure gold stuck under your toenails, but no one comes into my house threatening me with violence and making assertions about his sister what I haven't even held hands with."

"Pardon?" said Artie Shirtcliffe, and he began to back towards the door.

"And I'll tell you another thing — you lay another finger on Alison, you give her any more bruises on her face, and I'll knock the living shit out of you."

"Now then, professor, steady on," said Artie Shirtcliffe, stepping out of the lounge/diner and moving rapidly towards the front door.

Carter Brandon stood in the hall watching him. He fumbled with the latch of the front door.

"Give it a sharp twist, Artie. To the left. That's it, Artie. It's only a knack."

Artie Shirtcliffe walked quickly down the front path to his car.

Carter Brandon followed him and put his head through the window as Artie Shirtcliffe tugged at the starter button.

"Don't take the hump, Artie. We're still friends, aren't we? There's no need to part enemies, is there, Artie?"

"Get stuffed," said Artie Shirtcliffe and he stamped on the accelerator and roared off.

Just before he jumped out of the way Carter Brandon noticed something on the passenger seat next to the driver.

It was a length of nigger-brown braid.

Much to the surprise of the pundits and the Job's comforters the works football team was able to play a match that afternoon.

It was the quarter final of the Tufton Cup. The opponents were Cleansing Department Ramblers.

The pitch was covered in sleek, freshly-rolled snow. It was hard. It was slippy. It was difficult to control the ball, and the studs from the players' boots sent up hard, jagged splinters of ice.

Carter Brandon played in a fury.

He covered every inch of the pitch. He ran till his lungs ached. He tackled till every bone in his body throbbed.

He scored three goals, sent the opposing right half to hospital, and his side won by four goals to two.

"Great stuff, lad," said Eric Black, as he sloped wearily back to the dressing room. "Your wife's not going to recover too quick, is she?"

"Why?" said Carter Brandon.

"Because we want you available for the semi-final," said Eric Black. "Perhaps you could arrange for a relapse just to be on the safe side."

Carter Brandon showered himself quickly and caught the 18B bus to the hospital.

Pat welcomed him with an excited smile.

"I had another session in my womb last night, Carter," she said. "We held a union meeting."

"Pardon?"

"It was an emergency meeting. We had a card vote and the motion was carried unanimously."

"What motion?"

"The motion that mother be allowed to marry Mr Shirtcliffe," said Pat with a chuckle. "Won't she be thrilled, Carter? I bet Mr Shirtcliffe does a jig in the streets when he hears the news."

— What the hell's she on about, Daniel? What's this union she's talking about?

— The Amalgamated Society of Unborn Babies and Allied Trades. I'm the general secretary.

— You're off your chump, mate.

— No, I'm not. We're dead serious about it. We're going to be affiliated to the TUC next year. We've got metal badges to stick in our lapels.

Pat took hold of Carter Brandon's arm and pulled him onto the bed beside her.

"It was a right interesting meeting, Carter. It was very well-attended. We had fraternal greetings from behind the Iron Curtain, too."

— Come on, Daniel. What the hell's been going on?

— Simple, Carter. We held an emergency meeting in Pat's womb on account of a complaint received by one of our members — to wit, your baby. He said he had information to hand which led him to conclude that he was to be born with less than the agreed rate of grandfathers for the job — to wit, two. We put this to the management — to wit, your wife. And she confirmed that this was indeed the case. I pointed out to her on behalf of my executive committee that such flagrant breach of nationally negotiated conditions of birth could not be tolerated and informed her that unless the matter was rectified immediately, we should have no alternative but to withdraw her labour. Faced with these demands, I am pleased to say that the management recognised the justice of our case and agreed forthwith to put into immediate operation a unilateral round the board one hundred per cent increase in the number of our member's grandfathers.

"You see, Carter, you see, love, I think it's vital for baby's future development that he has two grandfathers to put in *Who's Who* when he's a High Court judge with a wig and a kindly twinkle to his eye," said Pat.

"Mm."

"And again, Carter, with Mr Shirtcliffe being a midget, baby won't feel out of things as regards size when we have family gatherings round the grand piano you're going to save up for from your overtime so baby can have lessons. Isn't he talented, Carter, playing so well at his age? Do you think he'll get curvature of the spine through sitting so long on the piano stool."

"No," said Carter Brandon. "But he might get piles."

"Good thinking, Carter," said Pat. "I'll get him a foam rubber cushion."

She laughed and rubbed her hands together with pleasure.

"Eee, Carter, I'd love to see Mr Shirtcliffe's face when he hears the news. I bet he'll be in seventh heaven."

Pat was wrong.

Mr Shirtcliffe did not even make first heaven.

Two days after the news of Pat's change of heart he presented himself at Carter Brandon's front door and begged admittance.

He was shown into the lounge/diner where he accepted a mug of cocoa and a plate of arrowroot biscuits.

"What can I do for you then?" said Carter Brandon.

"Well, I don't want to be a nuisance," said Mr Shirtcliffe. "But I'm here to issue you with a solemn threat."

"A threat?"

"Yes—a threat," said Mr Shirtcliffe dunking a biscuit into his cocoa. "Unless you use your influence to get the marriage cancelled, I shall be compelled to tell Pat of your association with my daughter."

"You what?" said Carter Brandon. "You bloody what?"

Mr Shirtcliffe smiled at him.

"I'll give you till the end of the week to find an answer," he said. "I don't want to impose."

*

—Bloody hell, Daniel, why is life so complicated? Why can't it be simple and uncluttered? Why have you always got to make decisions and take positive actions?

—What's up? What are you grousing at?

—Well, look at it. I'm held over a barrel of gunpowder by Mr bloody Shirtcliffe, and I haven't got a clue how to get out of it. Me mother's thrown me out of house and home. Me wife's stuck in hospital. Me father's miserable at work and ground down by love. Where's the sense in it, Daniel? Where's the simplicity?

—Simple, son—with Alison. Run off with her. Start a new life. Kick over the traces. See the world. It's simplicity itself, me old wingsy bash.

—But I don't want to run away. I want to stay here. I want things to be simple and clear-cut like what they used to be. I want it to be like when I was a nipper. I didn't have to make no decisions then. It was grey flannel shorts while April, and khaki shorts while the end of the school holidays. It were new potatoes in summer and old potatoes in winter. It were *The Rover* one week and *The Wizard* the next. It were Scouts on Friday and Crusaders on Sunday afternoon. If you didn't wash your feet in the slipper baths, you got polio, if you spent too much time in the bogs with *Health and Efficiency*, you went blind and got hairs on the palm of your hand. It were all simple, Daniel. It were all marvellously, wonderfully uncomplicated.

He picked up a half brick and hurled it savagely over the icy surface of the canal.

"You look as though you meant that one, kid."

It was Linda Preston.

She came up behind Carter Brandon and put her arms round his waist.

"What's up?" she said. "Feeling down, are you?"

"Aye," said Carter Brandon.

She spun him round to face her. She looked into his eyes earnestly.

"There's more wrong with you than not getting your oats, isn't there, kid?" she said.

"Aye. Mm. Maybe."

She linked his arm and led him along the tow-path as the hooter sounded to end the dinner break.

"I can't fathom you out, Carter," she said. "You had it for the taking at the jazz club, and you went and did a bunk. You know you've only got to ask, and I'll be there. Yet you haven't said a dicky bird, have you? You haven't made a move."

"Mm."

They turned into the factory yard.

"You're a rum bugger, Carter," she said. "Come back home to my place tonight, and I'll show you my appendix scar."

"No, thank you," said Carter Brandon. "I'm playing snooker with me dad tonight."

Carter Brandon and his father beat Teddy Ward and Emrys Tattersall by two frames to nil.

He slept well that night.

On Saturday it snowed.

In the afternoon visiting hour Pat said:

"Carter, which do you think is the more important attribute in the ideal family butcher—clean, white teeth or a hearty, infectious laugh?"

"Pardon?" said Carter Brandon.

On Sunday morning Alison called round at his house.

"You must be mad coming round here," said Carter Brandon pulling her hastily inside and glancing anxiously up and down the road. "What the hell will the neighbours think if they see you?"

Alison shrugged her shoulders.

She looked round at the furnishing and decorations in the hall and smiled. She followed Carter Brandon into the lounge/diner and looked around and smiled once more.

"I mean, that old faggot over the road'll shop me as soon as look at me. And as for . . ."

—By gum, Carter, just look at her, though. What a cracker. Hey up, she's taking her coat off. Now then, look at them knockers. I mean as regards size they're not up to much, but as regards shape they're a couple of little thoroughbreds. If there were a Crufts Show for titties she'd win Best Variety In Show every time.

Alison let her duffel coat fall to the floor and Carter Brandon sprang across, picked it up and arranged it neatly over the back of one of the low-slung imitation leather arm chairs.

"First it's your brother here, then it's your father and now you roll up out of the blue. I don't mind visitors. I've got plenty of biscuits in, but, I mean to say, when a bloke's in a house all

on his own and his missus is in hospital having a baby and a
single bird calls round while he's in the middle of his Hoovering
and . . ."

—And look at the mouth on it, Carter. By God, she could
suck iron filings out of a donkey's hoof with them lips of hers.

Alison stood at the french windows and looked out onto the
snow-laden garden. The weak winter sun glowed in her hair and
picked out the line of her thighs against the whiteness outside.

Carter Brandon's hands went moist and his mouth went dry.

"Aye. Well. Mm," he said. "What do you want then?"

Alison turned and smiled.

"I want you to take me out."

"Now?"

"Why not?"

Carter Brandon led Alison down the road at a skulking run and
did not breathe easily until they were on the back seat of the
single decker North Western Road Car Company bus bound
for the dales.

The sky was clear and the high crags clawed into it with gnarled
white knuckles.

The roads were stained brown and yellow by the salt and grit,
and the chains on the bus whined and whipped. Church bells
rang. Sheep bleated.

They got off the bus at a village with a stone well in the main
square. They went into a pub, which in the summer was draped
in wisteria and glowing ivy.

"I've not seen you two afore," said an old man standing at the
bar.

"We're strangers," said Carter Brandon.

"How do. You're very welcome," said the old man. "You'll
have to shout if you want serving. She's very hard of hearing, is
Mrs Peckitt."

From another room came the click clack of dominoes.

Carter Brandon ordered beer for himself and whisky for
Alison, and they set to with a will to tackle the mound of roast-
beef sandwiches made with thick fresh crusty bread and sharp
tangy dripping.

"What did my brother want at your house?" said Alison.

Carter Brandon told her, and she smiled.

"And what did my father want?"

Carter Brandon told her and she rocked with laughter.

"It's not funny. It's no laughing matter. It's landed me right in it. What the hell am I going to do?"

Alison stopped laughing. She looked at him seriously for a moment and then said quietly:

"Stop seeing me. Simple, isn't it?"

"Aye. Well. Mm," said Carter Brandon, and she laughed once more.

The pub filled up, and they were squashed together on the wooden bench beneath the window.

Carter Brandon eased himself sideways and ran his arm along the top of the bench. He kept it there for a while and then he lowered it and rested it on Alison's shoulders. She did not resist.

"How's the baby?" he said. "I mean, is it improving at all?"

"No," said Alison. "It's getting worse. Are we still drinking?"

Carter Brandon went to the bar and brought more drinks. When he returned, Alison turned herself to him so he could put his arm round her more easily. She responded to the pressure of his hand by moving closer to him.

"Do you like travelling to foreign parts?" she said.

"Yes. The ones I've travelled to I've liked. I haven't travelled to many, though. I bet I've not travelled to as many as what you've travelled to."

"I bet you haven't," said Alison, and she took a long sip of her whisky and sighed with pleasure.

"What was Norway like? I mean, I believe they've got a lot of fiords there. They say it can be very cold in winter, too. Is it cold?"

"Oh yes. It's much colder than Spain."

"Have you been to Spain?"

"Oh yes."

"They say it can get very hot in Spain."

"Oh yes. It can."

Carter Brandon nodded. Then he coughed and said:

"I hope you didn't go to Spain and lie on one of them beaches all day and eat fish and chips with the mobs and stay in a hotel like a hat box and drink Watney's Red Barrel and complain of the smell of garlic and then come home and say it's just the same as England only the weather's better and the drinks are cheaper."

Alison smiled.

"No, I didn't," she said. "I stayed in the mountains."

Carter Brandon nodded with satisfaction and drank his pint slowly and steadily.

"Have you been to Italy?" he said.

"Oh yes."

"And France, and Greece, and places like that?"

"Oh yes. Lots of places like that."

"Have you been to Vienna?"

Alison nodded.

"What colour trams do they have there?"

"Pardon?"

"I like to know what colour trams the various places have. It makes me visualise them better."

"I see."

"Aye. Mm. I'm buggered if I can remember what colour trams they have in Cologne. They're green and white in Blackpool, that I do know."

Closing time was called, and they caught the bus immediately.

They did not speak much on the journey back to the city. They sat close together on the back seat, and Carter Brandon had his arm round Alison's shoulders.

Just as they crossed the city boundary Carter Brandon coughed and said:

"Aye. Well. Mm. You can come back home with me, if you like."

"Oh no," said Alison. "Oh no, that wouldn't be a good thing at all."

They got to the bus terminus, and Alison was just about to step onto the bus that would take her home, when she stopped and turned to Carter Brandon with a broad grin on her face.

"I've got it," she said. "I know what you can do with my father."

"What?"

"Tell him to run away."

"He'd not do that. What about his Hoover?"

"He could still have it at the place he runs away to."

"Where's that?"

"Your home."

"Pardon?"

"Don't you see? It's a terrific idea. You tell this mother-in-law of yours that my father has run away from her, and she'll be so furious she'll never want to see him again. So all he has to do is lie low in your house for a few weeks until the fuss dies down and it's safe to come out again."

"It'll never work. Never in a million years."

"And here's another thing—you won't be alone in your house, will you? And when a bloke's not on his own in a house, it's perfectly safe for a bird to visit him, isn't it?"

She smiled and gave him a cheery wave of farewell.

Much to Carter Brandon's amazement Mr Shirtcliffe raised no objection when the plan was put to him.

"Can I bring my own Hoover?" he said.

"Yes," said Carter Brandon.

"Have you got a decent electric sewing machine?"

"Yes."

"What sort of washing machine have you got?"

"I don't know."

"Have you got your own spin drier?"

"Yes."

"I'll move in tonight then. It'll not be a nuisance."

Mr Shirtcliffe moved into the house under cover of darkness. He brought his belongings in a van from the snuff warehouse, and Carter Brandon sneezed violently several times as he helped carry them inside.

"Does Artie know where you are?" said Carter Brandon as they sat in the kitchen drinking a mug of herbal tea.

"No," said Mr Shirtcliffe, and then he wrinkled his nose and said: "Have you boiled your face cloths recently?"

"No," said Carter Brandon.

"Dearie me, fancy living in a household where they don't boil their face cloths," said Mr Shirtcliffe. "Right then, we'll soon change that."

Chapter Thirty-three

When Mrs Partington heard the news of Mr Shirtcliffe's defection, she was quite distraught.

Once again happiness had been snatched from her grasp at the last moment, she said. A great gaping chasm had appeared in her life. The future stretched out before her in a desert of despair. Her plans for re-lagging Mr Shirtcliffe's cock loft were of dust.

Mr Shirtcliffe did not bat an eyelid when he heard of her hysterical reaction.

He was far too busy re-organising Carter Brandon's house.

He re-arranged the furniture in the lounge/diner. He bought new curtains for the master bedroom. He got an estimate for re-upholstering the low-slung imitation leather suite.

"What the bloody hell are you up to?" said Carter Brandon. "Pat'll kill me if she finds out what you're doing to her house."

"She'd kill you even more if she found out you was going around with my daughter, wouldn't she?" said Mr Shirtcliffe with a smile. "Now, come on, eat all them prunes up and let's get some goodness into your blood stream."

And the cold weather continued.

It gripped the city tightly. The river was frozen solid from bank to bank at Hatton's Bridge and for two nights running the heating had failed on the midnight express for London.

One Wednesday morning Carter Brandon dragged himself out of bed and slouched into the bathroom to take his shower.

— I can't stand much more of this, Daniel. His bloody cooking's playing havoc with my liver. And as for laxatives and cod-liver oil, he's streets ahead of me mother.

— You know the answer, Carter. Do a bunk.

The shower gave him no relief from his tiredness. The breakfast of kedgeree, porridge and creamy cocoa gave him no relief from his liverishness.

—I feel right shagged, Daniel.

—Take the day off work then. Don't be a mug all your life.

—Good idea, I'll go for a walk.

He put on his donkey jacket and wound his muffler tightly round his neck and stepped outside into the sobbing cold.

Without thinking he made his way to the canal and began to walk along the tow-path into the countryside. The sky was leaden. It was bruised magenta and purple. Rooks croaked in it.

Carter Brandon walked slowly. His feet crunched into the crisp snow and left prints with mint-blue hearts.

He thought of Alison.

He thought of the evenings they had spent together in the lounge/diner while Mr Shirtcliffe did his dress-making in the kitchen.

She had sat on the low-slung imitation leather sofa with a soft smile on her face and a sharp glitter in her eyes. Sometimes she had inclined her neck and worked her slim fingers slowly round the small donkey-brown mole on her neck. He had felt at ease.

—At peace, Daniel. Safe. Secure. Know what I mean?

—Aye. I felt like that just after I'd snuffed it, Carter.

While she talked, he sat silent and motionless. She had spoken about the places she had visited on her travels. She told him of the village in France with its squat, crumbling, ivy-sheathed Saracen tower and the nearby woods full of sun and strawberries and lilies of the valley and snakes and oily beech nuts that tickled her throat and made her cough.

She told him of a dank, wet day in Paris, sad with the first cold rains of winter. She had taken shelter in a café on the Place St Michel. She had sat on her own at a table near the window. At the next table a man with a beard sipped at a rum St James and stared at her. Suddenly he had taken a notebook out and commenced to write furiously. From time to time he would sharpen his pencil, and the shavings would curl into the saucer beneath his drink. From time to time he would look up at her and then savagely he would rip out the pages of his notebook, on which he had written, crumple them up and hurl them to the floor. He had smiled at her after a while and spoken. He was American. "Pardon me, but I am trying to write one true sentence. I am trying to write the truest sentence I know." The look in his eye had disturbed her and she had left at once, but for weeks after the smell of old wet waterproofs and musty felt hats had wriggled in her nostrils at night.

She had told him of the boy friends she had had in Germany. One had a wonderful car. The other had an aeroplane. Another had fought seven duels. Another had a knack of putting out street lamps by giving them a smart kick in a certain spot. One night on the way back from a dance he and she had put out all the lamps in the neighbourhood.

Carter Brandon had listened, enraptured, enchanted, overwhelmed, and in the kitchen the sewing machine whirred and the kettle for the Instant Postum whistled.

Alison had said nothing about her baby. She had not mentioned running away. She had not spoken about Artie or the long strip of sticking plaster on her neck. She had not allowed Carter Brandon to touch her.

More rooks cawed, and a herring gull mewed.

Carter Brandon thought of his visits to Pat in the hospital. Mrs Frisby with the goitre said rude things in her sleep. The price of soup spoons was outrageous. What were the most important attributes of the ideal husband — a firm handshake, or the willingness to 'muck in' when unexpected guests arrived?

Carter Brandon thought of his father.

—Poor old son, Carter.

—Aye. Poor old devil, Daniel.

—Twenty-five years of married life, and I bet he's never once shook hands with your mother.

—Aye. Poor old devil. I'll go back and take him out for a pint.

It took him an hour of hard walking to reach the park where his father worked. Straightaway he went to the greenhouse. When he pushed open the double-glazed door, a puff of lazy sensuous earthy warmth lifted him gently under the arm pits and helped him inside.

His father was soaking a tray of newly-sown seeds in an iron sink half full of tepid water. There was a smell of paraffin and damp compost.

"We got a postcard from George Furnival," said Mr Brandon. "He's in Cairo. He says it's in Egypt."

"It is."

"That's what I told your mother."

He stared at the tray intently, and when the moisture began

13

to seep through to the surface of the soil and compost and turn it into a rich, chocolate brown, he picked it out of the sink and carried it back to his work bench.

"We got a postcard from your Uncle Mort, too," he said. "He's in Maryport."

"Where's that?"

"I don't know," said Mr Brandon. "But there were an English stamp on it."

"That's a good clue," said Carter Brandon.

"That's what I told your mother," said Mr Brandon.

He picked up another tray and began to sow more seeds. He whistled happily. Then suddenly he looked up and said:

"If it wasn't for this job, I'd slit me bloody throat."

"Still going well, is it?" said Carter Brandon.

"Not bad," said Mr Brandon. "They've just turned down my plans for converting the putting greens into a dolphinarium with killer whales provided."

"You'll get the boot if you go on like that."

"That's right," said Mr Brandon. "Do you fancy a pint?"

They went into the public house opposite the main gates of the park, where once Uncle Mort had taken Olive Furnival on an assignation.

Mr Brandon bought two pints of Stone's best bitter and lit his pipe. The blue smoke, attracted by the draught from the cold fireplace, swirled away over his shoulder.

He smoked silently for a while. Then he took the pipe from his mouth and poked inside the bowl with the spike from his smoker's compendium. He smiled.

"I tell you what, lad, why don't you and me do a bunk?" he said.

"Pardon?"

"Let's throw away our shackles. Let's run away and be a couple of devil-may-care vagabonds and roam the world."

"What are you on about?"

"It's our last chance, lad. A month from now, and I'll be swamped by all this Silver Wedding nonsense, and then I'll be stuck with love and kindness and sympathy and affection and Cheshire cheese and pickled bloody onions for the rest of my bloody life."

He clamped the pipe back between his teeth and sucked at it violently. Clouds of smoke gushed out of the bowl and were whisked away up the chimney. He leaned across the table and grasped Carter Brandon by the arm.

"Come on, lad. Let's be up and away. Thee and me. Father and son. A couple of mates. We'll show them who's master of their own destinies. We'll . . ."

Suddenly his mouth dropped open. He half stood out of his chair and pointed over Carter Brandon's shoulder.

"Bloody hell," he said. "It's your Uncle Mort."

Carter Brandon turned round to see Uncle Mort standing at the door, peering nervously round the room with bloodshot eyes. He called out, and Uncle Mort gave a weak grin and made his way to their table.

"I thought you was supposed to be in Maryport," said Mr Brandon.

"I was," said Uncle Mort. "But then Olive had an accident and got fatally killed."

"Oh dear," said Carter Brandon and he took Uncle Mort by the elbow and helped him into a chair. "What happened?"

"She fell off a bus," said Uncle Mort.

"That's what happened to your Edna, isn't it?" said Mr Brandon.

"That's right," said Uncle Mort. "I'm a bit of a Jonah with public transport, aren't I?"

Carter Brandon ordered three pints of bitter and a special triple rum and orange for Uncle Mort.

"Ta," said Uncle Mort, and he took a long gulp of the rum and sighed deeply. "What a time to fall off a bus. Why couldn't she have waited till after our world cruise?"

"World cruise?" said Mr Brandon.

"Aye. Olive come into an annuity from The Royal Liver so she decided to spend it on a boat voyage. We'd have gone by sea, too. By gum, I were looking forward to it. It were the chance of a lifetime—especially travelling by HMS *Cunard*."

"Cunard's the name of the company, pillock. What were the name of the boat?" said Mr Brandon.

"Eee, I don't know," said Uncle Mort. "I do know from the photos it had got enough funnels on it to sink a bloody ship."

"It'd be the *Queen Mary*," said Mr Brandon. "They were right profligate with their funnels in them days."

Uncle Mort nodded sombrely and sighed once more.

Mr Brandon tapped him sympathetically on the knee with the bowl of his pipe.

"Life's not worth living, is it?" he said.

"No," said Uncle Mort. "I wish there were summat else you could do with it."

Chapter Thirty-four

Mrs Brandon welcomed Uncle Mort with open arms. She kissed him and she cuddled him.

She gave him three laxatives, two dessert spoonfuls of Virol and sent him upstairs to a mustard bath and a rub down with Sloan's Liniment.

As soon as she had tucked him in bed he fell into a deep sleep. A tuft of his grey hair protruded from beneath the bedclothes and vibrated in time to his soft snores.

Mrs Brandon leaned down and kissed him tenderly on the top of the head.

"There, there, love," she said. "Isn't it a pity we're brother and sister? We'd have made a lovely husband and wife, if nature hadn't intervened otherwise."

Next morning she took him to the British Home Stores and bought him a complete set of woollen underwear.

"I don't like vests with buttons," said Uncle Mort. "They rattle when you're supping your ale."

"Nonsense," said Mrs Brandon, and she took him to Boot's Cash Chemists and weighed him.

"Good gracious, Mort, you're nowt bar skin and bone," she said, and straightway she led him to the UCP restaurant at the side of the covered market where she ordered pigs' trotters in mustard sauce, cow heel stew with parsley potatoes and cabinet pudding with white sauce.

That night in the back room of The Whippet Uncle Mort said:

"Isn't it rum the way women think catering's the way to a man's heart?"

"Aye," said Mr Brandon.

"And isn't it funny the way they're forever giving you laxatives?"

"Aye."

"Our Edna were a devil for laxatives. I could always tell when she were feeling a bit romantic—three spoonfuls of Turkey rhubarb root last thing on a Friday and that was that."

"What was what?"

"It was her sign for saying she wanted her nookie. If she just wanted a kiss and a cuddle, all I got were a sulphur tablet."

"Bloody hell," said Mr Brandon. "Annie's just told me she's taking three bottles of senna pods and a couple of packets of dried prunes on the honeymoon."

"Struth," said Uncle Mort. "It's going to be worse than the rape of the Sabine women."

The wind bent them double as they struggled through the freshly-fallen snow on their way home.

When they reached the lee side of Hankinson's Long Distance Removals in Derbyshire Road, Uncle Mort said:

"You want to ask Annie if she'll make alternate arrangements for the honeymoon."

"What alternate arrangements?" said Mr Brandon.

Uncle Mort told him, and as soon as Mr Brandon returned home he went into the kitchen and said to his wife:

"Listen. Why don't you go on the honeymoon on your own? I don't mind stopping at home. I'll not be lonely. There's bound to be a darts match on at the British Legion."

Mrs Brandon stopped dead in her tracks. She stared hard at her husband. Her lower lip quivered. A tear came to her right eye. A tear came to her left eye. And then tears spurted from both eyes and gushed down her cheeks.

"Oh Les, how could you?" she cried, and she fled out of the room and pounded upstairs to the bedroom.

"Now what have I said?" said Mr Brandon.

"Search me," said Uncle Mort. "She's not got an allergy to darts, has she?"

"Honestly, Carter, I'm right proud of you," said Pat. "All the overtime you've done this past three weeks. Sundays, too. You must have earned a small fortune for baby."

"Aye. Mm," said Carter Brandon.

It was three days since he had last visited Pat. Earlier in the evening he had received a message to say that Alison was unable to meet him.

"Now I hope you're not thinking of buying baby a Norton motor bike with all that money you've earned, Carter," said

Pat. "I've ear-marked that money for building a study for baby on top of the garage so's he won't have no disturbance when he's writing his symphonies and doing his sums homework for the grammar school."

Her cheeks were fattening out and her eyes were growing puffy.

"They're moving me into the maternity wing tomorrow, Carter," she said. "Only six weeks to go now, love. Are you getting excited about the prospect of becoming a daddy?"

"Mm," said Carter Brandon.

"Well, listen to me, Carter—when you are a daddy and you take baby to the rugby match, you'll not let him sit on them crush barriers, will you, Carter? You see, love, you see, he could easy get a splinter in his little bottie and it might go septic and he'd have to do his 11 plus sitting on a rubber ring, and if he overbalanced, he could easy break a leg and then he'd have no chance of playing in the 'varsity match, would he, Carter?"

"No."

Pat kissed him on the cheek.

"Oooh, Carter, you are a dull old stick," she said. "If only you'd got the imagination I'd got, we'd have the whole wide world at baby's doorstep."

"Mm."

"Never mind, love. You just do the day-to-day slogging and leave the creative part to me, eh?"

"Hullo, professor. You got the message about Alison, then?"

Artie Shirtcliffe loomed up out of the darkness as Carter Brandon stepped out of the hospital at the end of visiting hours.

Carter Brandon stopped. He stared at Artie Shirtcliffe. He said nothing.

"Look, professor. I'm sorry about what happened at your house. It were daft of me. I'm sorry. Honest, professor, I'm right sorry."

Carter Brandon stared at him for a moment. Then a smile came to his face.

"That's all right, Artie. I forgive you, Artie."

Artie Shirtcliffe clapped him on the shoulder, tickled him under the chin and led him to the car. It was a pale-green Daimler. He drove it quickly into town and then took Carter

Brandon into The Griffon where he bought him a pint of beer. He had a double whisky himself.

"Why couldn't Alison come tonight then?" said Carter Brandon as he was halfway through the pint.

"She was called to hospital, professor. The nipper. Getting worse, you see. No hope now."

Carter Brandon nodded. Artie Shirtcliffe coughed and said tentatively:

"Does Alison . . . well, does she ever talk about me? I mean, does she ever mention me in conversation?"

"No," said Carter Brandon. "Not even when you wallop her."

"Wallop her? Me?"

"Yes, you. What about that plaster on her neck? That didn't get there by itself, did it? She didn't put that on just for the sake of it, did she?"

Artie Shirtcliffe gulped back his whisky and then he shook his head.

"Oh, professor," he said. "Oh dear, professor, you've really fallen for it."

"Fallen for what?" said Carter Brandon irritably.

Phil Swindells, the Rugby League correspondent of *The Morning Argus*, brought over a glass of whisky. Artie Shirtcliffe took it and said:

"Ta, Phil, and a pint of bitter for the professor, eh?"

"Fallen for what?" said Carter Brandon firmly and deliberately. "What are you talking about?"

Artie Shirtcliffe waited until the pint arrived and then he said earnestly:

"I want to do you a favour, professor. I like you. I always have done. That's why I'm warning you again—stay away from Alison. Get shut of her. Have nothing more to do with her. If you carry on the way you're going, she'll destroy you."

"Bollocks!"

"She's done it before, professor. She's destroyed better blokes than you."

"Bollocks!"

"She'll destroy your home for you. She'll destroy your family. She'll destroy you."

Carter Brandon took a slow sup of his beer.

"Do you want to give up your family? Do you heck as like. You're not a roamer. You're a stick in the mud, professor. You're a stayer. You're a family man born and bred. You're a man destined to be ordinary and hum-drum and down-to-earth for the whole of your days, and, by God, do I envy you."

"You? What do you envy me for?"

"Being settled down and all that rubbish. Having a wife and all that balls ache. Going to become a dad and all that load of crap. That's what makes me envious."

"You?" said Carter Brandon. "You?"

"Aye. Me. And there's only one way I can get it, professor — become a punter. I'll have to destroy meself and become a punter like all the other silly buggers."

His shoulders sagged, and he picked up his glass and rolled the whisky dregs round and round.

Carter Brandon went to the bar and brought back more drinks.

"You're a good 'un, professor. You're the best," said Artie Shirtcliffe.

When Carter Brandon returned home after closing time, he found Alison waiting for him in the lounge/diner.

"And where the hell have you been?" she shouted.

"To the hospital," said Carter Brandon. "Then I went for a pint. What are you shouting at?"

"I've been waiting for you here since six o'clock — that's what I'm shouting at."

"But Artie rang me at work to say you'd been called to the hospital. He said the nipper had been took badly. He said you'd been called away urgent."

For a moment Alison's face crackled with anger. Then quite suddenly a smile came to her face and she sank back gently onto the low-slung imitation leather sofa.

"Good old Artie," she said. "Trust our Artie, eh?"

"Now what the devil's going on round here?" said Carter Brandon, grinding his fists and beginning to quiver with rage.

Alison laughed.

"Sit down," she said quietly.

Carter Brandon sat down.

"Give me a fag," she said.

Carter Brandon gave her a cigarette.

"Light it for me."

Carter Brandon lit it.

"Run away with me," she said.

"What?"

"You're fed up with life. I can see that. You're fed up with the cold. Let's find some sun. Come on, Carter—run away with me. Here's your great chance."

Chapter Thirty-five

—Course it's your great chance, Carter. It's the best chance you'll ever get. Do it, lad. Do it now. Run away while you can.

—How can I run away, Daniel? Where am I going to get the money from?

—Sell the house.

—I can't sell the house. What about Pat?

—Bugger Pat.

—What about the baby?

—Bugger that, too.

—I suppose I'll get insurance money on the car. But that won't come to much. I mean, it'll only be in the region of a hundred quid, and I've only got thirteen pounds ten in the savings bank. Bloody hell, you can't get far on thirteen pounds ten.

—You can get as far as you want, Carter.

—But what'll I do when I get there? I don't speak no foreign languages. How could I get a job when I don't speak the bloody lingo?

—Job? Who's worried about work? Who's worried about security and pensions and annuities and insurance policies and Welfare Committee holiday clubs when the whole world's at your feet?

—I am, mate. I'm worried about it.

March progressed. The day of the Silver Wedding came nearer and nearer and the cold grew even more intense.

Points froze on the railways. Midnight shunters cursed.

The migrant birds grew restless on the savannahs and mud swamps of Africa. The swallows and swifts sensed the distant northern cold, and they would not move.

Neither would Mr Brandon and Uncle Mort.

Nothing would budge them of an evening from the fire in the back room of The Whippet.

"This bloody weather makes you feel right hemmed in," said Mr Brandon.

"People like us are born to be hemmed in," said Uncle Mort. "We're doomed to a lifetime of being hemmed in."

"Aye. Look at me," said Mr Brandon. "I've got a Silver Wedding to contend with. I've got to celebrate twenty-five years of being hemmed in."

"Aye," said Uncle Mort tossing half a beer mat into the heart of the roaring fire. "I tell you what—marriage wouldn't be half so bad if you could keep it in the family."

"In what way?"

"Well, I reckon that bugger Oedipus had got the right idea. He wanted to keep it in the family. I bet he wanted to marry his mother for the sole and simple reason he were used to her cooking and he knew she'd iron his shirts proper and not singe his singlets."

"Aye, you've got something there," said Mr Brandon.

"I mean, regardless of the fact she's my sister, I'd have married Annie, if it wasn't for the way she's always humming out of tune when she's dusting the landing."

"It drives me mad, does that humming."

"Precisely. And if you'd been her brother, you'd have known all about it, and you'd not have entertained the idea of wedlock. The whole trouble with marriage is that nine times out of ten you find yourself marrying a total bloody stranger."

"Or a woman," said Mr Brandon.

"Certainly," said Uncle Mort. "Marriage is the last thing you'd keep a woman out of."

"You know who I'd have married, if it hadn't been customary to wed a woman?" said Mr Brandon.

"Who?" said Uncle Mort.

"King George the Sixth."

Uncle Mort nodded wisely.

"Aye. Aye. You could have done worse for yourself," he said. "You'd never have gone short of a ticket for the Lord's Test, would you?"

Mr Brandon nodded and went to the bar to fetch more drinks. When he returned to the snug, fuggy corner in which they had established themselves, Uncle Mort looked up and said shyly:

"If I'd been available, Les, would you have married me?"

Mr Brandon handed him his pint pot, sat down and said after puffing solemnly at his pipe:

"I don't know. Can you darn socks and use a dolly blue proper?"

"No," said Uncle Mort.

"Sod it then," said Mr Brandon. "If I'd married you, you'd have sent me out to work looking like a bloody rag-riser."

"Well?" said Alison. "Have you made up your mind?"

"I don't know," said Carter Brandon.

They were sitting in the lounge/diner. It was the fourth successive night that Carter Brandon had failed to visit Pat. That morning she had sent him a card, which read:

"Your overtime makes me very proud. You do more overtime than any other husband in maternity. I'm top of the league. Baby's delighted with the Austin Reed mohair suit in grey you're going to buy him out of all the extra money you've earned. Love Pat. P.S. Could you buy baby a matching cravat, too?"

Carter Brandon looked across at Alison and smiled weakly.

"We've got to go, Carter," she said, and there was a note of urgency in her voice. "It's all this cold. It's like an omen saying something terrible's going to happen to us. I can feel it in my bones. I've got to get away before it happens."

Carter Brandon stood up and walked over to the low-slung imitation leather sofa. He put out his arms to comfort her, but she brushed him away.

"Make up your mind, Carter," she said. "And quick. And quick."

She left shortly after, and Mr Shirtcliffe came in with two mugs of Instant Postum and a plateful of buttered water biscuits.

"I couldn't help overhearing," he said.

"Oh aye?" said Carter Brandon.

"I'm her father, lad, and I'm warning you—don't do it. She'll destroy you. She will—she'll ruin your life for you."

"Mm."

"Just think of it, Carter—wouldn't it be a terrible nuisance to have your life ruined?"

Carter Brandon grunted, and Mr Shirtcliffe fussed round him as he made his way upstairs to the bedroom.

"There's a terrible gale blowing," he said. "Do you think I could sleep with you just for one night till the wind dies down."

"No," said Carter Brandon, and he slammed the bedroom door behind him.

Within seconds he was fast asleep and dreaming.

He dreamed of a village square in the high Sierras. There were cool arcades and mules dozing in the sun and hairy-chested men sitting in wicker chairs drinking tequila. And there was a bedroom in the inn with its shutters drawn and a pitcher of ice-cold water on the dresser.

He dreamed of a Greek island with the sun stinging off the rocks and at night the sea was luminous and fireflies twinkled among the gnarled old olive groves and cicadas chirped at the side of the goat tracks and deep inside the thickets of myrtle. And there was a bedroom in a crumbling old house with vines rasping at the window and creaking springy floorboards and in the morning there was cold fresh orange juice to drink in bed.

He dreamed of eating fat carp. He dreamed of Schlagober and grape tartlets. He dreamed of Munich beer, of Koelsch, of Kirsch, of heuriger Wein and Foster's lager.

He dreamed of Trondheim in the autumn, and he walked among the leaves by the wooden houses and he watched the mist coiling above the fiord and he fed the eider ducks at the quay where the coastal steamers called.

When he awoke he felt refreshed.

— Course you do, Carter. You feel like a new man. You would be a new man, if you upped and offed while you've got the chance. All those places you dreamed of what Alison told you about in the lounge/diner — they're all yours, mate. You can visit them all. And more. Heaps more. Hundreds and thousands more.

— How can I? I haven't got the money. I haven't got the bloody money, Daniel. I haven't got a chance.

At half past eleven that morning the personnel manager, Mr Leatherbarrow, called Carter Brandon into his office. He introduced him to a stout man with heavy black eyelashes and a red nose.

"This is Mr Wormersall. He wants a few words with you."

Mr Wormersall's few words were potent and startling.

He was the chief fitter and maintenance man in Wagstaffe and Broome's foreign sales enterprises. He needed a new man. Carter Brandon had been recommended. He accepted that recommendation.

"Pardon?" said Carter Brandon.

There was a team of three engineers, a chief fitter and ten ordinary fitters and maintenance men. They travelled the world. They had been to South America, Canada, Southern Rhodesia, Austria, India, Italy, Libya, Persia, Pakistan and Dahomey.

Their next job was in Norway. They would be away three months. Carter Brandon had until the end of the week to decide whether or not to accept the job.

"Take my advice, Mr Brandon—accept it," said Mr Leather-barrow. "It's the chance of a lifetime. Goodness knows what it could lead to in time."

He patted Carter Brandon on the shoulder and smiled.

"I'm delighted for you, lad," he said.

—Yippeee, Carter. Bloody yippeeeeeeeee, me old wingsy bash.

—I can't believe it, Daniel. It's got me all in a dither.

—All in a dither? What's there to dither about? Good God, man, the job's come just when you need it. It's in Norway, too. You couldn't get a better omen than that.

—Omen?

—An omen to tell you to pull your finger out and accept the job. Don't you see, Carter—you've got it made, lad. Wherever you work abroad, you set up Alison there. She goes with you. So then you've got the best of both worlds. You've got a nagging wife and an howling bambino at home and a beautiful mistress waiting for you in foreign climes. You're in clover, mate. You're King of the Punters.

—You're right, Daniel. I bloody am.

He could hardly wait until the factory hooter blew to end the day's work. He raced into the washroom, scrubbed himself down furiously, sent Sid Skelhorn flying as he dashed across the factory yard and arrived at the hospital forty seven-minutes later breathless but triumphant.

His eyes sparkled as he told Pat about the job. His heart thumped joyously as he waited for her reaction.

"You'll take that job over my dead body," said Pat, and every muscle in her face hardened, and the skin on her neck grew taut.

"What?" said Carter Brandon. "Pardon?"

"Your place is at home. Your place is with me and baby. Your place is doing a steady job leaving the home at eight in the morning and coming back for your tea at half past six. Your place is the family hearth and the domestic circle."

"But it's a chance of a lifetime, is this job," said Carter Brandon. "There'd be promotion. I'd get experience I could never get in the factory here. I could get the chance to see the world."

"The world?" said Pat. "The world? Your world is here. Your world is baby and me."

Carter Brandon lowered his head and shrugged his shoulders.

"I expect you to go in to see this Mr Leatherbarrow first thing tomorrow morning and refuse the job outright. I expect you to tell him you couldn't entertain the idea. I expect you to tell him it's utterly impossible with a baby what'll soon be going to grammar school and a wife what'll be going to all the Parent-Teachers' Association dances so's she can bolster baby's future by getting to know the headmaster in the ladies' invitation fox-trots. Do you understand me, Carter? Do you understand what I want from you?"

"Mm," said Carter Brandon. "Mm."

"That's right, love. I knew you'd see it my way," said Pat gently, and she snuggled up to Carter Brandon and said: "We had braised heart and onions for dinner today. It were right tasty. Does me breath still smell of onions, love?"

"Yes," said Carter Brandon.

— You're not taking it lying down are you, Carter?
— Mm. Aye. Mm.
— You're never backing down without a fight, are you, Carter?
— Mm. Aye. Mm.
— Well? Well, Carter? You're throwing in the towel, are you?
— What else can I do? WHAT THE HELL ELSE IS THERE TO DO, DANIEL?

Chapter Thirty-six

Carter Brandon slept badly.

He tossed in his sleep. When he awoke, he twitched and he scratched. As the cold night progressed his scratching grew more violent.

—For pete's sake, Carter, stop your scratching.

—I can't help it.

—Yes you can. Just lie still and fight it.

—I can't. I'm itching all over.

—Oh hell, Carter, pack it up, mate. Stop scratching. Let me get some sleep.

In the morning he stumbled downstairs, red-eyed, pale-faced and yawning. He had no time for breakfast. He rammed *The Morning Argus* into the pocket of his donkey jacket and hurried off down the road to catch the bus.

The bus was crowded. He had to struggle to open his paper to the sports page. When he did so he saw a large picture of Artie Shirtcliffe and underneath it in an article written by Phil Swindells was the news that he had been selected to join the party to tour Australia that summer.

—Australia! Now there's a place to visit, Carter.

—Aye. They've still got trams there, haven't they?

—Take the job, son, and you'd soon find out. They're bound to be going to Australia soon. Just imagine you and Alison there, Carter. Just imagine all the places you could see. You could see the outback and dingoes and red mountains. You could see the Great Barrier Reef and the Great Dividing Range and Wally Grout.

—I'd sooner see Ernie Toshak.

He got off the bus outside the factory gates and joined the stream of workers shuffling into the yard and their designated clocking on points.

—So what have you decided, Carter? Are you going to give in

to her? Are you going to fight her and tell her to stuff it? What have you decided?

—I don't know. I haven't a clue. It's good news about Artie, isn't it?

He clocked on, hung his jacket in his locker, collected his tools from the cabinet and then joined Sid Skelhorn and Terry Dunphy in trudging along the echoing, green-distempered corridors to Dispatch where they were to repair a broken conveyor belt.

"When do you start your new job then?" said Sid Skelhorn.

"Who told you about that?" said Carter Brandon.

"I heard Leatherbarrow's typist talking about it at the bus stop last night. Hasn't she got odd-shaped knees?"

"She's no right to talk about it. It's supposed to be secret."

"What's the point in being secret? You're going to take it, so why not spread the news and cheer us all up?"

"I don't know whether I'm taking it yet."

"You what?" said Terry Dunphy.

"You're undecided?" said Sid Skelhorn. "You've got a chance to get away from your missus and kids and mother-in-law and Sunday dinner with burnt potatoes *and* get paid for it, and you can't make up your mind?"

"That's right," said Carter Brandon.

"You want your bloody bumps feeling," said Terry Dunphy.

—That's what I say, Carter. Them's my feelings, old son.

Sid Skelhorn put his hand on Carter Brandon's shoulder and stopped him just before they turned into Dispatch.

"You're not sickening for something, are you, Carter?" he said. "You've not got a fatal disease, have you? I mean, if you have, you'd best tell Eric Black and he'll not pick you for the semi-final."

Carter Brandon pushed him away and stepped inside to begin work on the conveyor belt.

He worked hard all morning. He cursed at Terry Dunphy, when he mislaid a spanner. He shouted at Sid Skelhorn for skulking off to the lavatory to smoke a dimp.

"I can't stand to see a bloke being enthusiastic about his work," said Sid Skelhorn. "It's against the law of nature, is that. It's like smiling when you do the rumba with your missus."

When the hooter blew for dinner break, Carter Brandon

bought himself a pork pie and a bar of peppermint-cream chocolate and went out onto the canal tow-path.

—You see, Carter, you're weakening. You've not seen Leatherbarrow yet, have you? You know bloody well you're not going to neither, don't you? You know you'd be a laughing stock with your mates if you turned it down, don't you?

—Aye. Mm.

—What a chance, Carter—travel, sun and a beautiful bird. What more could a bloke want?

—Give over. Leave off.

The canal tow-path was deserted. The surface of the snow was streaked with rust and coke dust.

Embedded in the rumpled and chipped ice on the canal were tin bath tubs, half bricks, spent condoms and a newly-dead herring gull, its neck bloated and twisted by the fishing line entwined round it.

"Looks a bit acky, doesn't it, Carter?"

It was Linda Preston. She pointed at the herring gull and pulled a face.

"Poor sod," said Carter Brandon.

Linda Preston linked his arm and they began to walk slowly back to the factory.

"By God, it's cold, though, isn't it, Carter? It's getting worse every day. I'm bloody sure there's icicles clinging to me suspenders."

Carter Brandon grunted.

"What I wouldn't give for a bit of sun, Carter."

"Aye."

"If I won the pools, I'd be up and off tomorrow. You'd not see my backside for dust. I'd stretch meself out on a beach on the Costa Brava and I wouldn't budge till I were as brown as Thornton's treacle toffee."

"Aye. Mm."

A sudden cold blast of Arctic wind hit them as they passed from the shelter of the high wall of the steam laundry. They shivered.

"I'd take you, too, if you wanted, Carter. We could stay in one of them modern hotels like what they have in the brochures with a balcony. And you wouldn't have to eat Spanish grub neither cos they've got special menus for them what doesn't like olive oil and garlic. And you could get English beer, too, Carter, and they have all the latest records in the cellar bar what you can twist to. Would you fancy that, Carter?"

"Aye. Mm."

Linda Preston huddled more closely into him as the wind grew fiercer.

"Your mate, Artie Shirtcliffe's bound for the sun, isn't he, Carter? Lucky bugger going to Australia like that."

"No, he deserves it," said Carter Brandon. "He's been playing well. He'll be a real hit in Australia when he gets there."

"Aye. And I hope he bloody stays there, too," said Linda Preston. "I hope he gets savaged by a boomerang."

"Why?"

Linda Preston stopped and turned Carter Brandon to face her. Her eyes narrowed.

"You've not seen much of him lately, have you, kid?" she said.

"No."

"Do you know why?"

"No."

"Because he's ashamed."

"What of?"

"His bird."

"What bird?"

"Don't you know?"

"No."

"You poor devil," said Linda Preston as they began to walk across the factory yard. "You poor bugger."

She gave him a quick peck on the cheek and waved to him as she went in through the door of the Paint Shop.

"Don't forget, kid—I'm waiting for the call," she said. "Any time, any place, and I'll be there."

When Carter Brandon got back to the conveyor belt, he found Eric Black, the supervisor, haranguing his two colleagues.

"Ah," he said to Carter Brandon. "Here's the other bloody skiver turned up."

"What?" said Carter Brandon.

"Look at this work here," said Eric Black pointing to the innards of the belt's main motor. "It's a bloody disgrace."

"Disgrace?" said Carter Brandon. "What are you talking about? It's nearly repaired, is that motor. We've been working our balls off all morning over it. We've never stopped."

"That's just the point," shouted Eric Black turning red in the face. "You're working too hard."

"Pardon?" said Terry Dunphy.

"Good God alive, man, we've got the semi-final of the cup tomorrow," said Eric Black. "I don't want two of my key men knackering themselves up by working too hard. Take it easy. Have a skive. Smoke a couple of dimps in the bogs."

"Spot on, Eric," said Sid Skelhorn. "I kept saying we was taking too much out of ourselves."

"Hey up, you're only the trainer, matey," said Eric Black. "There's no need for you to skive. When you've finished on that belt, you can come to my office and fix up the lid of me snap tin."

"Pillock," said Sid Skelhorn, when he had gone. "He doesn't realise the energy involved in carrying a wet sponge."

At four o'clock Carter Brandon suddenly stopped work.

"I'll not be a minute," he said. "I want to see someone."

—Hey up, Carter, you're not going to see Leatherbarrow, are you?

—Wait and see.

—Don't be a bloody fool, Carter. Don't be hasty. Don't do nothing you'll regret come this evening when you've a skinful of bitter inside you at The Tinker's Bucket.

—Shut up, Daniel. Mind your own business.

Carter Brandon came to the personnel block. He marched through the doors and strode purposefully down the corridor to Mr Leatherbarrow's office. He knocked on the door, and the secretary bade him enter.

"Hullo, Mr Brandon," she said with a smile. "What can we do for you then, Carter?"

She wore a tight navy-blue jumper which revealed the shape of two plump breasts. She had a large mouth with bright red lips. The lips were moist.

"Aye. Well. Mm," said Carter Brandon shuffling his feet. "I've come to speak to Mr Leatherbarrow."

"Oh dear, I'm afraid he isn't in, Mr Brandon. He's not expected back while tomorrow late. Can I take a message, Carter?"

"Aye. Mm. I don't really know really."

"Is it about the job, Mr Brandon?" said the secretary. "My word, aren't you lucky, Carter? Just think of all them gorgeous girls you'll meet on your travels. Oh, you'll go down a treat with them girls on the continent. You're just the sort what'll knock them flat in the aisles. Is your wife still in hospital by the way? Are you still living on your own, Carter? Don't you find life very lonely with no feminine company to keep you company? I would, Carter. I'd be on the look-out for someone to keep me company."

She pulled down her jumper and stuck out her chest. She parted her lips slightly and ran her tongue slowly from side to side.

"I think I'll wait while tomorrow, ta all the same," said Carter Brandon, and he turned quickly and beat his retreat.

"Well?" said Pat as soon as he walked into the ward that evening. "Did you tell him?"

"Yes," said Carter Brandon.

"What did you say?"

"I said: 'Thank you very much for your kind offer, but I can't take it cos' me wife won't let me.'"

"You never said that, Carter? Fancy dragging me into it like that. They must think I'm awful. They must think I'm a right tyrant. Why didn't you say it was your own decision? Why didn't you say you was doing it out of consideration for baby and having to save up for his books what'll teach him how to become a brain surgeon?"

"I did. Later on. That's what I said. I told them it was baby what was the fly in the ointment."

"That's right, love," said Pat. "I knew you'd turn up trumps in the end."

She was growing fatter each day. She was wearing a primrose yellow nightie with bottle-green frills at the neck and the wrists. She wriggled in bed to find a comfortable position for her belly.

"Now then, Carter, I've been doing some thinking," she said. "From henceforward we've got to plan our lives meticulously. With a baby in the house it's vital that we map out our lives to the last dot and make a timetable what we stick to through thick and thin. Don't you think I'm right, love?"

"Mm."

"Now as regards food I've made out a day by day menu for the week. We'll have roast brisket on Sunday, and we'll have it cold on Monday with fried left-overs. On Tuesday we'll have sausages and mash, on Wednesday we'll have liver and bacon, on Thursday we'll have cottage pie, on Friday we'll have hake and have you any preferences regarding Saturday?"

"No."

"I thought you wouldn't so I've already wrote in fish fingers with tinned garden peas. Now then what sort of car do you think we should get?"

"I don't want a car. I can't stand the bloody things. What do we want a car for?"

"So I can get around with baby and take him to school when he goes to Summers Park Infants so he won't have to cross that busy main road and risk being knocked down by a drunken commercial traveller. You don't want baby going through life with one leg shorter than the other, do you?"

"No."

"Good. Well, we'll have a Morris Minor estate in navy-blue," said Pat. "And there's another thing, Carter, what are your feelings as regards baby sitters?"

"Baby sitters?"

"For when we go out on our once monthly treat to The Scented Lotus Garden and you buy me a bunch of flowers and a box of fudge."

"I see."

"Now then, we could have Maureen Tobin, but she's Irish and she's got adenoids and I'd be worried sick that she'd stuff baby up with jacket potatoes while we was out. So we'll discard her, Carter, and turn our attentions to Mrs Winterbottom. Now I know she smells a bit funny, Carter, but she's very good with babies and I know for a fact she's not a fire risk. So shall we plump for Mrs Winterbottom, Carter?"

"Aye. All right."

Pat wriggled in bed once more.

"Eee, love, isn't it nice to map out our lives like this? Isn't it nice to know we're going to be together till Kingdom come? Do you like being together with me, Carter?"

"Mm."

"Do you wish you was me, love? Do you wish it was you in this bed about to give birth to baby instead of me?"

"No," said Carter Brandon.

"And why not?" snapped Pat.

"Because I'd feel a right bloody Charlie wearing that nightie with the frills round the neck."

The rest of the visiting hour passed smoothly and Pat decided that Carter Brandon should take down the Pluto wallpaper in the nursery and replace it with Clara Cluck.

He caught the bus back into town and went into the upstairs bar of The Furnace for a pint. It was empty. The barman scowled at him. There was a power cut, and the room was lit by hurricane lamps which hissed.

— What a life, Daniel. What a future, eh?

— Change it, lad. You can. Dead easy. Take the job. It's as simple as that.

— Pat'd kill me.

— Don't tell her. Take the job and present it to her as a fate accomplished.

— Mm. Mm.

He drank up his pint and walked down the road to The Drum and Fife. He drank three whiskies and passed on to The Three Tuns. There was no heating in the public bar. The beer was flat. A Scotsman asked him for half a crown for a cup of tea.

— It would be marvellous, though, wouldn't it, Daniel? I mean, really? It really would be bloody sensational, wouldn't it?

— A knock-out, lad.

— I mean, a bloke'd be off his chump to turn down a chance like that, wouldn't he? I mean, it'd be very educational for baby getting postcards from Norway, wouldn't it?

— Course it would, lad. And you could bring him back a knobkerry from Africa. They're very educational, are knobkerries.

— Aye, and I could bring him a Hohner harmonica from Switzerland.

— Spot on, Carter. He'd learn it bloody quickly, knowing baby, and then he could join Moreton Frazer's harmonica gang and make a fortune on the music hall.

— Course, he could. I bet Pat hasn't thought of that. I bet she didn't realise how educational a job like mine could be for a baby.

— Take the job, lad. Take it.

— Mm. Mm.

He swallowed his fourth whisky and weaved his way through the empty city streets to The Tinker's Bucket. Standing at the bar were Linda Preston and a squat, broad-shouldered, flat-nosed man who wore a powder blue suit with thin lapels and short jacket.

"This is Count Jugular—the wrestler," said Linda Preston jabbing her companion's barrel chest with her thumb.

"Pleased to meet you," said Count Jugular. "Haven't I seen you at the canary shows in the TA Drill hall?"

"No," said Carter Brandon.

"Oh, I beg your pardon. No offence," said Count Jugular. "I could have sworn you was one of the fancy."

He ordered a round of double whiskies and then smiled shyly at Carter Brandon.

"You don't breed white mice do you?" he said.

"No," said Carter Brandon, and Linda Preston giggled.

They took their drinks to a table that was awash with stale beer and sodden cigarette stubs. Linda Preston pressed herself into Carter Brandon and put her hand on his thigh while she gazed fondly into the piggy eyes of Count Jugular.

—Just imagine Alison's hand on your thigh, Carter.

—Give over, Daniel.

—Just imagine a lifetime with Alison's hand on your thigh.

—Give over. It's no use. Don't tempt me no more. I can't take that job. You know that. Deep down, Daniel, you know I'm not the sort for a job like that. I'm not a rover. I'm a stayer. I'm a sticker. I don't like yellow post buses and cold Munich beer and sizzling white sausages and pine woods and slate hung houses and dippers in mountain streams and spoonbills and curlews and whimbrels and empty beaches. I can't stand all that lot, Daniel. I'm a Clara Cluck man. I'm like me dad. We're birds of a feather. Two Clara Clucks in a coop. Two stop-at-homes. Persian rose gardens? Dutch West Indies? Bugger them for a tale, Daniel. They don't hold a candle to Douglas, Isle of Man, at honeymoon time and prawn crackers in the Scented Lotus Garden once a month. Bollocks to them, Daniel! They've won. The job's had it.

At that moment Mr Leatherbarrow's secretary walked in. She was with Phil Swindells, rugby league correspondent of *The Morning Argus*. A smile came to her face when she saw Carter Brandon, and she tottered across the room quickly to him on her high-heeled black patent leather peep-toes.

"I just thought I'd tell you, Mr Brandon, but Mr Leatherbarrow came back unexpected this evening, Carter, so I give him your message," she said.

"What message?"

"The message that you're going to take the job. That's what you come round for this afternoon, isn't it?"

Carter Brandon's face turned white. His knee joints locked.

And for the briefest of seconds there flashed before his vision a picture of myrtle groves, sampans, slow night rivers, clacking shutters, long silky blonde hair and green eyes flecked with tawny.

"What's up, Mr Brandon?" said Mr Leatherbarrow's secretary. "I've not done wrong, have I, Carter?"

Slowly Carter Brandon stood up. Slowly he moved towards her. Then suddenly a great beaming smile came to his face and he took her in his arms and hugged her.

"No, you haven't, sweetheart," he said. "You've done me bloody proud, me old ducks."

He turned to Linda Preston and Count Jugular who were watching him open-mouthed.

"Do us a favour, will you?" he said. "Run us to Artie Shirtcliffe's house, eh?"

"What for?" said Linda Preston.

"I've got some good news to hand over, kid," said Carter Brandon. "It's off and away time. It's tarra, Clara Cluck and how do to the biggest swallow of the summer."

"What's he on about?" said Count Jugular.

"Search me," said Linda Preston. "We'd best drive him out there and see what's what."

Count Jugular drove rapidly to Artie Shirtcliffe's house, giggling to himself when the car went into a skid and tittering softly when it hit the kerb and slithered onto the wrong side of the road.

Carter Brandon did not notice.

It was not a car. It was a gondola. It was a horse-drawn sleigh jingling on a mountain road. It was an airship floating silently above soaring, plunging pine woods. It was a caique motionless at anchor in a clove-scented, silver-mooned Arabian night.

The car hit the kerb outside Artie Shirtcliffe's house with a crunch and sent Carter Brandon crashing into the dashboard.

He did not notice.

He threw open the car door and bounded down the front path. He did not bother to knock on the door. He went straight to the uncurtained front window, blazing orange onto the snow, and looked inside.

What he saw froze him rigid.

Artie Shirtcliffe was on the sofa with a woman. The woman was naked to the waist. Artie Shirtcliffe was fondling her and kissing her.

Suddenly the woman caught sight of Carter Brandon. She screamed out.

Artie Shirtcliffe turned. A look of horror came to his face, when he saw Carter Brandon. His mouth dropped open. His eyes opened wide. He did not move.

—It's Alison, Carter. Bloody hell, it's Alison.

—It's Alison, Daniel. It's Alison, Alison, Alison.

He stumbled down the path. He fell head first into the car and shouted at the top of his voice:

"Come on. Let's get out of here. Come on. Please, please."

"What's to do with him?" said Count Jugular.

"Do as he says—drive," said Linda Preston, and she took Carter Brandon in her arms and gently ruffled his hair. "I told you, Carter. I told you as best I could."

Count Jugular looked at them in his driving mirror. Then suddenly he turned and said:

"I know where I've seen you before. You've won cups for breeding hamsters, haven't you?"

Chapter Thirty-seven

On the following day there was a shooting incident in a field at the back of Knap Edge Colliery.

Two people were involved.

One was Artie Shirtcliffe. The other was Alison.

Carter Brandon heard the news as he soaked in the bath after the semi-final of the Tufton Cup.

His side had won by two goals to nil.

Their opponents were Begley's Surgical Boots Villa. Both goals were scored by Ernie Cosgrove; the first with his right foot, the second with his left buttock.

Carter Brandon lay back in the hot water of the bath and let the steam rise round his ears.

He had played well. He had given his all to the cause. He had bruises on his shins and cuts on his elbows. He closed his eyes and felt the tautness slowly ebbing out of his muscles. He grunted with pleasure.

It was while he was in the deepest, snuggest part of this reverie that Sid Skelhorn shook him violently by the shoulder and thrust an evening newspaper under his nose.

"Here's a smashing bit of bad news, Carter," he said. "It's the best tragedy I've read about for donkey's years."

"Pardon?" said Carter Brandon sleepily. "What's that?"

"Your mate Artie Shirtcliffe's shot his foot off and killed his sister to boot."

"You what?" said Carter Brandon leaping out of the bath.

He snatched the paper out of Sid Skelhorn's hands. There on the front page was a picture of Artie Shirtcliffe under a banner headline with six consecutive capital S's.

Carter Brandon read the story quickly as the water cascaded off the protruding parts of his pink and naked body.

Sid Skelhorn was right.

Alison was dead, and Artie Shirtcliffe was minus one foot.

Their bodies had been discovered by 57-year-old shotfirer and deputy, Mr Raymond Tankersley of 267 Huddersfield Road, Donnington Common near Stocksby Bridge. Mr Tankersley, it was revealed, had once been on the books of Stockport County.

"Christ," said Carter Brandon. "Oh my God."

He dashed towards the changing room and Sid Skelhorn called after him:

"Hey up, give us me paper back. I've not read Curly Wee and Gussie Goose yet."

Carter Brandon towelled himself down so vigorously that he ripped the skin off his back and brought angry red blotches to his thighs.

He bundled himself into his clothes and sent Rudyard Kettle spinning as he rushed out of the dressing room and raced out into the bitter chill of the evening.

He flagged down a taxi and directed the driver to drive at top speed to the Memorial Hospital.

When he got there, he was told that Artie Shirtcliffe was recovering from an emergency operation. If he wished, he could wait outside the ward with the patient's father.

Mr Shirtcliffe was sitting on a metal chair outside the door of the ward. He grinned weakly when he saw Carter Brandon.

"He's just coming out of the anaesthetic," he said. "He's lost his right foot. Isn't it a nuisance?"

"And Alison?"

Mr Shirtcliffe gulped and hung his head.

"Dead," he said softly, and his shoulders began to heave slowly.

Carter Brandon coughed, stretched out his hand and patted him shyly on the back of the neck.

"There, there," he said.

Mr Shirtcliffe sniffed hard and then blew his nose noisily into a large khaki handkerchief.

"It *were* an accident, Carter," he said. "It were. It were."

"That's right," said Carter Brandon.

"What a day," said Mr Shirtcliffe. "First it's the bad news about Artie and Alison, and then it's bad news about the baby."

"The baby?"

"Aye. It passed on at half past three this afternoon. No, I tell a lie. It was half past two when I got the news. Just before serial time on Woman's Hour. Mazo de la Roche. Very nice. Do you like Mazo de la Roche, Carter?"

Carter Brandon coughed again.

"Hadn't someone better get in touch with Norway then?" he said.

"Norway?" said Mr Shirtcliffe.

"To inform the father."

"The father?"

"Alison's husband. He lives in Norway, doesn't he? She ran away from him with the baby, didn't she?"

Mr Shirtcliffe looked at him intently for a moment. Then he shook his head.

"You've got hold of the wrong end of the stick, lad," he said. "Alison's never been married. She's never been to Norway. She's never even set foot outside the country, lad."

"Well, who is the baby's father then?" said Carter Brandon. "Who is he for God's sake?"

Mr Shirtcliffe smiled sadly.

"Don't press me, lad," he said. "Don't push me."

The door to the ward was opened by a nurse.

"You can see him now," she whispered. "Only for a moment, though. He's not to be upset."

Mr Shirtcliffe nodded and crept into the ward. He beckoned Carter Brandon to follow.

The room was dark.

Artie Shirtcliffe smiled when his father sat down by the side of his bed. Suddenly he caught sight of Carter Brandon standing in the doorway. He raised his hand and waved him over.

He looked up at him with a wan, pain-creased smile.

"Hey up, professor," he said hoarsely. "This is a real one in the eye for the punters, eh?"

"I've no sympathy with them whatsoever," said Pat later that evening as Carter Brandon sat on the chair next to her. "What was she doing out in the fields, shooting, when she'd got all her housework to do? Why wasn't she at home scrubbing the tidemarks off the bath and dusting her skirting boards? People what dust their skirting boards regular rarely get killed in shooting accidents, and that's a fact, is that."

"Quite right, love," said Mrs Partington. "Thank goodness I never got mixed up in matrimony with that family. I'd never have been able to show me face again in the bird seed shop."

"Exactly. And just think of what it would have done to baby," said Pat. "It could have had a disastrous effect on his future to have a step-brother what goes and shoots his step-sister at the back of a colliery."

"It were an accident," said Carter Brandon.

"Maybe," said Pat. "But it could still count against baby when he comes up for election to the Royal College of Surgeons."

"What foot did you say he'd lost?" said Mr Brandon later still that evening as he sat with his son and Uncle Mort in the back room of The Whippet.

"His right one," said Carter Brandon.

"Ah, he'll not miss it then," said Mr Brandon. "He always were a terrible one-footed player."

Chapter Thirty-eight

Three days after the shooting incident the doctors took off Artie Shirtcliffe's other leg.

"I don't reckon much to his chances of touring Australia now," said Mr Brandon.

Two days later Artie Shirtcliffe was dead.

"Well, I hope that's convincing enough for the selectors," said Mr Brandon.

On the day after the funeral Carter Brandon climbed the hill to the windy cemetery and stood there with bowed head before the grave, in which both Artie and Alison were buried.

He was joined by Mr Shirtcliffe who stood by his side silently.

"They're together," said Mr Shirtcliffe after a while. "That's how it should be."

And then with hunched shoulders he walked away down the long main path with the snow creaking on the yews and a single sad sparrow croaking on the gravestone of Beth beloved wife of George.

The stone had not yet been placed at the head of Artie and Alison's grave.

The flowers and the wreaths were still laid out on top of the mound of frozen earth.

There was a wreath in the colours of the club Artie Shirtcliffe had once played for. There was a wreath in the shape of a rugby ball and a wreath shaped like a football pitch.

There was a simple spray of daffodils, on which was written: "From the biggest punter of them all."

—Good one, Carter. Well wrote, lad.

—Aye. Maybe. Maybe.

Slowly he turned away from the grave and began to walk to the main entrance.

—Wouldn't it be grand, if we could just mark time, Daniel?

—Aye.

—Wouldn't it be smashing if we could say: Right, from this time on there's to be no more change. No one's going to die. No one's going to be born. We'll stay as we are till the end of time. I'd like that, Daniel.

—What about your baby, though, Carter? It'd put the mockers on him, wouldn't it? And what about Pat? She'd be pregnant till Kingdom bloody come if you just held up time as it stands now.

—That's right, Daniel. Very true, old cock.

He bent down and scooped up a handful of snow. He hardened it and rounded it in his hands. He turned to hurl it at the cemetery notice board. But then he smiled and let it drop to the ground.

—From this moment on, Daniel, there's to be no change. No one's going to be born. No one's going to die.

And then he stepped outside the cemetery and bumped into Olive Furnival.

Chapter Thirty-nine

Carter Brandon took one look at her and fled.

His heart was still pounding and his knees still knocking when he arrived at his parents' house to bring them the news.

The doctor was there trying to soothe an anxious Mr Brandon.

Upstairs in the front bedroom Mrs Brandon was in a deep swoon. It was the third she had had since staggering home an hour previously and announcing to Uncle Mort that she had just seen Olive Furnival buying an apple tartlet in Jackson and Colclough's, the high-class bakers.

Immediately afterwards she had sunk to the floor and the doctor and Mr Brandon had been summoned.

"Who is this Olive Furnival?" said the doctor.

"She's the wife of my ex-boss," said Mr Brandon. "She died a couple of months ago as a matter of fact."

"Pardon?" said the doctor.

"She fell off a bus and gave her skull a nasty crack," said Mr Brandon and he pointed at Uncle Mort who was tip-toeing down the stairs with an anxious look on his face. "He'll give you more details than what I can. He were in at the kill when the fatality took place."

"Aye, well, that's just it," said Uncle Mort and he looked at the floor and shuffled his carpet slippers sheepishly. "The fact of the matter is, Les, that Olive Furnival didn't fall off a bus and kill herself. Quite the reverse. She got off it like a good 'un when it were stationary."

"You what?" said Mr Brandon.

"She's not dead at all," said Uncle Mort. "I made it all up."

"What the hell did you want to go and do that for?" said Mr Brandon three hours later as he waited to play snooker with Uncle Mort in the Liberal Club in Strachey Gardens.

Mrs Brandon had recovered sufficiently to sit up in bed with a glass of lemon barley water and a copy of *Pins and Needles*. Carter

Brandon had volunteered to stay behind and keep her company.

Uncle Mort coughed and looked sheepishly at the floor once more.

"I made it up because Olive ran off with another man."

"Another man? Who?" said Mr Brandon.

"George Furnival," said Uncle Mort.

Mr Brandon clutched hold of his billiard cue tightly.

"George Furnival?" he croaked.

"Aye," said Uncle Mort. "He contacted her in Maryport by telegram and asked her to join him in the South of France. He said it were very sunny for the time of the year, so she baked me a meat and potato pie with carrots and swede and upped and offed on the five o'clock bus. I carried her bags to the stop for her. She said she'd enjoyed the experience of being in my company even though I was thoroughly selfish and cantankerous, but she felt her place in life was at her husband's side even though he was a miserable bugger with nowt to commend him bar having all his own teeth. I've never felt so humiliated in my life."

He looked up at Mr Brandon and smiled feebly.

"And you made all that up about Olive snuffing it just so's you wouldn't be humiliated?" said Mr Brandon.

"That's right," said Uncle Mort. "Well, it's right humbling to be given the boot by an ugly woman, isn't it, Les? It'd do my standing no good at all at the Lacey Street Bowls Club. I'd be laughed out of bloody court at the Old Comrades' crib sessions."

"They'll be laughing even more now, owd lad," said Mr Brandon. "Teddy Ward'll piss himself when he hears what really happened. He's never forgiven you for the rude remarks you passed about his cap at Christmas."

"Oh dear," said Uncle Mort. "I wish I'd never set eyes on the woman. Do you know, Les, she's had a terrible effect on my snooker. I've not had a break in double figures since the night we first held hands."

They played snooker, and Uncle Mort cheered up a little when he made a break of thirty-five.

"I've just been thinking, Les," he said as they stood at the bar after the game. "If Joe Davis had been married to Olive Furnival, they'd have had to re-write the complete annals of the history of snooker. Even I could have beat him in a best of three frames. It's right interesting to surmise about things like that, isn't it, Les?"

Mr Brandon took a long sip of his pint.

"Aye," he said. "But if I was you I'd save me surmising for surmising what Annie's going to say to you when she gets on her pins again."

Surprisingly enough Mrs Brandon treated Uncle Mort with immense kindness when he returned from the Liberal Club at half past eleven.

He had brought her a conciliatory gift of a jar of cockles and a bag of crisps, and she accepted them with a smile and said:

"I'm not angry with you, Mort. It's sorrow what overwhelms me. My heart bleeds for you."

"Does it?" said Uncle Mort. "Why?"

"Because you've had love snatched away from you just at the very moment when it was about to blossom, ripen and fructify in a blaze of autumn colour."

"Oh," said Uncle Mort. "I didn't know that."

"Your whole world has come tumbling down in ruins just when it seemed you was entering a new era of glamour and romance like what me and Les'll have on the night of our Silver Wedding in Douglas, Isle of Man."

Mr Brandon coughed and said:

"Are you sure you're fit enough for that sort of thing? I mean, you've just had a nasty shock, haven't you? It might have affected your heart. Why don't we cancel the bloody thing and go on a cheap day excursion to Manchester?"

"Good idea," said Uncle Mort. "I think United are playing at home that day. I might come with you if it's not raining."

At this Mrs Brandon fell back onto the bed in another swoon.

It took the men three minutes to revive her.

They did so by opening the jar of cockles and waving it slowly under her nose.

The sky was clear when Carter Brandon began to walk home. There was a full moon.

It made the snow glow and the shadows brood blackly.

—Cheer up, Carter. It'll not be long before you're in Norway and then you'll be able to wash it all out of your mind.

—Norway? I'm not going to Norway. I'm not going nowhere, mate. I'm seeing Leatherbarrow first thing in the morning and telling him I don't want the job. I'm staying put, Daniel. I'm stopping where I belong – at the family hearth with a bottle of stout on a Saturday night and a chunky manly cardigan when the central heating goes wrong.

— Now, Carter, Carter, don't be a bloody fool, man. Listen to me and . . .

— I've listened to you long enough, mate. If I hadn't listened to you, I'd not have got mixed up with Alison, and she'd be alive today and Artie Shirtcliffe would be touring Australia come next summer. They was happy, them two. They'd got their own little number and they was content and not doing no harm to no one. Then I come along and wrecked it all. By God, I were warned often enough. The omens was all there. But I took no notice. And why? Because you kept egging me on all the time. Because you put all these ideas of grandeur into my head. Well, there's no room in my head for ideas like that. It's too small. It's too cramped. All my head can take is ideas like Woolworth's tumblers and Clara Cluck wallpaper. You've buggered it all up trying to stuff it with notions what don't fit it. And you've buggered up Alison and Artie by getting them involved with a stupid creep like me. You're a killer, Daniel. That's what you are, mate.

— Oh aye? A killer, am I, Carter? And what about Pat? What happened there, me owd lad, when she were lying at death's door? Who stepped in there to save the day?

— Sod you, Daniel. I don't care. It's what you done to Alison and Artie what matters.

By the time he reached home the moon had disappeared behind a cloud and the snow was a listless grey.

He went into the lounge/diner and saw at once the envelope propped against the electric toaster on the Scandinavian tea trolley.

He ripped it open and read the contents of the letter inside: They were as follows:

Dear Carter, just a line to let you know I am leaving you for good and all because I hold you responsible for the death of my son and my daughter and will you remember to iron the tea towels proper after I've gone. Owing to insurance policies which matured as soon as my two dear children passed on with the Royal Liver I am able to pay a visit to my dear sister in New Zealand which I hear is a very houseproud nation with excellent rail services and crisp juicy apples like what they used to be and at my time of life a man must take every chance he can to see the world, mustn't he, especially when his sister lives in a detached bungalow. Thank you for allowing me to share your home. I shall cherish the memories of your bolster all my life. Yours faithfully, Ernest William Malcolm Shirtcliffe.

Carter Brandon slowly crumpled up the letter.

And then he began to weep.

He wept until a quarter to two, and then he fell asleep in one of the low-slung imitation leather arm chairs.

As soon as he clocked on at work next morning he went round to Mr Leatherbarrow's office and left the message with his secretary that he had decided not to take the job.

"Good Lord, Mr Brandon, I am surprised, Carter," said Mr Leatherbarrow's secretary. "Did your wife put her foot down? I would, if I was in her shoes. I think a man's place is in the home with the woman especially when it's you. Any road, you're a real stop-at-home you, aren't you, Carter? I can see it in your eyes. Would you like to come with me to a party at Thelma Thurlow's tomorrow night?"

"No," said Carter Brandon.

He worked hard all morning, and when the lunchtime hooter blew he hurried outside to the canal tow-path.

An ice-breaker was at work carving its way into the ice and filling the air with acrid diesel fumes and the sound of searing, rending and cracking.

As it passed Carter Brandon it sent a large, triangular splinter of ice spinning onto the bank, and he had to jump backwards to dodge it. The man in the cast-iron cabin of the ice-breaker grinned at him.

He waited for a while, and then she came.

"I thought I'd find you here," she said.

"Mm," said Carter Brandon. "I knew you'd come."

Linda Preston linked his arm and they began to walk slowly towards the railway bridge.

"I heard about the job, kid," she said. "You was right to refuse it."

"Was I?"

"Course you was. You're not a roamer, Carter. You're a stayer, you are. You're like me, kid – you've got the urge but you've not got the energy. We could have been brother and sister, you and me, if it wasn't for the way I fancy you."

"You shouldn't talk like that."

"Why not? Brings back unhappy memories, does it?"

"Happy ones. Very happy ones if they wasn't so sad."

They stopped under the bridge. A freight train passed overhead, and the girders shook, and smuts and specks of ballast from the track fell about their heads.

"Stop at home with Pat, kid," said Linda Preston gently. "Take what you've got with a stiff upper lip and, if you want a bit on the sly, you know where to come, don't you?"

"Yes."

She put her arms round his waist and pressed her head into his chest.

"Do you fancy coming with me to Thelma Thurlow's party tomorrow?" she said.

"No, thank you," said Carter Brandon.

"Sod you then," said Linda Preston. "I'll go with Count Jugular and give him two falls and a submission on the back doorstep."

At the very moment that Carter Brandon was declining Linda Preston's kind invitation to accompany her to the party at the residence of Thelma Thurlow George Furnival stepped into the greenhouse where Mr Brandon was working on his chitties and his ledgers.

His desk was a litter of bulldog clips, bent staples, tattered order dockets, invoices, receipts, advice notes, bills of lading, cardboard files, blunt pencils and bundles of unopened letters.

His hair was awry, and his face was red as he struggled to fill in a large green indent form.

George Furnival watched him silently, and then he bared his teeth and let a faint narrow smile come to his long lugubrious face.

"Hey up, Les," he said. "I'm back."

"Hey up, George," said Mr Brandon. "I can see that."

George Furnival began to prowl round the office. He wrinkled his nose and clucked his tongue as he inspected the dusty chaos of scattered papers and twisted elastic bands.

"How's the job going, Les?" he said.

"Not bad, George," said Mr Brandon. "What was the world like?"

"Over-rated," said George Furnival. "I didn't see much evidence of thrift."

Mr Brandon looked at the rumpled indent form once more and scratched his head and sucked the end of his pencil furiously.

"Bugger it," he said screwing it up and tossing it into the over-laden waste paper basket at his feet. "I can't make head nor tail of it."

George Furnival clucked his tongue once more. Then he bent down, rooted through the contents of the basket, took out the form, flattened it on the desk, scribbled on it rapidly and neatly for five seconds and then inserted it into the pink cardboard file marked "Balls – Putting. Replacements – New".

He smiled smugly at Mr Brandon and said:

"It's only a knack, Les. It's green fingers what do it."

Mr Brandon grunted and poured George Furnival a mug of tea from his billy.

"You shouldn't be using a billy in your position, Les," said George Furnival. "You're in the china beaker class now with arrowroot biscuits on a plate. It doesn't do your standing with the men no good at all to be seen drinking tea from a billy. You never mash it yourself, do you?"

"Course I do," said Mr Brandon. "Letting another man tamper with your billy is worse than letting him tamper with your missus. It's streets worse."

George Furnival sighed and clicked his tongue.

"I wish I were in your shoes, Les," he said.

"Do you?"

"Aye. While I were away I visited some of the world's greatest gardens. You should see the benches in the Tuileries, Les. Not a spot of paint out of place. You should see the grounds at Schön-brunn – wonderful notice boards they've got there, Les. Immaculate. And you know what impressed me most of all about Kew Gardens?"

"No."

"The offices. They've got some of the finest ledgers there I've ever seen in a lifetime of gardening," said George Furnival and a glazed nostalgic look came to his eyes. "Aye. All the time I were away I kept thinking of this little park here and wondering how me chitties was getting on and if they'd produced a new colour for the indent forms."

Mr Brandon blew at the tea in the lid of his billy. He took a sip of the strong sweet tea and added another spoonful of condensed milk from the sticky tin on his desk top. He took another sip of his tea and this time he smacked his lips noisily.

George Furnival winced.

Mr Brandon looked at him over the top of his billy and smiled.

"So you want your job back, do you, George?" he said.

George Furnival shot up from the seat and put his hand to his chest.

"Me, Les? Want my job back, Les? What ever gave you that idea, Les? Whatever put that foolish notion into your head?"

"You can have it," said Mr Brandon softly.

"Pardon?"

"If you can guarantee to get me my old job back on the bowling greens, you can have the job tomorrow."

"Oh, I can guarantee that all right, Les," said George Furnival promptly. "Well, as a matter of fact, Les, I just happened to bump into the Parks Superintendent in his office this morning and I put that very idea to him – quite by chance and on the spur of the moment, of course, Les – and he concurred at once. And, Les, *and* he said you can have a new stove for your hut and two new refuse bins for your number two green. Now then, Les, how does that strike you, Les?"

Mr Brandon nodded his head slowly.

He stood up, opened the door and looked into the greenhouse.

Stretched out before him were the rows of seed trays he had sown and tended throughout the winter. There were the bedding plants lined up neatly ready for planting out in spring. There were the potted plants he sent to the municipal banquets and the judges' lodgings. There was the smell of musty soil and cool damp gravel walkways.

Then he turned and looked round his office with its rows of ledgers, its dusty dockets and its smell of indelible pencils and inking pads.

"The job's all yours, George," he said. "Don't forget to water your bulldog clips, will you?"

Mrs Brandon said very little when Mr Brandon told her somewhat fearfully what he had done.

"Right," she said. "Right. We'll see about that, won't we?"

Mr Brandon looked at her suspiciously.

"I know what your little game is, Leslie Brandon," she said. "Well, I've rumbled it, and it doesn't wash with me."

"What do you mean?" said Mr Brandon.

"You'll see," said Mrs Brandon and she went into the kitchen to take the cheese and onion pie out of the oven.

Uncle Mort said nothing about the job until he and Mr Brandon were safely ensconced in the back room of The Whippet.

"You'll not get away with it, Les," he said. "Retribution's bound to rear its ugly head."

"Mm," said Mr Brandon gloomily, and when Carter Brandon came to their table to join them, he looked up and gave him a sad nod of the head.

"What's up with you?" said Carter Brandon.

"He's jacked in his job," said Uncle Mort. "He's going back on the greens."

"You did right," said Carter Brandon and then he told them of the job he had been offered and how he had rejected it that morning.

"You bloody fool," said Uncle Mort. "Fancy turning down a chance to see the world at your age in life. Just think of all the places you could have gone to — Atletico Madrid, Borussia Dortmund, Shamrock Rovers if you don't mind bacon and cabbage. You must be off your bloody beanpole."

"No, he's not," snapped Mr Brandon angrily, and then he turned to his son and said gently: "I understand, lad. Thee and me — we know about these things, eh?"

"Mm," said Carter Brandon. "Mm."

When Mr Brandon and Uncle Mort arrived home, they found Mrs Brandon in triumphant mood.

"You're not going back to those bowling greens, Leslie Brandon," she said, eyes glowing, hands firmly on hips.

"You what?" said Mr Brandon.

"I thought something like this might happen so I made contingency plans."

"Contingency plans?"

"When you come back from the honeymoon in two weeks' time there'll be a new job waiting for you."

"Where?"

"In the snuff warehouse," said Mrs Brandon. "You'll be taking Mr Shirtcliffe's job. I went down and fixed it as soon as I heard George Furnival was back."

Mr Brandon collapsed back on the sofa.

"Sweet God," he said. "A snuff warehouse!"

"I thought that'd excite you, Les," said Mrs Brandon. "It's a white-collar job and you wear an alpaca jacket so's you'll not stain your cardigan and your boss will be Mrs Brassington's husband from the dry cleaners who fixed it up for me when I happened to mention by chance you was looking for a new job when I took in your navy-blue suit to be cleaned for the Silver Wedding."

"Oh hell," said Mr Brandon. "What a life."

He dragged himself to his feet and made for the door. He was halfway there when he doubled up and let out three billowing, echoing sneezes.

"Hey up," said Uncle Mort. "You've not even started in the warehouse yet. Don't be so prior."

Chapter Forty

The week of the Silver Wedding celebrations dawned with the most violent weather of the winter.

Gales swept in from the far north flattening flowering cherry and snapping weeping almonds.

They howled into the city from the snow-stooped crags and peeled back corrugated iron roofs, knocked bricks off the rims of mill chimneys and blew down a signal gantry outside the Midland Station.

Mr Brandon greeted Sunday morning with a volley of sneezes, and he was still sneezing intermittently when he went out to The Whippet with Uncle Mort at lunchtime.

"Look at this terrible bloody weather—Atishooo," he said. "It's an omen of doom for the Silver Wedding."

"Aye, that's right," said Uncle Mort. "I remember it pelted down cats and dogs the night before Bolton beat Manchester United in the Cup Final of '58. I knew we'd had our chips when I come down next morning and seen Edna had left the parrot out all night."

On Monday the snow came.

It brought down telephone wires and rusting weather cocks. It buried leverets in their forms.

Mr Brandon sneezed on, and in the evening he heard that Albert Everett with the squint and the club foot had been given his job on the bowling greens.

"There's another bloody omen for you," he said. "Atishooooo!"

On Tuesday morning Uncle Stavely arrived from the Old Folks' Home. He was clutching a cardboard gas mask case tightly to his chest.

"Whatever have you got in that box, Stavely?" said Mrs Brandon.

"Corporal Parkinson," said Uncle Stavely. "He's my oppo. Pardon?"

"But I thought Corporal Parkinson was dead, Stavely."

"He is," said Uncle Stavely. "These are his ashes. Pardon?"

Mrs Brandon took three brisk steps backwards.

"Ashes?" she said.

"That's right. I carry them everywhere with me. They're right good company, are Corporal Parkinson's ashes."

Mrs Brandon stared hard at the box. Then she flicked her shoulders and sniffed.

"Well, Stavely, I hope you keep them well clear of the ham sandwiches at the reception," she said.

On Tuesday evening Cousin Marion arrived from Burslem. She brought with her three cats in baskets and an aged Staffordshire bull terrier.

"They're my children," she said to Uncle Mort.

"Aye. I can see the likeness," said Uncle Mort, and in the back parlour Mr Brandon sneezed yet again.

"Perhaps you've got an allergy to something," said the doctor next morning to Mr Brandon after he had examined him.

"I have," said Mr Brandon. "To snuff warehouses. Atishooo."

The doctor wrote out a prescription for tablets and medicine and advised him to spend the next two days in a darkened room.

"Next few days?" said Mr Brandon to Uncle Mort. "The rest of my life's going to be no better than a darkened room."

Half an hour later the three great-aunts from Glossop arrived.

"What sort of carriages are we having to take us to church?" said the eldest. "I hope we're having Humbers."

"Lanchesters will do at a pinch," said the second great-aunt.

The third great-aunt smiled coyly and said:

"Could we have Daimlers with glass partitions?"

"Oh bloody hell," muttered Mr Brandon to Uncle Mort. "Do you fancy a pint?"

"Not half," said Uncle Mort.

They trudged through the snow to The Whippet and bought themselves foamy pints of Oughthwaite's Best Bitter.

"The house is getting more like a menagerie every day with all these bloody women," said Uncle Mort. "How many more's coming to stay?"

"God knows," said Mr Brandon.

"I bet he doesn't," said Uncle Mort.

On Wednesday afternoon the works football team had a

training session in the Palmerston Street Drill Hall in preparation
for the Cup Final against Cheesewright's Currants a fortnight
hence.

Carter Brandon played with reckless fury.

After ten minutes he had cut Maurice Buckle's lip, dislodged
Ernie Cosgrove's left molar and ripped Rudyard Kettle's flan-
nelette vest clean off his back.

"Steady on, Carter," yelled Eric Black clinging desperately
to the wall bars to keep out of his way. "Don't crock all the bloody
team for me. Save your venom for Cheesewright's Currants, will
you?"

"If you don't like the way I play, you can lump it," said
Carter Brandon and he booted the ball away angrily and stalked
out of the gym.

He changed quickly and without speaking to Eric Black or his
team mates walked out into the street. The wind whined relentlessly with icy flecks of snow on its breath. Great leaden-bellied
clouds rumbled across the skies. He found himself in Halifax
Road looking into the travel agent's window, where he had
stopped and spoken to Alison.

The posters had not been changed.

He stared hard at them and in one of the gondolas he saw a
blonde-haired girl with green eyes flecked with tawny. He
blinked his eyes hard. When he opened them he saw the girl
coiled in the stern of the white yacht in the azure sea. And then
she was everywhere. She was in the cable car on the snow-capped
mountain. She was on the beach under the parasol. She was
walking down a forest glade hand in hand with a man. It was
her brother. And on her face was a mocking grin, which turned
to scorn when she looked at Carter Brandon.

He shook his head and stumbled away through the crowds of
workers streaming home from the pickle factory.

"Why aren't you doing overtime tonight?" said Pat when he
went to the hospital that evening.

"I don't know," said Carter Brandon.

"You've not done no overtime for a fortnight or more. It's
only a month before baby's due. You should be working flat out
to earn all the money you can get. I mean to say, Carter, gram-
mar-school blazers cost a fortune these days, and when baby
starts playing cricket for the first team, I'll want him to have his

own pads. I mean, you can easy pick up something nasty wearing strange cricket pads, can't you, Carter?"

"Mm."

Pat had grown even podgier during the previous week. Her eyes were mere slits in her bloated face. Her fingers were the shape of sausage rolls and her stomach made a soaring round hummock in the bedclothes.

"What's up with you? Why don't you talk to me?" said Pat.

"I've not got much to say," said Carter Brandon.

"And I know why. It's because you're hiding something from me, isn't it? Oh yes you are. There's no point in denying it. You've got a terrible guilty secret. I can see it in your eyes. I can see by the way you're sucking the end of your tie. You've broken that vase me mother brought us from Skegness, haven't you?"

"No."

"You've never bought a cat, have you? You have. I know it. I can see it in your eyes. Well, you can damn well get rid of it. You know cats make me allergic. You know . . . "

"I haven't got a bloody cat."

"Ooooh, language," said Pat. "How dare you swear in the presence of maternity. You've picked that up from playing football, haven't you? Don't bother to deny it. You're playing football again, aren't you?"

"No."

"How dare you play football when baby's got no one to help him with his homework. Your place is in the home teaching baby how to play with his educational toys. Your place is . . . "

"For Christ's sake, shut up, woman," shouted Carter Brandon, and he stood up and stormed out of the ward.

All through the night the snow fell unrelentingly.

In the morning it lay thick and rippled by the sharp east wind that had sprung up just before dawn.

During the course of the morning the Brandon household was swelled by the arrival of Gertie Foreshaw and her handbags, Cousin Danny and his children and Cousin Doreen and her spotty shoulders.

Mr Brandon peered at them from behind his *Amateur Gardening* and sneezed.

"Oh my God," he groaned. "Oh dear, oh dear."

In the evening Pat apologised profusely to Carter Brandon for her aggressive behaviour of the night before.

"It's because of my condition, love," she said. "You get to imagine things when you're pregnant, you know. You get to imagine your husband's being unfaithful or that he finds you unattractive and wants to run away and roam the world. Do you understand what I mean, love?"

"Mm."

Pat smiled at him and spread out a newspaper on the bed.

"Good," she said. "You can help me with this competition. You see these pictures of places in foreign parts. Well, you've got to say what they are and then make up a slogan about why foreign travel broadens the mind."

Carter Brandon looked at the pictures. He recognised them all. There was St Mark's Square in Venice, the Eiffel Tower, the Matterhorn, the Prinzengracht in Amsterdam, the leaning tower of Pisa and the great wheel of the Prater in Vienna.

"I can't recognise a single one of them," he said.

"Oooh, Carter, you are a dull old stop-at-home, aren't you?" said Pat. "Look at that one there. Anyone can see that's the tower at Blackpool. I wonder what that mountain is? Do you think it's Scafell or is it Snowdon?"

"I haven't a clue."

"Well, what about a slogan then?"

"Oh, I've got one of them," said Carter Brandon. "Large or tall, big or small, travel the world and you'll have a ball.'"

All through the following morning Mr Brandon sat hunched up in a corner of the back parlour, sneezing and glowering as more friends and relations arrived, and Mrs Brandon dashed hither and thither making the final arrangements.

At half past six in the evening he was packed off to Carter Brandon's to spend the night before the day of the Silver Wedding and the service of rededication in St Winiefried's the Blessed Martyr.

Mrs Brandon held him tightly to her bosom on the front door-step and kissed him noisily on the mouth.

"Oh, Les, isn't life marvellous? Isn't love a many-splendoured thing?" she said. "Now you'll not forget to tie your spats proper tomorrow, will you, Les? We don't want them flapping all round your ankles. It'd spoil the tone, wouldn't it?"

Mr Brandon broke away from her and shuffled off through the snow with the suitcase containing his morning suit and his pyjamas banging sullenly against the side of his leg.

When he arrived at his son's home, Carter Brandon led him into the lounge/diner and took out a bottle of whisky and two tumblers.

"I don't fancy a pub tonight, do you?" he said.

"No," said Mr Brandon. "It'd be a sin to ruin a place of happy memories on such a morbid occasion as this."

They drank their whisky in silence.

Mr Brandon stared at his thumbs.

Carter Brandon stared at the patterns on the wallpaper. After a while he saw the face of a beautiful woman. It was the most beautiful face he had ever seen. She had green eyes flecked with tawny and long blonde golden hair.

Mr Brandon sighed long and loud.

"You're looking at a beaten man," he said.

"Mm," said Carter Brandon.

"Do you realise I might survive another twenty-five years of this misery? I'm young enough for it. I'm fit enough apart from me hammer toes. What a prospect. It'll be a Golden Wedding next time. She'll be wanting to book Wembley Stadium for it. I hope it's not on the day of the Cup Final . . . I'd feel a right bloody chuff trotting out of the players' tunnel in top hat and spats."

"Mm," said Carter Brandon.

His mind was miles away.

He was thinking of narrow streets with mattresses slung out over wrought iron balconies. He was thinking of larch forests and yellow post buses. He was thinking of salty strands and stiff-winged fulmars.

"I'm too old to make a break for it," said Mr Brandon. "But you're not, lad."

"Mm," said Carter Brandon.

He was thinking of the village with the crumbling, ivy-sheathed Saracen tower, which the girl with the long blonde hair had never seen. He was thinking of the café on the Place St Michel, which the girl had never been inside.

"Go on, lad—do a bunk. We'll not think any the worse of you. We'll think of you as an hero. Bugger what the women think. It's what the men think what counts. Pack up your bags and bugger

16

off out of it. Do it now. Do it for me. Do it for your Uncle Mort.
Do it for all us blokes what are hemmed in and bowed down and
defeated. Do it for us, lad."

"Mm," said Carter Brandon. "Mm."

Mr Brandon hauled himself to his feet and looked down at his
son.

"Chuff me. He's not been listening to a word I've said," he
said, and clutching the half-empty bottle of whisky to his chest
he staggered upstairs to bed.

"Mm," said Carter Brandon. "Mm."

He looked into the curtains and he thought he saw a flash of
golden hair. But he could not be sure.

Chapter Forty-one

"Struth," said Carter Brandon next morning when he looked through the bedroom window. "Bloody roll on, eh?"

During the night the thaw had burst upon the city.

The snow had disappeared completely.

The sky was mellow.

The air was filled with the sound of running water.

It dripped from the leaves of ornamental shrubs.

It gurgled down gutters.

It pattered on fanlights. And in the country it hurled itself through culverts and roared, deep-throated, over weirs.

Everything was sodden. But the birds sang.

Robins preened themselves. Blackbirds drank greedily from puddles. Sparrows squabbled.

The grass on Carter Brandon's lawn was lush and rich green. The bark shone on the flowering cherry. There was a light green sheen on the standard roses.

"Hey up, the thaw's come," he shouted to his father. "It's spring. It must be an omen for you."

He went into the spare bedroom, but his father was not there.

The bed was made, and the suitcase was gone.

He called downstairs, but there was no answer.

He bounded down the stairs and looked in all the rooms, but there was no trace of his father.

He opened the front door and looked up and down the street, but there was nothing to be seen.

"Oh hell," he said. "Oh bloody hell."

Then the phone rang. It was his mother. She wanted to speak to his father.

"Er . . . er . . . he's otherwise engaged at the moment."

"Pardon?" said Mrs Brandon. "What's that?"

"Er . . . er . . . er . . . he's in the bath," said Carter Brandon. "Aye, that's right. He's having a good old swill and scrub."

"Champion," said Mrs Brandon. "And tell him not to forget to pumice stone his knee caps, will you, love?"

"Righto."

"Isn't it a smashing day, Carter? Isn't it right gorgeous? It must be an omen. It must be God's way of saying: 'Go forth and multiply and there's no need to take an umbrella neither.'"

"That's right," said Carter Brandon and he slammed down the phone.

— Oh hell, Daniel. What am I going to do now?

— Sort it out yourself, lad. I'm not sticking me nose in after the way you treated me. You should be ashamed of yourself the things you said to me.

— Oh hell, Daniel. Oh hell.

He went into the kitchen to put on the kettle, but then he changed his mind and switched on the shower. He was just about to get under it, when he changed his mind, dashed downstairs and started to make toast.

— Come on, Carter. Pull yourself together, man. Take some action.

— What action?

— Stone me, Carter, what a gormless prat you are. Get your clobber on, get your bike out and get looking for your father. Search all the pubs. Scout round the railway station. See if he's floating face down in the reservoir at Mosscroft Edge.

Carter Brandon pounded upstairs and dressed himself quickly.

He was halfway down the stairs when the phone rang again. It was his mother. She wanted to speak to his father.

"Er . . . er . . . er . . . er . . . he's gone out to buy a new pumice stone," said Carter Brandon. "Aye, that's it. The old one was a bit clapped out so he nipped to the chandler's to buy another. I'll give him the message."

"I haven't given you a message yet," snapped Mrs Brandon. Then she said suspiciously: "You're not hiding anything from me, are you, Carter?"

"Pardon?"

"Your father's not gone off boozing with his cronies at the bowls club, has he?"

"No. No. Any road, it's not opening time yet. No, it's not. Not yet."

"Good. Well, that's the message I want to give you — no boozing and make sure you get him to the church on time.

Twelve o'clock. Bang on the dot. Can I rely on you, Carter?"

"Yes," said Carter Brandon, and he slammed down the phone.

He rammed a crust of dried bread into his mouth, raced out of the house, leapt onto his bicycle and pedalled away furiously in search of his father.

He went to the park where Mr Brandon had worked. He looked into the greenhouse. He looked into the greenkeeper's shed. He looked under the bandstand. He looked through the dripping shrubberies and the sopping rose gardens.

There was no sign of his father. It was ten o'clock.

He searched the Old Comrades' Club in Nelson Street, the Working Men's Club in Bullions Road, the British Legion Club in Musson Terrace and the Labour Club in Leuty Street.

There was no sign of his father. It was eleven o'clock.

Perspiring and panting he cycled to the Midland Station and said to the man at the ticket barrier:

"Excuse me, have you seen a bloke passing through here wearing a morning suit, top hat, dove-grey spats and a check muffler?"

"Piss off," said the ticket collector.

It was a quarter past eleven.

Desperately he made a swift tour of the pubs in the city centre.

He went to The Griffon, The Tinker's Bucket, The Engineers' Tavern, Topley's Wine Lodge, The Three Tuns, The Devonshire Arms, The Drum and Fife, The Dog and Partridge and The Swan With Two Nicks.

There was no sign of his father. It was a quarter to twelve.

—Well, that's it, Daniel. Hold onto your hat and wait for the fireworks.

He arrived at the church just as the large black Lanchester limousine containing his mother and Uncle Mort drew up.

Hot and flustered he stepped across the pavement and clutched his mother by the flowing sleeve of her long white satin dress with its broderie Anglaise bodice and its bolero of Macclesfield silk.

"Carter! What are you doing wearing bicycle clips in your best suit?" said Mrs Brandon. "Get yourself inside that church at once. Your place is at your father's side giving him comfort and stopping him playing with his tie pin."

"That's just it," said Carter Brandon. "He's not there. He's done a bunk."

"Grand," said Uncle Mort. "Let's cancel the service and have a few pints."

Mrs Brandon caught hold of him by his jacket collar and tugged him back.

"The service goes on," she said firmly. "I'm not backing down now. I've set my heart on standing in front of that altar re-affirming my wedding vows with the man in my life standing beside me repeating those vows of twenty-five years ago in a clear, loud, ringing voice."

"But that's the whole point, woman," said Uncle Mort. "The man in your life's scarpered. There's no one to stand next to you in front of the altar now."

"Oh yes there is," said Mrs Brandon. "You!"

"Me?" said Uncle Mort.

"You," said Mrs Brandon. "And you can fill in for Les at the honeymoon, too. It'll be good for your dandruff, will Douglas, Isle of Man."

"Oh hell," said Uncle Mort limply and then he turned to Carter Brandon and said: "You don't happen to know if the TT races are on, do you?"

Chapter Forty-two

When Carter Brandon walked up the front drive of his home after the reception he heard someone sneezing violently in the lounge/diner.

The room was in darkness. He switched on the light. His father looked up from one of the low-slung imitation leather arm chairs and blinked at him.

He was dishevelled.

His top hat was squashed at the back of his head, his shirt collar was torn, there was a large green stain on his jacket and his spats flapped loose at his ankles.

"You've been and gone and done it now, haven't you?" said Carter Brandon.

"Aye," said Mr Brandon.

Carter Brandon made a pot of tea and told his father what had happened at the service and the reception and how Uncle Mort had hunched his shoulders and wobbled his Adam's apple as he was led away to the honeymoon.

"Oh dear," said Mr Brandon. "I won't half be for it, when she gets back."

"What made you do it?" said Carter Brandon.

"I don't know," said Mr Brandon. "I got all dressed up before dawn like what they do in the condemned cell and then the sun came out and I thought Chuff me, I can't stand that bloody thing shining in me eyes so I packed up me suitcase and set off walking and I got lost at half past ten so I hitched a lift on a laundry van and come back here. I'd have made a pot of tea, but I couldn't find the caddie. Oh hell, Carter, what am I going to do?"

"Go to bed," said Carter Brandon. "We'll think of something in the morning."

The father and son went up the stairs to bed.

"Aye. Well. Mm," said Carter Brandon. "You can come into bed with me, if you like."

"Ta," said Mr Brandon. "I hope you don't snore."

Carter Brandon did not snore. He fell soundly asleep within seconds and within minutes he was deep in dreams.

At first they were vague and confused, but then it all came blindingly clear.

He was in Pat's womb.

It had french windows and low-slung imitation leather arm chairs.

The baby was sitting in his baby bouncer playing the 'cello. Pat was sitting on the sofa knitting an Oxford University boat-club scarf. Alison was laid out on the table among the shattered remains of the heavy cruiser *Prinz Eugen*.

She was dead.

He looked down on her pale white face. It was serene. A tear fell off his cheek and splashed onto the small donkey-brown mole on the side of her neck.

Suddenly she opened her eyes and smiled.

"Go on, Carter," she said. "Do it."

He was woken up in the morning by his father who brought him a cup of tea.

"I would have brought you a cake, but I couldn't find the tin," said Mr Brandon.

Carter Brandon yawned and smiled at him.

"I've decided what you'll do," he said.

"Oh aye?" said Mr Brandon, and his eyes lit up. "What?"

"We'll run away," said Carter Brandon.

"Now?"

"No on Saturday. After the Cup Final against Cheesewright's Currants."

"Whoopee," said Mr Brandon, and he tipped the scalding hot tea all down the front of his vest.

Carter Brandon worked hard on Monday and Tuesday.

He whistled while he worked and gave Sid Skelhorn his egg sandwiches without being asked.

"Do you think you could put more salt on them tomorrow, Carter?" said Sid Skelhorn.

On Wednesday morning his father, radiant of face and sparkling of eye, said:

"I've worked out the plan of campaign. We'll leave for London on the quarter past six, we'll take the night ferry to

Dunkirk and we should be in France by then. After that we'll see if there's a bus to Sicily, and if there isn't, we'll start to walk it. How does that strike you?"

"Champion," said Carter Brandon.

"And I'll tell you summat else, Carter," said Mr Brandon with a broad grin. "I've stopped sneezing, too. How about that for an omen?"

Carter Brandon smiled and left the house.

He decided to take the day off work.

For most of the morning he strolled round the streets where he had played marbles and conkers and hopscotch as a boy, and he looked in at the front parlours where as a youth he had kissed thin girls with cold freckles.

He sat on a bench in the park where his father had worked, and he thought of the woods where he had hunted for birds' eggs and the dens he had built with milk crates and sappy grass and the temperance bar where he had drunk cool, dark, glowing sarsaparilla.

In the afternoon he walked out to the hospital. The sun blazed down. Birds sang.

Daffodils trembled in the light spring breeze. Lenten roses glowed in woodland gardens. The hedgerows were tumbled with wake robin, dove's foot, crane's bill and herb Robert. In the coppice glades there were great filmy drifts of bluebells, red campion and yellow archangel.

"I hate this time of the year," said Pat. "It's neither one thing nor the other, is it? It's too early for short-sleeve blouses, yet it's not late enough to do without a petticoat."

She was plump and bloated.

She was glutted with happiness.

"Did you miss me at the service of rededication, love?" she said. "Did it make you feel all gooey and romantic?"

"Mm."

"You and me'll be like that when we celebrate our Silver Wedding, Carter, only baby won't let us hold the reception in a public house. He'll put his foot down and insist we have it in the marquee he'll put up in the grounds of his country residence with music by Mantovani and a running buffet with no crusts on the sandwiches. Isn't baby thoughtful to us in our old age, Carter? Doesn't he do us proud?"

"Mm."

"I didn't like his wife's dress, though, did you, Carter? Fancy showing all that much bosom with the Archbishop of Canterbury present."

"Mm."

"Do you love me, Carter? Are you excited about becoming a daddy? Are you looking forward to feeding our little bundle of joy and changing his nappies while I'm getting me hair done at Maison Enid's? Are you looking forward to giving him a spoonful of gripe water when he gets an attack of the windy wobblers?"

"Mm."

"Are you happy and contented, love?"

"Yes."

"You look it, too. I've never ever seen you looking so contented with life," said Pat. "Give us a cuddle while Nurse Balderstone's out emptying the bed pans."

He kissed her and then the buzzer went to end the visiting hour.

"Aye. Well. Mm," he said. "I'll not be seeing you while next Sunday. I've got a lot of overtime on, you see."

"That's all right, love. I don't mind. I'm proud of you doing all that overtime. And so's baby. He'll be born into this world with a grin from ear to ear at thought of all the hard work you've put in."

"Aye. Mm," said Carter Brandon.

He paused at the door and looked back at his wife. She smiled at him and blew him a kiss.

"Ta ta," he said.

"Ta ta, Carter," she said. "I do love you. Honest."

—Are you sure you're doing the right thing, Carter?
—Certain.
—No second thoughts?
—None.
—No cold feet?
—No.
—Good for you then. Stick by your guns and give the punters the biggest bloody broadside they've ever had in their lives.

On Thursday afternoon Eric Black called the team together for a talk on tactics.

"The main tactic, lads, is this—there's to be no getting your ends away on Friday night. It is a well-known fact of medical

science that having congress with a woman on the night before an
athletic function is tantamount to insuring that you'll be clapped
out and coughing your guts up. With this end in view I have
therefore arranged for us to stop the night at a secret destination
like what Inter Milan does. There'll be no spare birds there, and
as I'm the only one what knows where it is, you can't make
arrangements for your own personal crumpet to sneak in round
the back while I'm not looking, thus handing victory on a plate
to Cheesewright's Currants.''

The first person the team met when they walked into Eric
Black's secret destination—The Commercial Hotel, Stocksby
Bridge—was Linda Preston.

"Hey up, lads," she said. "What a coincidence. The works'
ladies' netball team's having its annual night out here
tonight."

"But the works hasn't got a ladies' netball team," bellowed
Eric Black.

"Eee, Eric, you're a bugger for getting bogged down wi'
irrelevancies what don't matter," said Linda Preston.

Eric Black groaned, and at that the night's entertainment
commenced.

Rudyard Kettle was sick three times and stained his singlet
with dandelion and burdock. Stewart Woodhead fell off a bench
locked in the arms of Thelma Thurlow from Ventilation. Ernie
Cosgrove cut his lip on Connie Watkinson's curlers and Tommy
Rowley slept happily on the floor at the back of the upright
piano.

At midnight Carter Brandon crept away with Linda Preston to
her bedroom.

She undressed him slowly.

He made love to her fiercely.

"By God," she gasped. "You certainly needed that, didn't
you?"

She blew into his hair.

The bed was hot. The sheets lay rumpled on the floor. Carter
Brandon ran his nose over her breasts and she tickled the skin at
the base of his spine with her heel.

"I'm running away from Pat tomorrow," said Carter Brandon
after they had made love once more.

Linda Preston stiffened.

"Oh aye?" she said, blowing a thin stream of cigarette smoke out of her nose.

"I've had enough. I can't take no more."

Linda Preston propped herself up on one elbow and looked down on him.

He smiled.

"I'm making the break, kid. Isn't it bloody marvellous? I'm going to roam the world and see the sights and drink the wine and love the birds till I'm blue in the face."

Linda Preston rolled over onto her back.

"Oh aye?" she said thoughtfully. "Oh aye?"

Cup final day!

Elopement day!

A scorcher!

"Now there's one man we've got to keep nailed down for ninety solid minutes," said Eric Black in the dressing room during the pre-match tactical talk. "And that man is Count Jugular."

"Count Jugular?" said Bernard Garside. "I thought he were a wrestler."

"Only part-time, Bernard," said Eric Black. "His main source of income is pipping currants. And I tell you this—if he pips any of you lot, it'll be a good three months flat on your back in the Royal Infirmary."

Louis St John groaned and clasped the wet face cloth tightly to his forehead.

"Oh dear," he said. "I wish I hadn't eaten that bowl of tulips last night."

Eric Black fussed up and down the dressing room with bottles of liniment, strips of sticking plaster and packets of chewing gum.

"Hey up, Rudyard, you're never playing in your underpants, are you, lad?" he said.

"I've got to," said Rudyard Kettle. "Me mum's watching."

They trotted onto the scrawny pitch in the middle of the greyhound stadium and were greeted by a scrawny cheer from Linda Preston and the girls.

There were small knots of spectators patchworking the terracing.

Carter Brandon saw his father standing on his own under the tote indicator board. He waved to him, and his father waved back and pointed happily to three suitcases and the knapsack at his feet.

Just before the kick-off Count Jugular trotted over to Carter Brandon and said:

"Grand day, isn't it? Are you sure you don't breed guinea pigs by any chance?"

The whistle blew and the game commenced.

Carter Brandon flung himself into it with passion.

After three minutes he took a through pass from Ernie Cosgrove, dummied past the centre half, pushed the ball through the legs of the left back and hit it hard and true into the top left hand corner of the net.

"Great goal, lad. Fantastic," screamed Eric Black.

—It *was* a great goal, too, Carter. By God, you played as though you meant that.

—I do, Daniel. I bloody do an' all. I'm going to go out of here with a bloody great bang. I'm going to give them something to remember me by. This time tomorrow I'll be gone. This time next year I'll be forgotten. Well then, let's make sure they don't forget me this afternoon. Let's give them something to shout about.

They were indeed given something to shout about.

After ten minutes Carter Brandon called for the ball from Rudyard Kettle. He brought it under control with his left foot, transferred it swiftly to his right foot, passed it to Terry Dunphy and then ran into the open space for the return pass.

It came.

So did Count Jugular.

He launched himself at Carter Brandon from three feet and hit him full speed ahead with head, knees and feet.

Carter Brandon was catapulted backwards. As he hit the earth Count Jugular landed on top of him and ground his elbows deep into his ribs and rubbed his wiry, close-cropped hair into his face.

"Sorry about that," he said. "But I'm doing it under orders."

"Orders?" gasped Carter Brandon fighting for breath.

"From Linda Preston. She told me to crock you up so's you'd not be able to walk for a good three month," said Count Jugular, and he stood up, looked down on Carter Brandon, nodded and said: "I seem to have made quite a good job of it, too."

Carter Brandon heard nothing more. He passed out as a searing, screaming pain wracked his body.

When he came to, he was on a stretcher and Sid Skelhorn was grinning at him.

"By gum, Carter, that's a smashing fracture you've got in your shin. And them two broken ribs are bloody classics. Well done, lad," he said. "I shall never forget those injuries as long as I live. You can't lend us half a bar while Monday, can you?"

Carter Brandon passed out once more.

He came to briefly as they were transferring him to the ambulance.

He looked up and saw the weary, wretched, withered look in the eyes of his father.

"Atishoo," he went. "Atishooooooooooooooo!"

On Linda Preston's face was a look of radiant happiness.

Chapter Forty-three

The effects of the drug wore off at half past eleven on Sunday morning.

The doctor smiled.

"Well, young man, you've done well for yourself, eh? You've a fractured shin bone in your left leg, two broken ribs, severely strained tendons on your right leg and multiple bruising to your left shoulder," he said. "And, ah yes, I almost forgot—you've also got a son."

"Pardon?"

"Your wife gave birth to an eight-pound-four-ounce baby boy at seven-fifteen this morning," said the doctor smiling. "We'll take you across to see them both as soon as we've tidied you up. You're in the same hospital. Isn't that a stroke of luck, eh?"

They wheeled Carter Brandon on a trolley to the maternity ward and showed him the baby.

It had a wrinkled skin and large ears.

"Isn't he gorgeous, Carter? Isn't he a little pearler?" said Pat.

She was pale. She was tired. She was happy.

"Are you proud of him, love?" she said. "Do you feel all maternal looking at him?"

"Mm," said Carter Brandon.

Pat smiled and said softly:

"Thank you for giving me such a smashing little baby, Carter."

"That's quite all right," said Carter Brandon. "Think nothing of it."

Pat cradled the baby in her arms and said:

"Who do you think he looks like, Carter—a chartered accountant or a commissioner for oaths?"

Just as they were wheeling Carter Brandon out through the door Pat called out.

"Oh, I almost forgot, Carter. We won first prize in the competition for Corbishley's Travel."

"Oh aye?" said Carter Brandon.

"It's a fortnight for two," said Pat. "Guess where."

"I can't," said Carter Brandon.

"The Costa Brava in Spain. It's a smashing hotel, Carter. They've got a balcony to each bedroom with individual maid service and there's a cellar bar what serves Watney's Red, and we can lie on the private beach all day and there's special English menus and it'll be just like home only it'll be much hotter," said Pat and she sighed with happiness. "Eee, Carter, isn't it romantic?"

"Mm," said Carter Brandon and they wheeled him across the lawns back to his ward.

A bird flashed across his vision.

It shimmered with iridescent blue.

He thought it was the first swallow of summer back from distant climes.

But he could not be sure.